# SIX WEEKS IN
# RENO

# SIX WEEKS IN RENO

A NOVEL

## LUCY H. HEDRICK

Text copyright © 2025 by Lucy H. Hedrick
All rights reserved.

Published by Lake Union Publishing, Seattle

www.apub.com

Amazon, the Amazon logo, and Lake Union Publishing are trademarks of Amazon.com, Inc., or its affiliates.

ISBN-13: 9781662525711 (paperback)
ISBN-13: 9781662525728 (digital)

Cover design by Faceout Studio, Jeff Miller

Cover image: © Alexia Feltser / Arcangel; © Alis Photo, © Ana Hollan, © Kirk Geisler, © madjdi vector, © Rubanitor, © Scott Book, © vso / Shutterstock

Printed in the United States of America

*For Evelyn*

# THE TRAIN GOING WEST

# CHAPTER 1

*Sunday, September 27, 1931*

Today my new life begins. I will board a train in Newark, New Jersey, for a trip to Penn Station in New York City. There I will connect to a cross-country journey that will upend my world. I'm leaving the East as Mrs. Dean Henderson of Hackensack, whom I've been for twenty years. Who will I be when I return?

As my sister, Marion, drives me and my luggage to the first leg of my travels, she clenches her jaw, thrusts her chin forward, and says, "I'm driving you to Newark because you're my sister, but I am, and always will be, *appalled* by your decision."

I say nothing.

The tires spit gravel when she speeds away from the station. While my heart gallops in my chest, I close my eyes to concentrate on calming myself. Inhaling and exhaling, my lungs meet resistance from my corset. A lot of modern girls have done away with girdles, but I am a John Robert Powers model, and a flat stomach and good posture are de rigueur. I don't wish to be anyone important on this journey, so perhaps an erect carriage will help disguise my apprehension. With my luggage handles wanting to slip through my perspiring hands, I walk to my train and ride to New York City.

At Penn Station, a sea of faces of many colors floods my vision. Who *are* all these people? Will they be on my train? I've been in this building many times but never in the long-distance section.

I purchased my round-trip ticket weeks before, but now I must find the sign for my train's platform. The shouting, pushing, and barking over the loudspeaker make me dizzy. Finally, between trying to hear and squinting to read the numbers over the departure doors, I locate the correct gate. Marching forward, eyes locked straight ahead, and praying not to see anyone who knows me, I take my place in line. Women—well dressed, hatted, and gloved—also burdened by several pieces of luggage—surround me, all straining to get through the same door. Several complain out loud.

"What's the holdup?"

"The train's here. Why can't we get on?"

"I should have gotten a porter."

Please, God, let me get on the right train. Inching through the door, I teeter as if I am about to faint. A trainman in a blue uniform and a railroad cap grabs my elbow and escorts me up the steps of my car. A Pullman porter, in his white coat, takes my bags, leads me to my seat, and stows my luggage underneath. My accommodations consist of a small section with two plush red bench seats facing each other. They convert to upper and lower beds when the berths are made up. The space opens to the aisle, but there are privacy curtains for use at night. I swallow a lump of fear. I am, and always have been, a modest woman.

The passenger who will share my section is already settled. She squeezes her knees to the side as I collapse onto the opposite bench. Removing my new cloche hat, I lean back and close my eyes. I made it. Then anxiety returns as I remember there are four days and three nights of travel to Reno, Nevada, ahead of me. According to gossip columnist Walter Winchell, I'm traveling west to get "Reno-vated."

While my section mate leafs through a copy of *Woman's Home Companion*, I am certain she is sizing me up. A quick glance tells me that she pencils her eyebrows. Not my taste. My modeling agency doesn't allow us to indulge in this fad, but it is now all the rage, thanks to Clara Bow and Greta Garbo. This one is plain featured, her traveling costume a gray tweed suit, which adds to her dull pallor. When I get a chance, I will suggest some makeup to give her some color.

As I turn the page of my Somerset Maugham short story, she looks up and extends her hand. "How do you do? I'm Tessa Marquand."

"Evelyn Henderson." Tessa wears a wedding ring. Mine is back home.

"How far are you traveling?"

I hesitate, then whisper, "All the way."

Tessa winks. "Me too."

What do you know—two of us going to Reno?

"You're very beautiful. Are you famous?"

A smile teases my lips. I'm not famous, but before I married, I modeled in John Wanamaker's fashion parades at the Philadelphia store. After my husband lost his job, I wanted to return to the modeling I'd done before I had my children. If Dean couldn't find a job, well, by golly, I could, but my parents forbade it.

"It's unseemly for a young mother to work," my mother said. "What will the neighbors and our friends at church think?"

"You have no need to worry about money," my father added. "I can support all of us."

"But there are opportunities for me," I protested.

"It's out of the question," Mother said.

In fact, after ten years of my husband's unemployment, I defied my parents. Slowly, carefully, I made trips to Philadelphia under the pretense of lunching with friends. Betsy and Sally, my two oldest and dearest friends and my coconspirators, visited museums or the theater while I went back to the runway at Wanamaker's, where I was discovered by John Robert Powers, who had a modeling school and agency. I had no desire to be a Hollywood actress—John's specialty—but the runway was fun, and John secured other jobs for me.

My mother figured out what I was doing, but mashing her lips and turning away, she left me alone.

To this day, I love wearing fine clothes and hats, using makeup—in short, enhancing my feminine attributes—but on this trip, I do not want to call attention to myself in any way.

Tessa is waiting for my reply.

"Thank you. And no."

"Your hair color. Is it natural?" she asks.

"Yes." I am blessed to be a strawberry blonde.

"I love your suit. What color do you call that?"

"Aubergine," I say. For my traveling outfit, I have chosen a sheer wool dress with a matching jacket.

"Aubergine," Tessa repeats with reverence. "And your skin. You don't look a day over twenty-five."

I pretend to read. In truth, I'm thirty-nine.

"What's your secret?" whispers Tessa, inching forward on her bench.

"Pond's Cold Cream."

"Is that all?"

"That, and never, *ever* exposing my face to the sun."

Tessa nods.

I return to my story. Tessa seems several years my junior. Still, she doesn't seem the least bit anxious. I, on the other hand, flinch at every noise and look for something to grab on to. I assume every woman in this car is as frightened as I am.

My determination to make this crossing is the result of the chasm that grew between me and my husband due to his inability to find a job—that, and the death of my disapproving mother. Not being strong enough to oppose my parents' wishes, I had been forced to marry Dean.

In secret, I had followed the vacillating moves of the Nevada Legislature, always chronicled in East Coast newspapers, as are all the celebrities who go to Reno, "the Divorce Colony." For many years, the residency requirement to secure a divorce was six months.

As I sat under the hair dryer at my local beauty salon, skimming the *Trenton Times*, I gasped. What was this? The legislature had reduced the required stay in Reno to six weeks. Shielding my face with the newspaper, I reread the paragraph to make sure I was not just imagining things. Then I felt my forearms turn to gooseflesh: my children, Charlie and June, were grown and in college, and I needed to stay for only six weeks, not six months. And thanks to the money my parents left to me and Marion, I could afford to make the trip. In short, I could get free.

No longer would Marion and I sit at the supper table with a ghost—a man who ate little and said less.

I must give Marion some credit. She, too, had tried to engage Dean in conversation, talking about stories in the newspapers or what Charlie and June had written in their letters from college.

"I read we have a new national anthem," Marion had said. "'The Star-Spangled Banner.' We'll have to ask June to play it on the piano for us when she comes home from school."

Dean had chewed slowly, mute.

"Oh my gosh, did you hear about Scottsboro?" I'd said. "And the Midwest and the Plains seem to be getting more dust storms."

We'd both looked at Dean.

Nothing.

⌒

"Sallyanne, Sallyanne," I called to my hairdresser. "Please comb me out. I have to leave right away." I was in my lawyer's office the next day.

Al—short for Aloysius—Gardner had managed the legal affairs of our family for years. As he looked fixedly at me from across his desk through unruly eyebrows, he asked, "Are you certain?"

I had anticipated much greater resistance from him. As I gripped my hands to quiet them, I said, "*Very* certain."

Al sat up straighter, tugged his vest down, and outlined the necessary steps and papers I would need. I took notes.

When we both stood at the end of the meeting, Al handed me a copy of George W. Bond's 1921 divorce handbook, *Six Months in Reno*. *Months* was crossed out and *Weeks* scribbled above. As I turned to leave,

Al held on to my hand and said, "Your new identity may prove to be a heavy cross to bear. The securing of this divorce decree is amazingly simple, but the label you will wear will follow you forever."

I stared at Al for a moment, my heart in my throat. "No more so than my daily despair."

Would I ever recover from a morose husband who had withdrawn from me into silence? Secretly, I prayed I could abandon my need to regurgitate. I lifted my chin and marched forth.

Hiding in corners at the Hackensack Library, I read up on Reno. I was well aware that the country was in the middle of a depression, but Reno, an old mining town, was booming, thanks to the divorce seekers. The ranchers, who had lost almost everything, rented their guest rooms to the "six-weekers," and lots of Hollywood actors came north to gamble and enjoy the dance halls.

Thoughts of casinos and dancing scared me enough that I wanted to abandon the idea, but I was determined to at least understand more. I telephoned the Chamber of Commerce in Reno to learn about the climate during autumn and began to set aside my clothes accordingly. I checked references for the Flying N Ranch, wired my deposit, and bought traveler's checks. My Hackensack lawyer, Al Gardner, prepared the necessary documents for me to carry. Every time I was consumed by my fears, Dean would return to the house, but as soon as he saw me, he would turn away, further confirming the breakdown of our communication.

The Lord knows I want no part of Reno nightlife, or horseback riding, or cowboys, or any of the other aspects outlined in the lurid tales in the newspapers. I am traveling this incredible distance and devoting two months of my life to securing one piece of paper—the decree dissolving a loveless marriage. At thirty-nine years old, I am determined to live the rest of my life on my terms.

My sister, Marion, warned that my divorce will bring incredible disgrace to our family. There have never been any divorces in our Dutch Reformed Church, she reminded me. "We have a position in this town," she argued. "Moore Street was named after our father, who was a deacon."

"Our parents are dead," I countered.

Marion wouldn't let it go. "We're a churchy family. It isn't done, Evelyn."

Yes, we were churchy, sometimes attending church four times on Sunday—Sunday school, the regular service, Bible study, and often a deacon or trustee meeting after supper. We said grace before meals and very much observed the Sabbath. The sewing machine was closed up, Sunday's foods were prepared the day before, and our entertainment was singing hymns around the piano. And I had contemplated all these things.

However, I came to realize that my sanity was at stake. Sally and Betsy had caught me blotting away tears, which came on at the most unexpected times. I felt so lost. On a recent trip to Philadelphia, as I lifted my teacup in the Crystal Palace, Betsy observed, "Evelyn, your hand is shaking. Are you all right?" I returned my cup to my saucer and broke down into convulsive sobs. Would they understand my panic about going to Reno? Would they abandon me if I did?

Dabbing at my eyes with my linen hankie, I recognized their concern for me. Scandal or not, I *had* to take charge of my future.

∽

Sadly, my fact-finding and planning did not allay all my fears. I have never been farther west than Toledo, where I visited my cousin Alice years ago. Yes, I am a mature woman with considerable poise, but who knows what I'll encounter in the "Wild West"?

A conductor stomps through the car shouting, "All aboard. Last call. All aboard!"

Finally, the train chugs away from the station as we begin the first leg of the trip—an overnight to Chicago. All the passengers fall silent. I sense that we are holding our collective breath as we leave behind our former lives. The two women across the aisle sit upright, stiff as boards, clutching their pocketbooks. Tessa and I do the same.

Today, the poor families who live close to the train tracks are a sorrowful sight. Children stare at us with sunken eyes, wearing clothing that is too thin for the late September temperature. Their backyards are dirt, some bounded by chicken wire, others filled with broken toys and trash. One boy gazes vacantly as he pushes an empty swing that hangs from a single chain.

I have seen newspaper accounts of the breadlines in New York and other big cities, but what about the children whose parents have no work? I have read, too, about the migrant farmers who moved west to find a better life, only to be buried by dust storms. I realize I have lived a comfortable life in Hackensack. What I read in the newspapers didn't touch my family. We always had enough to eat, all the clothing we needed, and my father always went to work. Since our mother died, Marion and I have kept on as we always have—church work, the Ladies' Aid Society, writing letters to the children, and having friends in for tea. My only escape in Hackensack was going to the movies with Betsy and Sally.

What am I going to find in Reno? More poverty and homelessness? From what I have read, the casinos are paying their "entertainment taxes" so that Reno can pave roads and build schools. Please, God, don't let me find myself in a wasteland. My window gazing is interrupted when a conductor comes through the car to punch our tickets. Then I lean back and close my eyes again.

I jump when an African American waiter strikes the xylophone-like plate chimes right beside me, signaling that we can make our way to the dining car.

Tessa says, "I'm *starved*."

We stand in unison, along with the two women across the aisle, and inch toward the dining car. I can't refrain from wrinkling my nose at the clash of perfumes and sour body odors. Someone stinks of tobacco, and hat feathers poke my eye.

Tessa shows good manners, hanging back and waiting until a white-coated steward gives us menus and extends a hand toward a table with two empty seats. Crisp white linens, heavy silverware, and bone china greet us. I had no idea that the dining car would be so elegant. Perhaps this adventure isn't going to be so uncomfortable after all. This gentility reminds me of my parents' home.

Conversation in the dining car begins as a murmur. I'm guessing that none of us are used to eating with strangers. Tessa breaks the ice, introducing herself to our tablemates. While she shows surprising confidence, my stomach is churning from both hunger and nerves. I am not accustomed to making small talk or, heaven forbid, unburdening myself to people I don't know. It's not the same as eating at home with my sister, my husband, and my children. Sometimes my husband's brothers and their wives would dine with us, but they weren't outsiders.

Across from Tessa and me are the two from the other side of the aisle: Madeline Abel from Manhattan, buxom and on the portly side, and Candace Niven, as slender as a thread, with short-cropped, tomboyish hair. All four of us are headed to Reno.

Tessa probes where each of us will reside during our six-week sojourn. She is boarding at the Del Monte Ranch, while Madeline is staying with me at the Flying N. Candace reveals that she is a photographer on assignment and is booked into the Colonial Apartments in town.

"What will you photograph in Reno?" Tessa asks.

"Everything that's happening there."

I gasp and quickly conceal my mouth with my napkin. For almost twenty years, the *New York Times* has front-paged the names of prominent divorce seekers who go to Nevada. I can see it—the dissolution of my marriage for all to see. Divorce is still uncommon in 1931, and the newspapers love to highlight these shameful misdeeds. Wouldn't seeing my name send Marion and the rest of Hackensack over a cliff? I have no intention of being on such a list and resolve to always avoid Candace and her lens.

"I feel as if I've seen your picture before," Candace says to me.

"I doubt it."

"I told her she's very beautiful," Tessa says. "I asked if she's famous."

I glower at Tessa. "And I replied, 'Thank you, and no, I'm not famous.' I do a little runway modeling." And I have every intention of returning to it if they'll still have me.

"I knew you looked familiar," says Candace.

A waiter appears to take our order, and I'm grateful to change the subject.

Madeline wipes her eyes with a lace hankie and stares at her lap. She is one of those girls my mother would say could be uniquely beautiful if she'd only reduce. She has a peaches-and-cream complexion and the latest bob with a Marcel wave, but with her head lowered, she has three chins. What has she lived through to cause those tears? Poor dear.

The meal is surprisingly satisfying, my stew hot and well seasoned. The diners' voices rise in volume as they become more acclimated to their tablemates. Tessa gives a running monologue of her marriage, her husband's infidelity "with the blonde down the block," and her decision to go to Reno.

Madeline continues to mop the corners of her eyes. Perhaps her husband is also an adulterer.

"If your husband is the one who wants the divorce," Candace says, "why are *you* the one who is going to Reno?"

"I'm the one who's available," says Tessa. "My husband is a doctor, and despite this blasted depression, he still earns a living. He's paying all my expenses for this trip, and I'm getting a paid vacation. We have a son, but he's at boarding school."

Tessa sounds so flippant. Maybe she doesn't care that her husband has fallen for another woman.

"My attorney tells me that adultery is grounds for divorce in New York," I say.

"I know," says Tessa between bites, "but which would you choose—a nasty trial where you live or a vacation out West? I'm looking forward to this."

Maybe Tessa is a true adventurer. And fearless.

"How does your family feel about your getting a divorce?" I ask.

"My parents are gone, and I'm an only child."

No acrimonious sister Marion.

"But I'm sure I'm the top subject in the gossip mill on the Upper East Side of Manhattan," she says, chuckling. "It's pretty obvious, when I approach the cashier at my market, that all the customers are whispering about me. When I glance at them, they snap their mouths shut and look the other way. The same thing happens when I go to my local bakery. And my hair salon? Oh, golly. When I go under the dryer, the other customers convene at the pay station to gossip and point."

To which she seems impervious. Can I learn to be as invulnerable as Tessa?

I can hear fragments of nearby confessions—"abused me," "drank too much," "disappeared one day"—and I feel uneasy about justifying my decision. My husband has done none of these things.

"How about you?" Tessa asks Madeline. "Is your husband an adulterer?"

"If only he were," she replies, looking off into space. Each of us stops chewing and waits for her explanation, but it is not forthcoming.

"And you, Evelyn?"

I pretend to look confused.

"Madeline," says Candace, "if your husband isn't an adulterer, then what is he? Why are you getting a divorce?"

Doesn't she know a lady doesn't ask personal questions? I'm shocked by Candace's directness.

"He hits me," whispers Madeline, while more tears pour forth down her cheeks.

"No! You poor thing," I say, reaching across the table to touch her hand. "Of course you must divorce him."

"A lot of my friends wonder what's taken me so long." Again, Madeline looks down at her lap.

"But you're doing it," I say. "Aren't we all at the point where we say, 'Enough'?"

Inside, my stomach is doing summersaults. I have never known anyone who's been abused by her husband. Madeline appears very fragile, but by golly, she has left him. She deserves credit for that.

"I had to escape during the day when he was at work," Madeline says. "My parents gave me the money."

"And you will succeed and be safe," says Tessa. "Won't she?"

We all nod, and Madeline tries to smile. Does she share Tessa's confidence? Not yet, I am certain. This is an intimate conversation to be having with strangers, but ill-fated Madeline? She deserves our support.

"That leaves you, Evelyn," Candace says.

I set down my fork, clear my throat. "Dean lost his job five years after we married—long before the Crash. We had to move back in with my parents. He never worked again."

"Did he look for work?" she asks.

"Every day . . . for a while." There is so much more I could say, but I have revealed enough.

Candace continues to stare at me, her fork poised in the air, while I focus on applying butter to my roll. She won't get another word out of me. More importantly, I don't know any of these women and have no intention of sharing confidences with them. To be sure, we are all in the same boat, or the same train, and my experiences with my church friends remind me that women tend to open up to one another more readily than do menfolk. Nevertheless, I reach for my glass of water, determined to keep the details of my marriage off the record.

Candace lowers her fork with a defeated sigh and resumes eating her stew.

My thoughts return to the day that Dean came home to tell me of his dismissal from the Lawrenceville School, where he served as secretary. "Evelyn," he said, "I don't have enough money. I can't afford to buy us a house while I look for my next job." His hands were trembling, and I knew he fought back tears. Since we were living in Stone Cottage, a house owned by the school and used for faculty and administrators, we had no choice but to move in with my parents in Hackensack.

Mother tried to comfort me by saying, "This is the happiest day of my life. I will hear the sounds of children again. Meanwhile, we must do everything we can to be supportive of Dean." Wasn't that a loving thing for her to say? I know she missed my deceased brothers immensely and adored our children. I needed to feel grateful that I had parents who could take us in. I was sympathetic to the shock Dean had received, but my world had collapsed too. I prayed this wouldn't be for long.

Charlie and June, both in grammar school at the time, adjusted to their new home more easily than I did. Charlie, who is athletic, could frequently be found playing baseball with neighborhood boys in the vacant lot on the corner. June, very shy, took longer to find playmates. I would often find her in the branches of the large maple tree reading a book of poetry. She is also a natural musician, and my mother paid for her to take piano lessons. June used her piano ability to overcome some of her shyness. "Please play for us" was often the cry from the neighborhood kids, who would gather around our piano.

No longer the first lady of my house, I observed my mother make all the decisions and my father pay all the bills. Every evening, I watched for Dean walking home from the train station. I opened the door for him, kissed his cheek, and hung up his coat. "Anything?" I whispered, praying for a reason to announce good news at supper. Eyes closed, he shook his head. Dolefully, he climbed the stairs to take a nap. His defeated posture reminded me of someone grieving at a graveside.

Everyone assumed that Dean would find another job, but as time wore on, I saw the truth—a frail, hopeless man who could neither compete nor cope. In truth, I suspected my parents saw it too.

At first, conversation at dinner revolved around the private schools Dean would apply to. Before the new headmaster had arrived at Lawrenceville, Dean had practically run the school, as the previous headmaster had been ailing. "You have vast experience," said my father. "Any school would be fortunate to bring you on board." In fact, he had served the school for thirty-one years.

As the days marched on, we all looked to Dean for encouraging news and were quietly troubled by its absence. Before we sat down to supper, Charlie would whisper to me, "Did Papa find a job today?" My father would ask him about new prospects or people he had met at educational meetings in New York. With weary eyes, Dean would shake his head and sigh. Gradually, I witnessed my father's optimism drain away.

A great chasm grew between Dean and me. It was as if rejection after rejection after rejection had created a cancer that he couldn't cure. We shared the same bed, but his depression formed an impenetrable wall between us. I felt such a profound loneliness—even though he lay inches away from me and I could hear his breathing.

The four of us dig into our dessert, a lovely *floating island*. While waiters refill water glasses and silver spoons scrape their bowls, my stomach is doing flip flops. Will my tablemates think my reasons for divorcing Dean are unjustified? He has never struck me, abused alcohol, or been with another woman—to the best of my knowledge. Is giving up on himself and his family reason enough? There's no way I will reveal the rest. I will take Dean's dirty little secret to my grave.

# CHAPTER 2

Candace, who boasts that she works close to the headlines, continues the conversation. "It's my unfortunate job to photograph when a manager locks his bank's front door," she says, "and there are too many of those." We nod in agreement.

"They sent me to Chicago to take portraits of Jane Addams, the woman who founded the first settlement house. I found her work at Hull-House to be extraordinary."

No one comments, but we nod again.

"After this trip to Reno, I'm stopping in the Midwest to capture the devastation caused by the grasshopper plagues."

Madeline and Tessa look away in disgust.

"What do you think?" Candace continues. "Will Congress do away with Prohibition anytime soon?"

We shake our heads in unison.

While we are in the dining car, our Pullman porter makes up our berths. As the passenger riding forward, I have the lower berth, Tessa the upper. I try to fall asleep, but my thoughts are all whipped up, as if spun by an eggbeater. The train rocks like a baby's cradle, but then there are stops with deafening bursts of steam and much shouting amid switching of cars and loading of coal and water. The first time the train stopped, I panicked. What was wrong? The cars were at a standstill, but no passengers got on or off that I could hear. Then travel resumed, and I lost all sense of time as my memories returned.

I recalled the winter morning five years ago when, feeling particularly despondent, I tapped on my mother's bedroom door. She opened it, looking elegant as always. Her brown hair was swept up from her neck and piled artfully on top of her head, a pendant with amethysts resting on her ivory skin.

"Come in, darling," she said. "I'm preparing a shopping list for the grocer. You're looking very glum. Come. Sit." With her hand at the small of my back, she led me to the damask-upholstered chair beside her desk.

Filled with gnawing despair in my gut, I wept. "I can't endure my marriage any longer."

My mother grabbed me by both shoulders. "Calm down," she commanded. "You had a very good life in Lawrenceville. You were happy. Now Dean has had a setback. We all encounter these kinds of troubles. God knows your father and I have had our challenges—we buried two sons. Your job is to be solicitous and supportive. I am confident his next position is right around the corner."

"But, Mother," I argued, "it's been almost ten years since he lost his job at Lawrenceville and we moved back in with you and Father. They say these are the Roaring Twenties and our economy is booming. Every other faculty member and administrator who was forced to leave the school has found a new job. Every single one. Lord knows I've tried so hard to be encouraging. I greet him every evening when he returns, wearing my most loving smile, listening to his report, sharing his disappointments, making gentle suggestions. But his demeanor—he's dour and withdrawn all the time. He won't admit it, but I suspect he's given up."

"Dean goes to New York to look for work every day," Mother said. "He's doing everything he can."

"Yes. Yes. He keeps up appearances. But I hear he sits in the New York Public Library and reads books. And there's something else, something peculiar. I've never told you this, but I have called on every trustee at Lawrenceville and begged each one to give Dean a job, or to think of someone who can. To a one, they are exceedingly polite but evasive. When I met with Horace Watkins, he kept changing the subject. And Merrill Essing? His remarks to me were vague, and I honestly felt he was stonewalling me. It's as if every door has been closed to Dean." Taking a deep breath, I added, "I want a divorce."

Eyes ablaze, Mother growled, "Evelyn, in this family, divorce is unthinkable."

I walked to the door, and she followed me.

I turned and hissed, "This is all *your* fault. You *forced* me to marry him."

She raised her palm, and I feared she was going to slap me. "Remember your vows and count your blessings," she said, and shoved her Bible into my hands.

I felt at a complete loss and feared that I, too, would give up, but I couldn't let Dean drag me down. Somehow, I had to find a path to freedom.

# CHAPTER 3

*Monday, September 28, 1931*

At breakfast on the train, everyone personifies "prim and proper." Gentlemen stand when a lady approaches a table. The few men to whom I've been introduced are universally presented as "my cousin who is accompanying me on this journey." I think, *How kind of him to take time away, to interrupt his life and accompany his female cousin to Reno.*

When we arrive at Chicago's Union Station around eleven o'clock, Tessa and I each give our porter a quarter, and he puts our luggage on the platform for us. Then the station's redcaps take our bags to the Parmelee Transfer vans waiting outside and make certain we get on the same vehicle as our luggage. Our only experience of Chicago, its pulsing, energetic commercial center, is seen from the van's windows. Immense buildings stretching to the sky block out the sun, and a cacophony of noises screams from the El cars overhead. No Al Capone sightings. Alas, whenever I think of Chicago, the first things that come to mind are gangsters.

At North Western Station, with the aid of more redcaps and porters, we connect to the next leg of our trip. This entire process would have terrified me, but there are hundreds of women making this transfer, and Tessa and I float along in the wave of cloche hats and follow the orders barked by the trainmen. Once again, Tessa and I share a sleeping section.

Several passengers warn us to beware of the stench of the stockyards when leaving Chicago, but the Windy City is cool today, so the train windows are closed, and we don't need to fear such unpleasantness. We are now on the longest leg of our journey, which will take us across the vast western states all the way to Reno. This is a "through train"—no more inner-city transfers—and we will arrive in Reno on the fourth day at 10:45 at night. The railroad companies will change names several times as engines are switched, but if I don't have to get off, it doesn't concern me.

Tonight at dinner, Tessa and I sit with two other six-weekers from our car whom we haven't met before: Beatrice Winters from Philadelphia and Florence Van Dyke from Ridgewood, New Jersey. It turns out that Florence, who insists on being called Flo, and I have some acquaintances in common through the women's aid societies of our respective churches.

I'm guessing I needn't worry about this coincidence, but it's as close as I ever want to get to being recognized in Reno. Also, Flo is very much a lady, a blonde like me, and the fine cut of her taupe suit tells me she has money.

Beatrice will reside at the Flying N Ranch with Madeline and me. She is a full-figured brunette, with perhaps too much makeup, who is also full of theatrical gestures. Much talking with her hands. I presume she has been on the stage.

As usual, Tessa inquires about each woman's marriage story by first revealing her own.

"My husband has had a breakdown," says Flo, who does not reveal further details. Her hand trembles as she brings her coffee cup to her mouth. Maybe he's in an asylum.

"I'm so sorry." A tear escapes from Beatrice's eye, and she gives Flo's hand a squeeze.

"Personally, I loved being married," Beatrice adds. She closes her eyes, hugs herself, and smiles as if lost in a delicious dream.

We all nod. I can relate to that, at least in the early years before Dean lost his job and when I was the mistress of my own home. Our children arrived quickly, and my parents, being generous, provided the funds for a nursemaid. I had to admit, those first five years were happy ones. However, after we moved in with my parents, there was never a question as to who was in charge.

"Then why are you going to Reno?" Flo asks.

"After our first child was born, my Francis became a Don Juan. Fooled around every chance he got."

I hear similar tales so often on this train. How would I feel if Dean had fallen in love with another woman? But no matter what our individual circumstances, each of us has experienced a huge disappointment and the pain of betrayal.

"I resisted coming to Reno for a long time," Beatrice continues. "I lost my mother when I was very young, and then my sister died. I tried hard to keep my marriage together."

Our heads bob in agreement. We had each wrestled with our decisions. I, too, lost my two brothers. Carlton, the oldest and first to pass, caught typhus, and Willie, the closest to me in age and the one I miss the most, died of pneumonia after swimming in the Hackensack River. I miss them every day. Mother turned to her Bible, and Father developed trigeminal neuralgia. The deaths of their favored sons forced my parents to pin their hopes on me for a marriage that would give them grandchildren.

After Marion and I graduated from high school, we were sent to the Dwight School for Girls, where we were taught the social graces—how to curtsy, how to prepare and serve tea, and how to answer wedding or other invitations. At home, we learned to sew and bake. And for as long as I can remember, our lives revolved around the Dutch Reformed Church and its missions. I had a small group of friends with whom I'd gone to public school. Most of us took ballroom dancing lessons in the church's basement, which were witnessed, of course, by adult chaperones.

In 1911, Mother, Father, Marion, and I attended a chamber music concert in the chapel at Princeton University. At the reception that followed, I met Dean Henderson, a tall, scholarly-looking gentleman who was secretary of the Lawrenceville School for Boys. I smiled up into his deep-blue eyes when he handed me a cup of punch. Without consulting me, Mother invited him to tea on Saturday. After that, she gave him permission to bring me to other concerts. Two months later, we were engaged.

At first, I was swept along by a flurry of marriage customs, but Dean's stiff, lockjawed kisses were awkward. This made me question my desirability. Confusion whirled in my head. Was there something wrong with me? I was young and inexperienced, but I had enjoyed passionate wet kisses from earlier beaus who were closer to my age—Robert, then Jonathan—in a motor car or two. I wanted tenderness. Soon, I concluded that I didn't really love Dean, who was twenty years my senior; I told my parents that I wanted to return the engagement ring. However, Mother commanded that I honor my commitment, because Dean was a gentleman and a scholar—"a good catch." In those days, young women followed their mother's directions—on how to get bread dough to rise, how to baste a hem, and whom to marry. I remember wondering, *Why are my parents in such a hurry?*

Now, almost twenty years later, I understand they had come to accept that my sister Marion would never marry. She pursued her interests, including women's suffrage, and had a group of friends, but she was adamant that she had no interest in getting married or having children. I was so young that I had yet to give any thought to what I wanted.

So Dean and I married and settled into what became, at first, a quiet but satisfying life. Housed in a cottage on the Lawrenceville School's grounds, I enjoyed socializing with the other faculty wives and gained confidence as a hostess. Soon our son Charlie arrived, followed by a daughter, June. We visited my parents and Marion often, and I knew that our little family made them incredibly happy. At times, I caught myself pining for more gaiety and laughter. Dean's idea of an evening's entertainment was gathering a few friends with their wives to read plays aloud. The works were seldom comedies, and I found the tragedies of O'Neill and Ibsen very depressing. Dean always argued, "But they are great literature."

"Your friend Thornton Wilder is writing plays," I said. "Perhaps he would like to hear them read." I liked Thornton, a French teacher at Lawrenceville. He had a contagious grin and loved to laugh.

"I'll ask him," Dean replied. But he never did, and his lack of initiative frustrated me. I didn't realize it at the time, but I was seeing forewarnings of what was to come.

Five years after our marriage, the headmaster passed away, and the trustees appointed a new man to head the school. His first act was to fire the entire faculty and all the administrators and replace them with colleagues from his previous school. We moved back in with my parents, and Dean began to look for his next position.

A waiter interrupts our memories, offering more water. "Meanwhile," Beatrice continues, "I am the laughingstock of West Philadelphia. I can't stand the finger-pointing, the gossip. My other sister is happily married with a brood of kids. She, my father, and my stepmother—they're the ones who insisted I leave him."

At this point, Beatrice's eyes well up, and she dabs their corners with her napkin. I wonder if she worries about her designation as "divorcée." If I listen to Marion, I'm already a marked woman, a headline for gossip. "You will bring unbearable shame to this family," she had said. "Not only will *you* be unable to walk the streets of town, but I, by being related to you, will not be able to hold my head up."

Beatrice lowers her voice to a whisper. "And then there's the other thing. I'm terrified of being alone," she confesses, sobbing into her napkin.

Tessa and I steal a glance at one another. She is looking forward to her western vacation. I'm looking forward to being alone by choice, free from the emptiness of my marriage and the burden of a broken man. Probably neither of us has thought about our solitary lives in the future. Perhaps Tessa's doctor husband will provide housing for her when she returns to the East Coast—a roof over her head and that of their son.

I will return to Hackensack and live in the family home with Marion—hardly ideal, but at least I have a house to come back to, no small feat in this depression. I pray that Charlie and June will choose to spend vacations with us, but I can't worry about that yet. They are mostly grown, which is all for the good. I can still recall the letter I sent to them.

> Dearest Children,
>
> I pray you've both settled into your college classes and routines, found your favorite friends or are making new ones. I am taking a trip at the end of this week. I'm riding the train from New York City to Reno, Nevada, where I will stay for six weeks. Aunt Marion will remain at home. There is no gentle way to say this. I am going to Reno to divorce your father. It is the quickest and quietest way to do this, and your father is cooperating. I'm quite certain that this news will shock and even hurt you, but I pray for your forgiveness. Please don't worry about your college or living expenses. Your grandparents have left the house to Marion and me, and income from other investments will keep us all comfortable, even in this blasted depression. Your father, who will always be your father, and I love you both to pieces. Please send me your news care of the Flying N Ranch, Reno, Nevada.
>
> I love you with all my heart,
> Mother

I added a postscript to the page addressed to Charlie at the University of Pennsylvania, asking for his help in sending monthly checks to his father.

Conversation hushes, drowned out by screeching brakes, and my contentment turns to more jitters at the prospect of what awaits me in the Divorce Colony.

# CHAPTER 4

***Tuesday, September 29, 1931***

In the morning, I'm exhausted, having hardly slept a wink. In the middle of the night, I was awakened by the train's strident brakes. Where were we now? As the train stopped, I was thrown against the head of my berth. After an interminable pause, loud footfalls pounded the floor outside our curtain. A man shouted, "Police activity! Remain in your berths."

Bile collected at the back of my throat. More running feet went by. I clutched my bedclothes to my chin, my eyes wide open in the semi-darkness. A disembodied voice asked, "What's going on?"

"Police activity," the authoritative voice repeated. "Remain in your berths."

Then silence.

Then more stomping came closer. "Here's the man, Officer. He's the one."

A loud thud, then something heavy scraped across the aisle carpet. I sat up in bed, biting my hand to keep from screaming. The unmistakable sounds of fisticuffs and knuckles on flesh were followed by "Ugh" and what sounded like a body falling to the floor.

"You're under arrest," a man said outside my berth. "Attempted kidnapping."

"Gentlemen," said another man in a syrupy but breathless tone, "this is a simple misunderstanding. This woman is my wife. We're getting off here in Omaha."

"Madam, you have a ticket to Reno, Nevada," the officer said. "Is it your desire . . . ?"

"Come along, dear," said the menacing voice.

"Wait a minute, mister. Ma'am, is it your desire to get off this train?"

"No," a woman's voice squeaked.

"You won't get away with this," said the man, whose threatening tone got louder.

I held my breath. Metal clicked—a gun? I dove under my covers. Many scuffling feet. Finally, curiosity got the better of me, and I parted the curtain. In the dim light, three men in uniform pushing a male passenger disappeared into the next car. My heart drummed in my chest, and I tried to moisten my lips. The curtain across the aisle rippled and then came to rest. Though muffled, the unmistakable sound of a woman crying reached my ears. Was it Madeline? I trembled all over. Would I survive this train ride? We hadn't even made it to Ogden.

"Evelyn," Tessa whispered, "are you all right?"

"Yes."

"This is only our second night on the train. What else is going to happen?"

I couldn't think of anything to say. Eventually, the train began to move. I lay awake for the rest of the night.

❦

I am astounded to learn at breakfast that Madeline's husband, Owen, boarded the train in Chicago, hid in a day coach, and planned to remove her at Omaha. She has chosen not to press charges, as it would mean getting off the train and abandoning her goal. Her wrists are bruised. Did he restrain her? What a beast of a man!

"I can't talk about it," she says.

I am horrified for her and lose my appetite. The poor dear. Words fail me.

Madeline and I share a table with Candace, who is irate that she missed the chance to photograph last night's events, and a woman named Ruby Alstead, who will spend her six weeks at yet another "divorce ranch." While I stare icily at Candace for wanting to exploit Madeline's misfortune, Ruby, a bleached platinum blonde from Long Island, provides a running monologue.

The front of her red dress displays too much of her ample bosom, and her long nails are polished a matching red. I glance at Madeline when Ruby uses her painted pinkie to dislodge food from her teeth. Madeline hides her smile behind her napkin. Good. At least Miss Ruby is providing some diversion.

"My next husband, Tony, is waiting for me in New York," Ruby says.

I suspect she will have many husbands before she is through.

"Ruby has also tried her hand at modeling," says Candace. "Where can I see your photos? Evelyn here walks the runways."

Ruby says, "I'm on calendars and postcards."

Madeline chokes on a piece of bread, and each of us offers her a glass of water.

"I've never been west of Chicago," Ruby continues. "I'm excited to go to Reno. I hear it's very prosperous."

"It's an old mining town," says Candace. "Gold, silver, and iron ore. When the metals dried up, people tried ranching."

"We've got a trainload of women," says Ruby. "I hope there's a cowboy for each one of us." She grins and puffs out her chest.

Madeline and I make eye contact. "What about Tony?" Madeline asks.

"Tony?"

"Your fiancé."

"Oh, *that* Tony. We're going to marry as soon as I get back to New York. But in the meantime, I'm going to enjoy myself."

Ruby says nothing about her soon-to-be ex-husband. Madeline, Candace, and I return to our seats while Ruby orders more coffee. Tessa comes up behind me and whispers, "I see you met Wild Ruby."

I roll my eyes.

Tessa squeezes my arm. "I suspect her stay will not be dull."

Later, when Madeline and I stand in line to use the WC, she tells me that Owen brought her a bouquet of roses and put forth all his charms to dissuade her from divorcing him. He said he had booked a "second honeymoon suite" in Omaha.

Madeline closes her eyes and sighs. "The last time he put me in the hospital, I reached a point of no return. I will *never* go back."

Madeline is as determined to complete this quest as I am. I pat her hand while my admiration for her rises several notches. What a life she has endured. My marriage to Dean has been so different and so calm—so bland—by comparison. I know wife battering exists. Through my church's missions and the Ladies' Aid, I have donated clothing and other items for runaways.

Do my reasons for divorcing stand up beside Madeline's? Feelings of guilt turn over in my stomach. When safely in the WC, I can't help myself—I stick my finger down my throat and bring up my breakfast.

In the beginning, Dean took the train into New York City every weekday. His office was the New York Public Library. I encouraged him at every turn. I listened patiently when he listed the school headmasters he had written to. No replies arrived in the mail. The telephone was silent.

Late one morning, Marion and I found him reading a newspaper—the sports section—in the waiting room at Penn Station. We had taken the train from Newark to shop the sales on the Ladies' Mile. Dean stood and stammered his excuses, insisting he searched for job leads in the daily papers and would now move on to the library. I clenched my teeth to prevent myself from releasing the anger I felt. I wanted to give him the benefit of the doubt, but his flush of embarrassment gave away his deceit. We had caught him.

Then my dear friend Sally revealed her encounter with Dean outside the Gramercy Park Hotel in June. It was pouring rain, and although Sally carried a large umbrella, she sought shelter under the roofed entry. Standing to the side, Sally bided her time by observing uniformed doormen open limousine doors for elegant women draped in furs.

Was that Ginger Rogers? she had wondered as a familiar face dashed from the revolving door to the back of a Cadillac. Ginger had recently starred on Broadway in *Girl Crazy*. Wait till I get home to Hackensack. I'll have something fabulous to tell the girls, Sally had thought.

Just then, Sally recognized Dean exiting the Gramercy, along with a young man who wore a black raincoat and fedora. Dean opened his large umbrella, grasped the young man's hand as one would a cherished child, and escorted him to the curb, where he entered a taxi. As the cab headed up Lexington Avenue, Dean lifted his hand in what Sally described as a wistful farewell.

"Hello, Dean," Sally called from her corner. Dean turned toward the voice and froze.

"Oh, Sally," he stammered, coming closer. "I didn't see you there. What brings you to New York on this foul day?" Sally said his eyes kept darting in the direction of the departed taxi.

"Doctor's appointment," she said. "Now Bill has promised to take me to lunch."

"I have an appointment too," said Dean. "Please excuse me. My regards to Bill." He tipped his hat and raced across the street, the peak of his umbrella pointed against the driving rain.

The next day Sally regaled Betsy and me, over tea in her living room, with her Ginger Rogers sighting. "Oh, and I ran into Dean outside the Gramercy," she said. "He was saying goodbye to a young man, and then he took off like a shot."

I looked at her quizzically. "I hope that young man was going to offer Dean a job."

Sally and Betsy nodded in sympathy. "More tea?" Betsy asked, teapot raised to pour.

What I didn't reveal was that I knew Dean had attended a meeting at the Gramercy Park Hotel the night before, a gathering of school directors and others looking for staff positions. "I will spend the night with William and Jane," he said. His brother and sister-in-law did, indeed, live at the hotel, so I had thought nothing of it.

By now, this train ride is tedious in the extreme. While I know Reno is on the other side of the country, I hadn't expected the monotony of the journey. Some of the women read books. I have those too, but when I try to absorb more than one page, the movement of the train makes me nauseous. Others pass the time by knitting or crocheting. One woman works on an elaborate petit point—the stitches are so small, it's amazing she hasn't gone blind. Others play cards in the dining car. Most of us stare out the window, lulled into yet more naps by the endless vacant farms, caved-in barns, and dust twisters.

We are headed to Cheyenne, Wyoming. After the interminable prairie of Nebraska, mountains would be a welcome change, but we are too far south to see the Tetons. On the outskirts of small towns, there are more worn-out families. One group in a buckboard is pulled by a sway-backed horse. Another—a mother, father, and two children—stand by the tracks, staring at us. The little boy, his hair hanging in his eyes, looks like Charlie years ago. All knees and elbows, scrapes and bruises, from playing baseball.

There is a pleasant hum of chatter in the various seats around me. By now, the passengers are on comfortable terms, and new friendships have been forged. However, I decline to discuss my life story. Many women are forthcoming with the details of their marriages, but to their credit, they respect those of us who prefer to keep our own counsel.

The daily headlines provide fodder for amiable conversation. Many gals buy and share newspapers in Chicago and Cheyenne, and when we arrive in Ogden, they will resupply themselves.

"No matter what Hoover tries, it won't work," says a man's voice behind me.

"He's trying to create jobs in public works," says another.

Women from New York City comment on the Empire State Building, which opened in May.

"Is it grand?" one asks.

"Oh yes. Grand, indeed," says another.

I choose not to remind them that the building is seventy-five percent empty. During the peak of this depression, it is paying its bills from the one-dollar fees it charges to ride to the top and view the city.

I must have nodded off, but not for long, as I am startled awake by a shriek. "Robbed! I've been robbed!"

Tessa and I stand and search up and down the car. Between the unscheduled stops for coal and water, attempted kidnappings in the middle of the night, and now this, I am ready to scream, but my throat is too dry.

I recognize Flo Van Dyke turning every which way in the aisle. She and Beatrice occupy seats farther forward in our car. Passengers pat their pockets and check their personal belongings. Compacts, lipsticks, combs, and glasses rain onto seats as women dump out the contents of their pocketbooks. With quivering fingers, I feel around my midriff—my money belt is secure.

Tessa and I run to Flo's side. Two conductors arrive, and Candace, camera in hand, tries to elbow her way around them.

"It's gone," Flo moans. "All my money's gone."

Her eyes wide, Beatrice leans toward one end of her bench and fans her face with a newspaper.

"Keep your seats," one conductor cries. "Everyone, keep your seats."

A second conductor, hurrying up the aisle, says, "Check your property, ladies. Make an inventory."

"Keep calm," Tessa says to Flo. "Where's your bag?"

Flo passes her a leather handbag. Tessa turns it upside down. Empty. Candace takes aim with her camera, but Tessa gives the lens a shove and scowls at her. Candace steps back.

"Do you keep money anywhere else?" Tessa continues.

"Only there, in a soft wallet," says Flo, her face as white as a cloud. She crumples into the aisle in a dead faint.

"Smelling salts," says Tessa, her volume rising. "Who has smelling salts?"

On my knees, I pat Flo's cheeks. "Wake up. Flo, wake up."

A third conductor appears at my side with a glass of water. I pull her to a sit and lean her against the armrest. Flo's eyes open, and she can take a sip. The conductor helps us lift her onto the seat while Beatrice continues to recline in her swoon. Tessa frowns at her. I search the floor under Flo's bench. "There's nothing here."

"What am I going to do?" Flo asks, looking as limp as a wilted flower.

"I bet it is one of those smelly, unwashed people from the day coaches up ahead," says Beatrice. "What's to keep someone from coming into these cars at night? Our porter is sound asleep on his little stool."

"Another theft two cars up," says the first conductor. The three trainmen run into the next coach. Candace follows them.

"Don't worry, Flo," says Tessa. "We'll think of something."

⸙

Tessa and I wobble back to our seats. "Do you have everything?" I whisper.

"Yes."

"Me too. I don't even remove my money belt when I sleep."

Seated again, I close my eyes, lace my hands across my stomach, and try to count backward from one hundred. Two criminal activities in two days. What else is going to happen? My resolve was firm on day one, but I am not prepared for kidnappings and robberies. As I try to calm my thumping heart, my courage wanes, like a slow drip of water from a leaky pipe. Perhaps this adventure is too hazardous.

The passengers are silent. I suspect many are in shock. Those who carry purses or valises clasp them to their bellies. Most people stare straight ahead. A few go over the contents of their bags again, checking and rechecking. One voice asks, "Is there a safe on this train?"

On my way to the WC, I encounter Ruby, flushed and fanning herself. She drinks something from a silver flask. Behind her, Candace is talking to the conductors and scribbling faster than a machine in her journalist's notebook. One conductor says, "No, there is no safe on the train. Everyone is responsible for her own belongings."

Candace asks, "Is anyone missing? Can someone come through the sleeping cars at night and snatch purses? Perhaps they jumped from the train."

"That's under investigation," says the second conductor.

The third quickly adds, "Those who have been robbed can send telegrams and pick up money at the bank in Reno."

He offers this solution as if robberies like this happen every day. How will those who have been robbed pay for their dinner tonight? We will all chip in and buy Flo her meal in the dining car, but please, God, get us to Reno soon!

Back in my section, my heart rate eventually slows, and I take stock. I will reach Reno tomorrow. With the social upheaval of this depression—desperate people committing desperate acts—I can't help but shudder as I wonder what lies in store.

On the other hand, the attempted abduction and robbery did not happen to me. I am safe, so far. Eyes closed and feigning a nap, I fixate on my inhales and exhales and retreat into a favorite daydream. I'm floating along a fashion runway, turning this way and that. I'm surrounded by a sea of enthralled faces looking up at me, delicate music in the background. The announcer describes the features of my chiffon gown while I gaze down and smile. No dreary husband, just admirers.

A screech of brakes interrupts my fantasy, and I bounce off the back of my seat. Regarding Tessa, who has also bounced, I wonder if she succumbed to her mother's wishes like I did when I agreed to marry Dean. Biting down on my bottom lip, I swallow a lump of rage. I tried to be a devoted wife. I tried *everything*. Today I am a woman of modest but independent means, and I am determined to do whatever it takes to shape the rest of my life. I say a silent prayer for the courage to see this through.

As the train slows in its approach to Ogden, I resolve to remain fixed on my purpose. I have come this far and will hang on until Reno.

# WEEK ONE

# CHAPTER 5

*Wednesday, September 30, 1931*

Our train pulls into the Reno station at eleven o'clock at night, fifteen minutes late, but we have arrived. When the conductor shouts, "Reno! Arriving in Reno, Nevada," there is an audible sigh of relief, like a whoosh of autumn wind. Despite the late hour, there is animated chitchat among the passengers—excitement masking fear, perhaps. I say a second prayer that I have seen the last of the unlawful happenings.

We put on our hats and gloves and touch up our makeup while assembling our belongings. After tipping our porter, universally called "George," he sets our luggage outside on the platform. Station porters wheel our larger suitcases on a pushcart to the building straight ahead. Now the talking ceases as four train cars of women, and a few men, move forward like the grazing herds of cattle we saw from the train. A few gas lamps light our way. The only sounds come from our shoes treading on the pavement and the *brrrr* from several women who audibly shiver.

*How will I find my ride to the ranch?* I swallow, and swallow again, trying to moisten my throat.

The station building is a large brick structure, but it can't accommodate all of us plus our luggage. The air inside is stuffy, so we continue to press toward the exit, where cars are waiting. Outside, drivers hold up roughly drawn signs identifying destinations—the Flying M E,

Washoe Pines, Donner Trail, Pyramid Lake. I purposely chose a small, unglamorous guest ranch. No Pyramid Lake for me. That one is full of Hollywood types and the very wealthy. The adventures of their guests there are regularly written up in the newspapers.

There are so many cars and signs that I am overwhelmed and stand frozen in the crush of bodies. Someone grabs my arm.

"Look there," says Madeline, pointing. "Flying N Ranch."

Beatrice pushes up beside us, and we move toward an unsmiling woman who has gray hair pulled back from her face and wears an elaborate turquoise necklace. She introduces herself as Ramona Anselm. She and her husband own the Flying N. Looking at a notebook, she calls out each of our names. We three are to ride with her in the Ford Model A passenger car, and our luggage is piled into the back of a pickup truck by a small Native American who is identified as Little Hawk. Beside us, I hear Tessa call, "Evelyn! Yoo-hoo, Evelyn!" before she disappears into the Model A Sport Coupe next to us.

I ride up front with Ramona. Beatrice relates our train adventures in dramatic detail—the attempted abduction by Madeline's husband and the robbery. Away from the lights of Reno, we are guided by an almost full moon and a brilliant display of stars. Stealing a look at our driver while Beatrice babbles, I can make out that she has a dark complexion—from Native American ancestry or the sun or both—and her profile is so striking that I can't take my eyes away. Her gray hair is gathered into one thick, long braid. The gray must be premature, as her figure is slender and youthful. She wears brown slacks and an embroidered white shirt under her chunky necklace. I have never seen anyone like her.

We drive south out of Reno on a paved road that soon turns to packed dirt with gravel. Ramona identifies the Sierra Nevada mountain range to the right. The headlights reveal a valley floor that is flat and dry, spotted with what Ramona says are various cacti and sagebrush. There are no signs of human activity in any direction. This austere terrain is vastly different from the lush lawns I am used to back East. The mountains here loom like demons, and yet the stars are breathtaking. Eventually, Beatrice runs out of stories, and we ride in silence, consumed with awe for these star-spangled heavens.

After half an hour, Ramona approaches a tall archway built of log posts. A sign across the top says FLYING N RANCH, with the *N* tossed up at an angle. I feel like that unanchored *N*—thrown into a new and quite different part of our country.

The main house stands on a slight rise in the distance. Lit windows hint at warmth inside. Split-rail fences create corrals on both sides of the long drive, but they hold no animals.

A man in blue jeans and a cowboy hat descends the steps from the front porch. "Welcome to the Flying N Ranch," he says as he opens the two passenger doors. "Arthur Anselm, at your service." As I stand to shake his hand, I see that his face, too, is tanned and rugged. I am immediately put at ease by his smile and the crinkles at the corners of his eyes that turn up with his mouth.

"Feels good to stand," says Madeline, adjusting her skirt. Little Hawk is already carrying our suitcases into the house.

Arthur ushers us through the front door into a large room with a high ceiling and knotty pine walls. The furnishings are built from varnished wood, upholstered in what resembles Native American blankets. In the center of the opposite wall, flames crackle in a tall stone fireplace. A giant antlered elk's head is anchored above the mantel. The elk's eyes leer at me. Little Hawk passes a tray of glasses filled with cold water. I have read that it is well water from the Sierra Nevada. I gulp mine down without stopping and ask for a refill.

Ramona stands behind a tall desk. We register, each on a separate page. She explains that our dated signatures will begin the affidavits that we will bring with us to the courthouse at the end of our stay. Thank goodness Ramona knows what we must do legally. While I admire the tidy room and comfortable furnishings, like the homemaker that I have always been, Ramona and her quiet efficiency remind me of why I'm here. In fact, one of my first missions in Reno is to deliver various documents to my Reno attorney. Al Gardner had introduced me to a Reno lawyer named Boyd Whitaker, and I carry forms for him—the paper pushing required for a New Jersey woman to get an uncontested divorce in Reno. After I'm settled, I hope I can ask Ramona more questions about what I can expect to happen in court. At this moment, exhaustion overtakes me like a noxious cloud. I feel as if I could fall asleep standing up.

Arthur and Little Hawk carry our suitcases up separate staircases, one at each end of the room, to the second floor. This living room will be a comfortable refuge in which to read by the fire, but my eyes are constantly drawn to the domineering elk's head. A faint smell of disinfectant mixed with a sweet spice permeates the air.

A young woman appears with a pitcher to refill our glasses. Her blue chambray shirt, which is tucked into her dungarees, complements her light-hazel eyes. Is she the Anselms' daughter?

"I'm Neppy Gunther," she says, bowing her head slightly. "That's short for Penelope. I'm a six-weeker too." She's a blonde with long, straight hair, and the dimple in her right cheek keeps her from being plain.

"Pleased to meet you, Neppy. I'm Evelyn Henderson." I turn and introduce her to Madeline and Beatrice.

"You hardly look old enough to marry," says Beatrice—too sharply, in my opinion.

"I'm old enough to have a son," she says with a lift of her chin. "His father made an honest woman of me, if you know what I mean, but I had to promise to come out here and divorce him."

"I'm sorry," I say.

"Oh, don't be sorry," says Neppy. "He's in jail now, and we don't ever want to see him again."

Jail? I have never met anyone who had a husband in jail. What kinds of women come to Reno? I guess I'm going to learn.

"May I have my room key?" Beatrice asks.

Ramona comes forward from behind her desk, her mouth fixed in a stern line. "You're safe here," she says. "You don't need to lock your rooms. No one enters this house except Arthur and me, Little Hawk, and Neppy."

Beatrice crosses her arms and harrumphs. "There was a robbery on the train."

"Follow me," Ramona says.

Beatrice and a mystery guest, who arrived earlier, will occupy the eastern guest rooms. I assume we will meet her in the morning. Neppy leads Madeline and me to the two rooms on the western side. As I put one foot in front of the other to mount the stairs, total weariness holds me in its grip. I want to sleep for a year.

I invite Madeline to soak in the bathtub before me while I settle into my space. It is small but comfortable, and I am blessed with two windows—north and west. As I put my clothing away in the armoire, my gaze keeps returning to the window facing west, where a small pine desk sits, the room's only chair tucked under it. I take a seat. The coarse mountains are now black, the sky ink blue. Again, the saturation of stars dazzles me. Is everything about this place gargantuan—the mountains, the sky, the distances?

Madeline knocks to tell me the tub is now mine. As I sink into the deliciously warm water, I close my eyes and concentrate on the sweet smell of lavender while I sponge off four days on a train. However rough the terrain may be outside, I can be soothed by a warm bath.

While I blissfully soak, I realize that I also have many questions. Who is the other six-weeker we have yet to meet? How will we occupy our days? In my mind's eye, I see the Milky Way again. I feel so small in this foreign land. Perhaps I will stay inside most of the time. Ramona seems remote, stoic, but Arthur has an easy way about him. After the nerve-racking surprises on the train, more than anything, I want to be safe.

Now warm and clean and tucked into my bed, I count my blessings—a comfortable place to sleep, two hot meals a day, and a snug sanctuary for the next six weeks. This room will be a cozy refuge. What more could I want?

I feel like I have been holding my breath ever since the train arrived in Reno. Now I can finally exhale. Lying under several quilts, I finally close my eyes, but memories capture me again.

On the night my father died—he was struck by a passing car whose approach he did not hear as he stepped off the curb—my mother took up the saber as matriarch, but toward the end, she ruled with a more loving hand. I realize her life did not turn out as she had planned and that she had endured with grace.

That's what she did—endured. The family did not experience financial hardships the way so many others did, the result of risky investing before the Crash, but the deaths of my two older brothers, Carlton and Willie, as teenagers, were devastating.

*Mother, I hope you can find it in your heart to forgive me for this journey.* I have tried to bear the brunt of Dean's unemployment and, these days, his complete lack of initiative. Day after day, week after week, his inability to find a new position piled up. He also stopped sharing anything with me. My shame was in what our friends and neighbors were thinking, but the ache in my heart was from how he shut me out. It was during these hopeless times that my need to regurgitate took hold of me. I felt powerless.

As the years moved on, Dean became sickly with "spells"—headaches that immobilized him for days. Conversations at home always began with "When Dean secures his next position," but I knew he had given up. Likewise, I began to give up on our marriage. All my reserves drained slowly away, like a narrow rivulet making its way to a water catchment after a rain. Our social life, outside of church meetings, evaporated. I wore two coats in those years—a coat of shame and a coat of rage. It took every ounce of strength I could muster to hold my head up in church.

My associations with the other Lawrenceville wives also withered away. We kept up at first, meeting in each other's homes for afternoon tea, but one by one, their husbands found work. I rejoiced with them while a sickening knot festered in my stomach. Time after time, I swallowed my pride and begged a wife to ask her husband to inquire on Dean's behalf. They promised their full support, always followed by nothing. And then I saw these same friends admiring someone's new hat, another's new shoes. I feigned enthusiasm while I fought nausea. Wobbly, I found the nearest chair.

# CHAPTER 6

**Thursday, October 1, 1931**

At breakfast on our first Reno morning, we sit at one long pine table with our hosts, Ramona and Arthur, at either end. Beatrice is across from Madeline and me, an empty chair beside her. Neppy and Little Hawk pass eggs, browned potatoes, and hot biscuits. I should be famished, but my stomach is a knot of nerves. I am only beginning to get my bearings here.

"Twice a day, you say?" says Beatrice. Anticipating her first visit to Reno, Beatrice is very elegant in a gold-toned wool suit and much gold jewelry. Her doeskin gloves and mink boa rest on the chair next to her. Ever the actress, she continues to talk with her hands.

"Standard procedure for our six-weekers," says Arthur. "We go in late morning and stay through lunch. This will give you a chance to get your hair done, have lunch in a tearoom, and go shopping—whatever you like. Then we make a second trip after supper."

"You go to the dance halls too?" Beatrice asks.

"Heavens no," says Arthur, winking at Ramona. "We turn right around and return here. You ladies will have to hire taxis when you're ready to come back to the ranch. They got plenty of those Chevy vans. Or our cowboys will bring you back."

"Cowboys?" says Beatrice, sitting up straighter and lifting her rich-brunette curls.

"Good morning."

We all turn toward the new voice. A tall, willowy beauty poses in the doorway from the living room, every bit an easterner in a navy-blue sheath and a single strand of pearls.

Arthur smiles his self-conscious grin and rises. "Allow me to introduce Thistlena Duncan, who arrived by plane at Hubbard Field yesterday."

By plane? Isn't that grand!

The statuesque Thistlena steps forward to shake everyone's hand. Her slender fingers are soft, her nail polish restrained. Her shoulder-length brown hair is held away from her ears by tortoiseshell combs, and her lipstick and rouge are subtle. This one knows a makeup trick or two. Is she a model? Perhaps a movie star or someone from an important family. She has the bones for it.

Beatrice scoops up her gloves and boa and pats the empty chair beside her. We listen to Arthur describe how tough the depression has been for Nevada ranchers. Between bites, I sneak peeks at Thistlena. *Who is she?*

There is a burst of laughter from the back room. A female voice says, "You're all rascals, the lot of ya." A large woman—very wide in the middle but narrow at her neck and ankles, with brown skin—comes in. Her smile reveals pearly teeth as she slaps a wooden spoon against her palm, laughing to herself.

Arthur says, "Savannah, say hello to our new guests."

As Savannah turns to face our table, I am stunned by a prominent scar that runs from above her left cheekbone all the way to the corner of her mouth. "Mornin', ladies," she says.

"This here is Savannah, our cook. The finest in Reno."

"Oh, boss, don't go giving them no inflated ideas."

"I've never tasted finer biscuits," says Madeline.

"I'm much obliged, ma'am." Savannah recedes into the kitchen as Neppy returns with more eggs. As she had said, Neppy is fulfilling her residency by working at the ranch.

After the hearty breakfast, we are eager to discover all that awaits us in downtown Reno. It is broad daylight, so we will be safe, and I will most certainly come back to the ranch after lunch. We climb into Arthur's sedan. Like Beatrice, but perhaps a bit more understated, Madeline and I choose to wear dress-with-jacket suits and matching hats. Gloves too, of course. If I didn't know different, I would swear we four are headed to the Ladies' Mile in New York City, where women can shop without male companions. A stiff breeze across the valley floor stirs up the dust. Madeline and I prefer the car windows rolled down, as the day promises to be warm, but Beatrice is aghast at the thought of dust in her hair. Thistlena withholds comment and sits as still as marble in front with Arthur.

"Dust is a way of life out here," says Arthur. "It's clean dust, though."

He parks the car beside the post office, north of the Truckee River. While we listen to Arthur's instructions, we put on our sunglasses, a required accessory in Nevada. He points out the Monarch Cafe for lunch, the beauty salon, the Gray Reid Wright department store, and the Reno National Bank, which is still operating despite so many bank closures during the depression. We are to avoid, at all costs, an area for prostitution known as the Stockade on East Second Street.

"Prostitution?" I repeat.

"The oldest profession," says Arthur, "is alive and well in Reno. But it's confined to one area. You don't have to go near it. One other thing: stay away from the casinos."

"Where are they?" asks Madeline.

"They are mostly up on Commercial Row near the tracks, but you can't miss them, as the air is thick with smoke."

When I turn around, all I see in any direction are women—all shapes and sizes, most in eastern attire, but a few have "gone western." They smile behind their sunglasses, nod to one another, and chat with friends as they move along, window-shopping or going in and out of the stores. They certainly do not appear frightened. Perhaps this is their first taste of freedom and they're finding it very agreeable. I know I am.

"Shall we explore?" I ask Thistlena.

"Another day, thanks," she says. "I have an appointment."

Madeline, Beatrice, and I look at each other and shrug as Thistlena heads across the river toward the Riverside Hotel. An appointment? *What is Thistlena up to?*

The streets are packed with tourists—are they all divorce seekers? There is so much to learn. Determined to explore the town, I lead the three of us to the shops on the west side of Virginia Street.

Through several doorways, we hear radios blasting the opening game of the World Series—the St. Louis Cardinals versus the Philadelphia Athletics. Makes me think of Charlie. My son is at college in Philadelphia, and he loves baseball. Perhaps he's listening too.

I have not heard anything from either Charlie or June. I hope they will write to me. Still, this is only the first week of my tenure here. I must be patient.

We enjoy our stroll, peering in windows and critiquing the outfits of passersby. I am aware of admiring glances from other six-weekers, which I am used to from my visits to New York and Philadelphia. Many of these women were on the train. They wear chic hats and the latest fashions, some with furs draped over their shoulders. And, of course, the requisite sunglasses. It's a party—it's a parade.

I spy a few timid souls, flush against a building, in drab attire— brown sparrows among tropical birds. Perhaps, like Neppy, they are working here.

We push north to the famous Reno Arch that reads RENO, THE BIGGEST LITTLE CITY IN THE WORLD, then cross the street and head south. At the Waldorf Hotel, a cowboy steps forward and offers his suntanned arm. "Show you the sights today, ladies?" he asks.

Madeline grabs my hand, and we take a step back.

A second, taller man joins the first and tips his hat to me. "Take you to the best place for lunch, miss?"

"Beautiful day in Reno today, miss," a third says, removing his hat and bowing. "May I show you around our fair town?"

Who are these men? Stage-door Johnnies? Madeline clings to my elbow while I smile politely and say gaily, "Busy today. Maybe on Thursday."

"Speak for yourself," says Beatrice, hooking her arms with two of the men.

"Remember the time for our ride home," I call to her receding back. Skipping away from us, Beatrice flutters her fingers goodbye. The rejected cowboy is already chatting with another six-weeker coming along behind us.

"How did you know what to say?" Madeline whispers as we continue south.

"Practice, my dear. Practice."

I've often been stopped on the street by gentlemen who pretend to want to know the time or the way to Broadway but who wish for more. I've learned to keep a ladylike demeanor, answer quickly, and march on with a straight back. What works in New York and Philadelphia will work in Reno, I hope.

I lead Madeline toward the river. At the post office where we began, Tessa Marquand appears beside us, along with Flo Van Dyke, she of the robbery and fainting spell on the train.

"Why, Tessa, you've gone Annie Oakley on us," I say, smiling at her denim skirt and cowgirl boots, her red-checkered shirt, fringed vest, and cowboy hat. She has even tied a red bandanna around her neck. Hasn't taken her long to jump into western ways. Are these costumes in my future?

"Look at you," says Madeline. "Where did you buy your clothes?"

"The nice folks at Burke and Short helped me," Tessa says, pointing across the street. "I tried to convince Flo to join me, but she said she wasn't ready."

Flo wears a lavender suit trimmed with a beaver collar. I am right. She comes from money. I imagine her eyes rolling behind her sunglasses.

"We're hoping you both will join us for lunch," Flo says.

I glance at Madeline and link my arm with hers. "That sounds lovely."

The din of chatting diners at the Monarch Cafe plays against the whirring of ceiling fans. Waitresses wearing black uniforms and ruffled white aprons bustle from the kitchen to tables while waiters in white jackets pour and refill glasses of iced tea and lemonade. Except for the absence of Irish accents and the addition of sawdust on the floor, I could be lunching at Schrafft's on Madison Avenue. Maybe six weeks in Reno isn't going to be so unpleasant after all.

As usual, Tessa leads the conversation, regaling us with tales of her ranch mates, who sound even more dramatic than our Beatrice. I can't help but notice through the front windows more and more six-weekers passing by on the arms of men like those we saw outside the hotel. They are smiling and laughing. Perhaps those women know something I don't, but in Hackensack, a lady is introduced to a gentleman by mutual friends and then properly chaperoned.

"Our ranch owners make two trips into town every day," Tessa says.

"So do ours," says Madeline.

"Are you both coming back tonight to go to the dance halls?" Tessa asks.

Madeline looks at me.

I shake my head. "I hadn't planned on it." Heaven forbid!

Tessa frowns.

"Who are you going to dance with?" I ask. "I've never seen so many women in one town. Haven't you noticed?"

"Our ranch owner says that at night all of the cowboys come into town to dance with the six-weekers in exchange for free drinks."

Madeline's eyes double in size.

"Well, where's the harm?" Tessa asks. "I'm not going home with anyone."

"Tessa!"

"Evelyn, it's only a dance."

Only a dance? My sister Marion would faint.

After lunch, we make our way to a beauty salon. I am desperate for a shampoo and set, and so are the others. The four of us step inside. The shop is deep, with a black-and-white linoleum floor and a long row of sinks lining one side, many hair dryers opposite. Almost all the stations are busy. One hairdresser, wearing a white shirt over black pants, runs forward.

"I'm Violet," she says. "How can I help you?"

"We all need shampoos and sets," Tessa says.

"All six-weekers, right?" Violet doesn't wait for an answer. "I would like to fit you in, but all the ranches bring their guests in for lunch, and we can't accommodate everyone before the cars go back. Sometimes you must get your hair done later in the afternoon and wait till the evening car or take a taxi."

Tessa pulls us into a tight circle. "I don't know about you girls, but my head is already full of Nevada dust. Why don't we see if she can take the four of us on the same afternoon?"

And so we are booked for tomorrow at 3:00 p.m. When we return to Arthur's car in front of the post office, Thistlena is talking to two well-dressed men. Both favor the new Prince of Wales drape cut for suits. These are worn on Park Avenue by the few unaffected by the depression. As Madeline and I approach, Thistlena smiles broadly.

"Evelyn, Madeline," she says, "I'd like you to meet my business associates, Raymond Sessions and Nathaniel Harrison. Evelyn, they're from New York, like you and me."

Business associates? What business? And I'm from New Jersey, but I am complimented that she mistakes me for a sophisticated New Yorker.

They both tip their hats and shake hands with us. "Call me Ray," says Sessions, who doesn't let go of my hand. He is the taller of the two and sports a Douglas Fairbanks mustache.

"Call me Nat," mimics Harrison with a small bow. His shirt collar is so tight that a bit of neck flesh folds over it. How does he breathe?

They completely ignore Madeline, which is rude, in my opinion. She may be shorter and rounder, but she is also Thistlena's ranch mate.

As a model, I am used to turning heads, but I learned to stand erect and walk purposefully so as not to encourage advances from strangers. Can I rest more easily if these men are Thistlena's friends?

"Ray and Nat want to take us to lunch," says Thistlena.

I open my mouth to speak but struggle for words.

"You too, Madeline," she adds hastily.

Ray adjusts his cuffs and straightens his tie. Nat opens both passenger-side doors of Arthur's car. "A pleasure to meet you, ladies."

Well, I can't fault their manners.

Thistlena slides in with Madeline and me and waves to the men. Beatrice comes running up, holding on to her hat and laughing. Her escorts hand her the shopping bags from Burke and Short.

"Wait till you see my new outfits," Beatrice says, sliding into the front seat next to Arthur.

I can only imagine.

Tonight at dinner, Beatrice, donning her newly purchased pink-lace-over-taffeta frock, keeps turning toward the sound of laughter in the back room off the kitchen.

"They're our wranglers," says Arthur. "They eat in that back room and sleep in the bunkhouse. We don't have many cattle left, but around this time of year, they bring them down out of those hills for the winter. Oh, and we have a couple of saddle horses if any of you ladies would like to ride."

"I might take you up on that," says Thistlena. "I grew up riding horseback in Central Park."

As I suspected, she was raised with advantages. I am determined to uncover more. Maybe I'll have to get back on a horse. I haven't ridden since finishing school. I don't have a lot in common with shy Madeline or dramatic Beatrice, but if Thistlena and I can establish a rapport, maybe we can be friends back East. On the other hand, we may share similar traits from our upbringings, but perhaps my fascination with her is one sided. I hope not.

"I'm game," adds Beatrice. "I haven't ridden before, but I'm assuming one of those cowboys will show me the ropes." She puffs out her bosom and shimmies her shoulders.

Ramona, always silent, reveals the hint of a smile.

"How 'bout the rest of you?" asks Arthur.

"Not for me," says Madeline.

Beatrice leans toward Arthur, eyelids fluttering, and asks, "Can we meet the cowboys?"

"Well, I guess that can be arranged. I'll bring them in while Little Hawk and Neppy clear your dishes." Heading for the door, he calls back, "Hope you saved room for Savannah's peach cobbler."

The four wranglers stride into the dining room, all dusty jeans and boots, hats at their sides. Each one has a noticeable tan line above his eyebrows where his hat would cover his forehead, and each is cowboy-actor handsome. Two of them wink at us.

Pointing, in turn, starting on the left, Arthur says, "This here is Henry, Smoky Joe, Zack, and Gerry."

"Pleased to meetcha," says Beatrice, pushing out her chest and primping her hair as usual.

The second one, Smoky Joe, winks again.

Thistlena and I glance at each other and struggle to hide our amusement. Madeline fiddles with the napkin in her lap.

"Okay, fellas," says Arthur, "go get your dessert." The men depart in single file, boots scraping the wooden floor, and redon their hats when they reach the door.

Wouldn't Marion have apoplexy if she knew about these cowboys?

Thistlena and Beatrice decide to head back into Reno with Arthur. When Beatrice asks why Madeline and I are not coming along, I make an awkward excuse about still recovering from the train ride. Madeline has attached herself to me—she looks to me for words and actions—but after everything she's been through, I accept her under my wing. Still, I want to get to know Thistlena and find out why she has come to Reno.

# CHAPTER 7

*Friday, October 2, 1931*

The next morning, I enter a narrow door off Virginia Street and climb a steep set of stairs to Attorney Boyd Whitaker's office. With each step, I am reminded of Dean's face when I told him I was going to Reno.

The front door in Hackensack opened, then closed with a heavy thud. Dean sighed loudly as he hung up his coat.

"I need to talk to you," I said, coming into the foyer. I flexed my fingers, hoping to steady my nerves.

"I want to change into my slippers," he said, one hand on the newel of the banister.

"This can't wait. Come into the parlor."

We sat opposite one another on either side of the fireplace. I remember thinking, *I must jump in, or I will lose my nerve.*

"I have to tell you that I am very unhappy—desperate, in fact—and I am going to Reno, Nevada, this Sunday to secure a divorce."

Dean sat motionless. No doubt, I was giving him the shock of his life. His widening eyes revealed alarm. But he must have felt the growing chasm between us, an emotional crevasse now so vast it was impossible to bridge the distance. I pressed on.

"I will be absent for almost two months while I reside in Reno for the requisite six weeks, and I will return with a final decree."

"Ev-ve-ve-lyn," he stammered, "I can't believe what I'm hearing. Twenty years ago, we exchanged vows before God. I have loved you always. You can't divorce me."

I inhaled and shifted forward. "I can, and I will. My mind's made up. I can't pretend any longer."

"Reno, Evelyn? That's for Mafia molls and Hollywood idols. And a well-bred lady doesn't divorce."

"*This* lady will. It's very simple, really. Al Gardner has prepared my papers. I have here a power of attorney for you to sign." I handed him the document, which he took with a trembling hand.

"The children. What about the children?" he asked.

"I have written to both Charlie and June."

Dean's chin fell to his chest, his eyes closed. Then he pushed himself to a stand. "How will I live?" he asked in a halting, raspy voice. "I don't have any money."

"Everything's been worked out," I said. "You'll receive a check every month. And I'm certain your brothers will help."

"Divorce, Evelyn? It's out of the question. You *must* reconsider," he said as he began to pace in front of the fireplace. "We're a family. Your sister lives here. When the children return from college, we'll celebrate holidays together, like we've always done."

I had to swallow twice. I couldn't play that "we're a happy family" role any longer. In the beginning, I was proud of his position at Lawrenceville, but through the years I had watched every one of my friends' husbands find new jobs. I had tried so hard to be encouraging toward his efforts, but as time wore on, he pushed me away. Like a pond whose water had evaporated, I felt our earlier connection dwindle to nothing.

I inhaled deeply and continued. "Marion and I will live in this house, and I pray the children will visit, and you will always be their father, but I am determined to live the rest of my life on my own. Now I'm going upstairs to pack."

Dean grabbed my arm. "What can I do? I'll do *anything* to change your mind. *Anything*."

I looked up into his wounded eyes and shook my head. I resisted the temptation to scream of his deceit. This decision was about *my* happiness. I had performed the role of devoted wife for twenty years. Now I would take center stage in my own play.

Climbing the stairs, I refused to look back, but I heard him collapse into his chair, exhale mournfully, and begin to sob.

I don't like having to support Dean, but if this is what I must do to secure my freedom, so be it. And even now, in this foreign land, I am filled with relief by his absence. At the top of the stairs, I arrive at the end of a long hallway dotted on both sides with smoky glass windows whose faded black lettering identifies the occupants, some more clearly than others. Into what Black Hole of Calcutta has Al Gardner sent me? Way at the other end, I find Whitaker's office.

After the dingy hallway, I am pleasantly surprised when I open the door to find a well-appointed reception room where four women sit. The room is as quiet as a church before a funeral. Whispering my name to the receptionist, I'm asked to speak up.

"Evelyn Henderson." I take my seat next to a woman dressed in an elegant cranberry suit trimmed with nutria. I mumble, "Good morning."

She holds her face rigid beneath the veil of her matching hat and does not reply. In fact, all the women sit stiff as wood.

When the door to the inner office opens, the women assume new postures of attention, as if to say, "Choose me. Choose me." A petite Jean Harlow–like brunette exits, followed by a man who must be Boyd Whitaker. The brunette blows her nose like a horn and leaves the office in haste, slamming the door. Was that actually Jean Harlow? A dead ringer, for sure, and she was crying.

Mr. Whitaker, with dark, wavy hair and a slender mustache, takes a folder from his receptionist, speaks a name I don't know, and extends his arm with a slight bow toward the woman in cranberry. His highly polished black shoes reflect the bright fluorescent light above. The only sound is the rubbing of silk stockings belonging to his client. The rest of us lean back in our chairs, accepting our fates of waiting our turns. The woman wearing cranberry also emerges from Mr. Whitaker's office in tears. Her silk blouse is untucked and her jacket askew. What happened in there? Mr. Whitaker joins her at the receptionist's desk, one hand on the small of her back, the other holding her elbow. His actions appear indelicate to me.

"Please wire Mrs. Dollier's attorney in Philadelphia," he says to the receptionist. "She has come unprepared." He turns the crying woman to face him, too closely I feel, and touches her eyes with his handkerchief. "It's not too late," he reassures her. "You are here, and you have begun your residency." The woman sobs and drops her forehead onto his shoulder. Mr. Whitaker wraps both arms around her. I look away.

I am the last woman to be called, and I brace myself—chin up, back straight, a thick folder of papers from Al Gardner held in front of my bosom. Mr. Whitaker takes a seat behind his large desk and gestures to the other chair in front.

"It's been quite a morning," he says, mopping his face. "So many six-weekers arrive in Reno with incomplete documents."

I have complete confidence in Al Gardner, but my heart pounds.

"Your folder, Mrs. Henderson."

Grudgingly, I pass him my paper shield. He puts on his glasses and examines each page. He makes notes on a pad to one side while he mutters to himself.

"This all looks very good," he says, removing his glasses. "Very complete."

I allow myself an audible sigh.

Having finished his duties, Mr. Whitaker leans back with a syrupy smile. His eyes move as if he is evaluating every inch of me. Anxious to take my leave, I stand. He hurries around his desk and tries to block my path. "You are my last appointment this morning. Allow me to take you to lunch so we can get better acquainted."

As he reaches for my hand, I fumble in my purse to retrieve my gloves and head for the door. "Thank you, but I'm busy today."

Mr. Whitaker follows close behind me. "Rain check? I would so love to take you to the Willows."

I pause, one hand on the doorknob. "The Willows?"

"Reno's most exclusive resort."

I have heard of the Willows, the glamorous resort on Verdi Road. I have read that it has become the most exclusive gambling house and speakeasy in all of Nevada. This is where ladies can gamble alongside men, whereas in Reno proper, only men are allowed at the gaming tables.

Why in the world would I ever want to visit the Willows? I loathe gambling in any form.

I close the door to the hallway, scurry to the far end, and fly down the stairs.

༄

That afternoon, Tessa, Flo, Madeline, and I sink back into our respective shampoo chairs and close our eyes. Is there anything more blissful than feeling warm water cascading over my scalp? The beautician, Serena, adds citrus-smelling shampoo and massages my head. Heaven!

Later, we each sit under a hair dryer, reading a glossy. A gripping *Hollywood* magazine story about Tallulah Bankhead's exploits captivates me. My attention is interrupted by the powerful perfume of a woman across from me who is having her hair brushed. She talks animatedly to her stylist. In the mirror, her makeup seems exaggerated, as if she is ready to go onstage. A Hollywood actress? Her fingers are covered with rings. Who is she? When she stands to leave, I admire her deep-rose-colored suit and mink boa. She tips the hairdresser and sashays to the front of the salon.

"Same time tomorrow, Miss Helen?" asks Violet.

"Same time," she sings as she blows a kiss.

Paying for my shampoo and set beside Tessa, I ask Violet, "Who is that woman in the pink suit? An actress, perhaps?"

Violet hesitates. "She goes by Miss Helen."

"Have I seen her at the cinema?"

"I don't think so, but she is one of the richest women in Reno. And also one of the most generous."

Outside the salon, I ask Tessa, "What did you think of Miss Helen?"

"I presume we have seen a member of 'the world's oldest profession.'"

I am struck dumb. Tessa is even more worldly than I imagined.

"Evelyn, a woman who is made up as if for the stage during the day . . . ," she says. "Skirt is a little too short. Bosom is a little too exposed." She quickly changes the subject. "Now that you're shampooed and curled, will we see you at the dance hall tonight?"

Madeline looks at me hopefully. Once again, I decline.

# CHAPTER 8

Later that night in my bed, in the half place between asleep and awake, I thrash to loosen myself from my twisted bedclothes. It is always the same dream. It takes me back to Hackensack on the day my mother lay dying.

I entered her bedroom, as I did so many mornings. Mother had been more tired recently, inclined to close her eyes and doze throughout the day. When I lifted the window shade, the sunshine spilled onto the pink flowers in the French hooked rug. There were neat stacks of bills and envelopes on the desk. A cloisonné fountain pen lay on the blotter, ready to take up its tasks. The scent of her favorite gardenia bath powder filled the air.

When I turned to my sleeping mother, her lips were blue, her breathing labored and irregular. One side of her face twitched.

I tried to wake her, jostling her shoulder. Sitting on the bed, I felt her forehead. In addition to the gardenia, there was a new, vile odor.

I screamed for Marion to call Dr. Ferguson. Sophie, our maid, entered, her brown hands clasped against her white apron. She sobbed as she took her hankie from her bosom and wiped her eyes. My daughter, June, about to leave for high school, came in with my husband. June clutched her father's hand.

Marion burst into the room while tying her bathrobe, her brown hair unpinned and flying in every direction. "I called Dr. Ferguson," she said, pacing back and forth, wringing her handkerchief.

Even though I often felt angry with my mother, I had accepted my lot and the rituals of our daily life. Ladies came to tea; the dressmaker, with pins in her mouth, knelt to take up our hems; and we went to church. I wasn't prepared for it to end.

She was demanding, but she was loving. When I thought of the losses she had endured, I suspected she had a backbone of steel. She knew I did some modeling, but we didn't discuss it. Was there a part of her that envied my moments of independence?

"She's still breathing," I said, "but she won't wake up." I brushed Mother's forehead with the backs of my fingers and kissed her cheek. I slid off the side of the bed onto my knees while clasping her hand.

Dr. Ferguson, who always smelled of pipe tobacco, came into the room. He listened to Mother's heart and took her pulse. He lifted each eyelid and frowned. He said she'd had a small seizure because of a cerebral hemorrhage.

Marion asked, "She *is* going to wake up, isn't she?"

Dr. Ferguson shrugged his shoulders and frowned.

"What can we do, Doctor?" Marion asked.

"You can pray."

Sophie began, "Our Father . . ."

The others intoned the Lord's Prayer, but grief and fear balled up in my throat. Mother and I had our conflicts, but she was the matriarch. She took care of us. Who would fill her shoes if she died? I glanced at my husband, thin and pale, motionless. His brown leather slippers showed the white cracks of age. It was clear that Dean didn't have the fortitude to pay bills, negotiate with the butcher, or initiate or reply to invitations. As I exhaled, my whole body shuddered. I would have to make the decisions now.

❦

This is where I always wake. Feeling the Reno night's chill, I uncoil my legs from the covers and reassemble the bedding. Shivering, I consider closing the windows but instead reach for the extra quilt at the foot of my bed. I have replayed my mother's final days so many times. They haunt me. How can I stop the dreams?

Today, Mother would condemn me for my actions, as Marion does. She forbade me to divorce Dean, and yet here I am. Mother did not live long enough to see my final breaking point—the deception that demanded I divorce him. Will there be some future retribution in store for me, a hand from the grave flogging me for my sin? *Oh, Mother, I can't tolerate my desolate marriage any longer. I will always conduct myself as the lady you raised me to be. I don't know my future, but my destiny will be my choice. I pray for your forgiveness.*

Rising from bed, I take in the view from the window of the desk alcove. As far as my eyes can see, up to the foothills of the Sierra Nevada, the desert is rugged, the vegetation haphazard—so unlike the manicured lawns back home. Aside from the cacti and sagebrush that dot the valley floor, nothing else grows. My marriage had become like this panorama—an arid wasteland. I would never develop or flower if I remained in it.

### Saturday, October 3, 1931

At breakfast, Beatrice talks nonstop about dancing at Belle's Barn on the Hall Ranch last night. To hear her tell it, she was the star on the dance floor. I had read all about Belle Livingstone, who after several run-ins with Prohibition agents in New York City, set up shop in Reno, much to the dismay of neighboring ranchers.

I have never danced in a barn and don't intend to try, but a tiny part of me catches Beatrice's enthusiasm. She is full of joy this morning. Perhaps it's not so disgraceful if one behaves like a lady.

I hope for a chat with Thistlena this morning, but she leaves the table halfway through the meal when Nat and Ray honk their car horn. In fact, she runs to the door, her pearl string swinging, as if being chased by dogs. What are they up to? She certainly spends a lot of time with them.

I go back to my room to prepare for my desert walk. All of a sudden, my breakfast whirls in my stomach, and I rush to the bathroom. I push my finger down my throat so I will vomit into the toilet bowl. Madeline opens the door and gasps. "Are you all right? Do you need a doctor?"

I insist I am fine. A slightly upset stomach.

# CHAPTER 9

Setting out on my morning walk—a daily habit I'm finding soothing as well as invigorating—with the requisite sunglasses and a wide-brimmed hat, I circle the ranch house, not letting it out of my sight, weaving around boulders and half-dead desert plants. The last thing I need is to get lost. I am also terrified of rattlesnakes, and I watch the ground for them. My shoes fill with sand. With all my planning, I hadn't considered what footwear would be appropriate for a ranch. Now I have something to shop for in Reno. I might have to "go western"—not cowgirl boots but something flatter with closed toes.

The mountains to the west pull my eyes like a magnet. They appear blurred in the distance, but their size and expanse are so foreign to what I have known in the East that I can't stop staring. There is always a wind here. Small twisters of dust pop up suddenly, move several yards, and then dissolve as quickly as they form. Will I ever get used to this parched landscape? Shivering, I fasten all the buttons on my Persian lamb jacket.

As I stand, mesmerized by the barren peaks, Thistlena and Gerry, one of the ranch cowboys, cross my path on horseback. I hold on to my hat as I look up at her on the horse. What a spectacle she is—imposing with her erect posture and handsome black velvet riding attire. How regal she appears! Not like Ramona, whose beauty is rugged. The planes of Thistlena's face are delicately chiseled, like the aristocrat she must be. I have had my share of approving glances, but everyone would notice this woman.

Both riders circle their horses around and face me.

"What a glorious place to ride," Thistlena says, her brown curls lifted off her shoulders by the wind. "Evelyn, you have to come! We've got so much space." She strokes the stallion's brown neck over his black mane. "Anytime here is a good sport to put up with this eastern-trained gal."

"That's why we call him Anytime," says Gerry. "He accepts all riders whenever he's called."

I can tell that Anytime is a real working horse but very handsome. He would measure up against any of those I rode at finishing school.

"Ray and Nat want to take us to lunch on Monday," Thistlena adds. "Madeline too. Told them we'll meet at the Grand Café on Second Street at twelve o'clock. You'll like it. It's a little off Virginia Street." With that, she turns her horse and canters off from whence she came.

Gerry kicks his horse. "C'mon, Sadie, we gotta keep up with that gal."

I sneeze from the desert dirt kicked up by the horses and feel annoyed. Thistlena doesn't ask if we *want* to have lunch with them. She demands it. What do she and her partners have up their sleeves? In the distance, the two riders withdraw farther into the hills, galloping hooves leaving clouds of dust.

Savannah puts bread, cheese, and fruit on the sideboard so we can help ourselves to a light lunch. We are admonished to drink lots of water, as the air here is so dry, and I concur. My jar of Pond's Cold Cream isn't going to last my stay.

Alone at the dining room table and munching on an apple, I contemplate Monday's meeting. On the one hand, I am peeved by Thistlena's insistence. She doesn't extend herself woman to woman the way I've become accustomed to, the way the women on the train shared confidences.

On the other hand, where is the harm in having lunch? Madeline will be with me, and we might learn something. We will keep it brief— we will say we have to rendezvous with Tessa. But, meanwhile, perhaps I will uncover more about this businesswoman from New York.

The rest of the day and Sunday were uneventful.

# CHAPTER 10

*Monday, October 5, 1931*

I hear a knock on my bedroom door. "Telegram for you, Miss Evelyn." Frightened out of my wits, I scramble out of my bed and grab my robe while my heart beats double time imagining what unwelcome news has come for me. The children, Charlie or June? Marion? I have given everyone my mailing address and phone number out here, but I have received no mail or calls. Who could possibly need to send me a telegram? I open my door, and Neppy, wearing worry on her face, hands me a Western Union envelope.

COUSIN ALICE DEAD. STOP. LEAVE RENO AT ONCE. STOP. MEET ME IN TOLEDO. STOP. FUNERAL ON FRIDAY. STOP. FAMILY COMES FIRST. STOP. MARION.

I pour a glass of water from the pitcher on my bureau and sit down on my bed to think. Neppy is still standing in my doorway.

"Bad news, Miss Evelyn?" she asks, her eyes wide with alarm.

"No . . . no," I stammer. "Not really."

Is Marion crazy? I feel sorry about Alice's passing, but I hardly knew her. Does Marion honestly think I am going to interrupt my residency here to attend the funeral of a cousin I have met once?

But wait a minute. How is this going to look in Toledo if I do not attend? Only Marion, my children, and a couple of close friends know about my trip out West. Mother and Father are gone now. Charlie and June are at college. That leaves Marion and me as first cousins, as family. My attorney emphasized that Reno's six-week residency requirement is just that—six weeks. No interruptions. After all, Ramona will have to swear an affidavit at the courthouse. That settles it.

I don't doubt that Alice died, but I know Marion sees this as a chance to sabotage my plans. This is further proof that she will do anything to divert me. Let *her* take the train to Toledo. If I decline to go— and I *will* decline—I wager that Marion won't make the trek by herself.

It would be different if Mother and Father were still alive and we were required to be present as a family. But I wouldn't be here if my parents had not passed. I hope Marion knows enough not to bother Charlie or June. I can imagine my anxious daughter's reaction to getting such a telegram. I will go to the Western Union office in Reno this morning and send my reply. I will have to word it carefully.

When I come downstairs for breakfast, all eyes turn to me. Palms up in protest, I assure everyone that no one important has died. "An older cousin whom I only met once," I say. The table is quiet—the only sounds are fork tines spearing hush puppies on stoneware plates. Perhaps the others are conjuring up who might send them telegrams. I prefer animated chatter, but my stomach turns summersaults while I try to hold my resolve against Marion's strike. Before heading into Reno, I feel compelled to bring up my meal over the toilet bowl.

Thistlena leads the way to the Grand Café on Second Street, the seams of her stockings as straight as rods, her firm calves kicking up the pleat at the back of her herringbone skirt. Madeline and I follow. Ray and Nat emerge from the restaurant to greet us. They remove their hats and shake our hands.

The café is a pleasant surprise. Though it has a dark-wood interior, it is brightly lit and uses crisp white linens. They say this is the "headquarters" for the Divorce Colony. A lady could do worse. It is what my mother would have called "very genteel." I smile at the agreeable surroundings while fighting the knowledge that I am lunching with strange men. Back in Hackensack, as an unmarried girl, I would have always been chaperoned by one or both parents. However, they're gone now. Perhaps I must reimagine myself as an independent businesswoman. I'd like to get used to that.

Now I take a longer look at Thistlena's business associates. Nat, the smaller and pudgier of the two, appears to be about forty. He wears an olive-toned poplin suit that complements his auburn hair. But that hair is so lacquered it looks artificial.

Ray is taller, leaner, and suntanned. He is dressed in a dark-blue suit, but I can easily imagine him on horseback. He has a lot of creases around his blue eyes, but he could be a couple of years younger than Nat. Are they what I would call refined? I can't be certain yet. There is something that makes me wary, but I can't dispute that they have perfected their social graces.

We are seated at a front window table, and Thistlena leads the conversation about insignificant things—the weather, her horseback ride, the crowds on Virginia Street. She appears enlivened by Ray and Nat's company, and her brown eyes sparkle. The men, too, are animated. Are they smitten with Miss Duncan? Well, who wouldn't be?

When our lunches arrive, Ray stretches his arms up and out to push back his jacket sleeves, revealing fine gold cuff links, and addresses us. "As you know, Thistlena, Nat, and I are business partners, and we want to tell you about an investment opportunity here in Reno. Many of the six-weekers have joined us in our venture."

Madeline and I put down our forks. Ray looks to Nat, who reaches beneath his chair to retrieve folders. He hands one to each of us. "This is a prospectus that describes the plans for our hotel and casino, Twin Arches."

Madeline opens her folder. My jaw is locked by the word *casino*, and I take a long drink of water.

Much to my surprise, my timid Madeline says, "Tell us more. What is your budget? Your timetable?"

I can't believe my ears. I nibble my chicken pot pie while my eyes dart between her and Nat, as if I am watching a tennis match. It turns out that Madeline's father worked in real estate in New York City. She continues to ask pointed questions.

Swiping his mustache with his index fingers, Ray says, "You've got to see our plans in person. When can we take you ladies to the building site?"

Golly, he's a fast mover. I jump in. "I would like some time to look over your materials."

"Any day works for me," says Madeline.

Ray's and Nat's eyebrows lift simultaneously over their broad smiles.

"It's not like we have anything else to do," says Madeline, searching my face.

I want to tell her that I have an aversion to gambling of any kind, but I must bide my time. I hope she reads a hint of my mistrust in my pinched mouth and squinting eyes.

"It goes without saying that we will pick you up at the Flying N, drive you to the site, and return you safely," says Nat. "Sometimes, we make several trips a day to the site. We're showing it all the time, aren't we, Thistlena?"

"All the time."

I am astonished. I assumed she was horseback riding. I know she isn't relaxing by the fire or shopping in town like the rest of us. I want to get to know her better, but she is always away. Now I know why.

"My family's never been much for real estate investments," I say.

Nat's pupils slide to Ray's. He is relaying an SOS.

"Miss Evelyn," says Ray, "have you looked around Reno? I mean, really looked?"

"Yes, yes," I reply, "the economy is strong here, but there are already many hotels and casinos."

"And the demand is growing," adds Nat. "Have you seen the crowds at night?"

I shake my head.

He regards Ray. "We must get these girls to a dance hall. Let them see how busy, how prosperous, the ballrooms are."

I pat my mouth with my napkin and take another drink. I am feeling the pressure of their sales pitch and need to hold my ground. "Why do you propose to build your hotel and casino on the outskirts of Reno when all of the activity is in town?"

"It's a question of space," says Thistlena. "There is no more room in town. And wait till you see the site. It's glorious." She draws out the *o* in "glorious." In puppetlike unison, Ray and Nat nod their agreement.

"We want to offer our guests all the amenities with lots of room," Ray says, sweeping out his arm.

Before returning to the ranch, I had reluctantly agreed to visit the Silver Slipper tonight. Ray and Nat had offered to escort "the Flying N girls"—Thistlena, Madeline, Beatrice, and me. It is flattering to be referred to as a girl. I live in fear of looking too old to continue modeling. I haven't made up my mind about the men yet, but I will be more comfortable having them along. Tomorrow, I will have been in Reno for a week, and time is already weighing heavily on my hands. So, after dinner, I will visit a real Reno dance hall for the first time. Will I ever tell Marion? Not ever!

The Silver Slipper is, indeed, elegant, much to our delight. Ray and Nat tip their hats, murmuring "Felix" to a mustachioed gentleman in a cutaway who is welcoming guests. After some indecipherable sign language from Felix, Ray and Nat lead us to our table. Though the dining room is dimly lit, the china, silver, and crystal reflect their high polish. Ray and Nat take our coats, and my eyes gradually adjust to the dark interior. I'm wearing an emerald-green silk sheath with a gathered bodice and long sleeves. I've learned that strong colors always flatter me.

I can't help eyeing the other patrons, noting glamorous dresses and high-fashion hats. I have intentionally left my important jewelry back in Hackensack, but I see that many of the six-weekers from the train are wearing exceptionally fine brooches, pins, and bracelets. Thistlena takes no notice of anyone else and in fact appears tired and uninterested. To her regular navy sheath and single strand of pearls, she has added a wide-brimmed straw hat that matches the color of her dress. The chandelier lights, though faint, reveal a shabby weave in her hat's crown. If it were mine, I would have tossed it long ago.

Nine o'clock is early by dance-hall standards, but it looks as if all the chairs are occupied. A waiter comes up to our group. Since we have already had supper at the Flying N, Ray selects some desserts and a cheese plate to taste. I order a lemonade.

The waiter snarls, "With or without gin?"

"Without."

"*With* gin," says Beatrice with a flick of her hand to fluff her curls.

Thistlena and Madeline indicate the same.

No doubt they think I'm a prude. Perhaps some will call me a lady, but I'm not stupid. I know that Prohibition doesn't allow the sale of alcohol, and that the government does little to enforce it. In New York City alone, there are tens of thousands of speakeasies. Surely Reno is no different. However, I come from an abstemious family, and drinking can lead to undesired outcomes. We kept a small bottle of brandy in the medicine cabinet "for medicinal purposes only," but that was all.

I watch many men and some women climb the stairs to the second floor. Ray follows my eyes and says, "They're going up to the gaming tables."

I can't help myself and grimace as if I've suddenly smelled a foul odor.

Ruby Alstead, dressed in fuchsia pink and holding her glass in the air, breezes up to our table. Beatrice rises to greet her, and they leave us, arms wrapped around each other's waists. Tessa, whom I scarcely recognize in her champagne silk sheath and long pearls, waves to us from the far end of the room. Grinning broadly, she pulls up a chair to join us, and several from her group—Margaret, Elena, and Abigail—stand behind her. Ray and Nat quickly locate a second table and move it next to ours. Our waiter brings extra chairs.

"The more the merrier," says Thistlena, suddenly perking up. Thistlena, Nat, and Ray make a point of reassigning seats, each sitting between Tessa's friends. Every six-weeker is a potential investor, I gather.

"The band is taking a break," Tessa says. "They're terrific. They sound like Paul Whiteman."

In this setting, Tessa is not the nondescript woman I met on the train. She has changed her hair and perhaps bought a new dress. Tonight she approaches glamorous, and I am a witness to her transformation. Maybe it is her newfound freedom, or her absence from an adulterous husband, that lights her face with such obvious elation. I envy her joie de vivre. What magic is in store for me?

It's too soon for me to adopt Tessa's high spirits. I've never been to a dance hall like this, and I don't know what to expect. Further, I still carry the burden of my marriage, my deceitful husband. It rests on my shoulders like a yoke. Do I also harbor some guilt?

Yes, to be sure. But I honestly believe I tried my best, and I kept trying until the fateful encounter at the Gramercy Park Hotel. I haven't yet shaken that massive millstone, but I'm on my way.

High-pitched laughter interrupts my musings. Turning around, I see Ruby and Beatrice in the corner with Smoky Joe and Gerry, all drinking champagne. It must be as Tessa says—free drinks in exchange for dancing with the gals.

The band members—eight in all—saunter to the stage, a raised platform with an upright piano, and retrieve their instruments. The musicians wear white shirts, western bolo ties, and cowboy boots. I wonder if these men are ranchers, cowboys, or full-time players. I fear enduring endless rounds of cowboy songs, but much to my delight, the band launches into another Paul Whiteman standard.

Marion and I were sent to dancing school in Hackensack, and I always enjoyed it. I loved the waltzes and foxtrots, played at an upright piano by an older lady whose upper arms flapped with the music. We changed partners with every new dance—monopolizing any one girl was frowned upon—and the boys were taught to bring us to the punch table, pour the beverage into a crystal cup, and hand it to us without spilling on our party dresses. The lessons were abandoned after eighth grade, but the dances continued right through high school and finishing school.

Someone taps my shoulder.

"Care to dance, miss?" a man young enough to be my son asks. I take a gulp of lemonade and stifle a giggle. Perhaps there is no harm in one dance. And this fellow is a child!

"I'm Larry," he says as he takes my hand.

"Evelyn." I have every intention of sticking with first names.

He is tall, sandy haired, and has a generous sprinkling of freckles across his cheeks and nose. He has tobacco-stained teeth, but he is scrubbed clean, smells of aftershave, and knows how to hold a lady for a dance. He compliments my footwork, and I blush. Soon the dance floor is very crowded, and one must step lightly or be stepped *on*. Over Larry's shoulder, I can see broad smiles on the faces of Tessa and Madeline, while Thistlena dances a little too closely to Ray. But they are business partners after all.

We are destined to enjoy more Whiteman standards as the band moves into a lively number. No sooner does the tune change than Larry is replaced by Smoky Joe from the Flying N. Relieved by a familiar face, I lower my chin to one side and flutter my eyelashes. He grins from ear to ear, gathers me in, and spins me out. I laugh despite myself. Before the set is over, I dance with three more cowboys and finish up with Ray Sessions.

We return to our tables and order more drinks all around. Thistlena is missing. Perhaps she is gambling.

I am beginning to understand the way of things here—keep the six-weekers dancing to keep them thirsty so they drink more. Judging by the boisterous merriment coming from Beatrice and Ruby across the room, the dance hall's approach is working.

Thistlena returns to the table looking ashen. Ray stands immediately and adjusts her chair. He offers her the drink he ordered, but she waves it away. "I'm a little overtired."

I'm not convinced. She appears sick. Conversation ceases while we avoid staring at her. I don't want to seem unconcerned and ask, "Glass of water?"

"I'll be fine," she insists and moves to the dance floor with Nat as the band takes up their instruments.

How I wish that Dean would have taken me out dancing. Several of our friends went to regular tea dances. But no—reading those darn plays was his idea of an evening's fun. And now here I am in Reno, dancing with cowboys I have not been properly introduced to. I have never had so much fun.

Another young man asks me to dance, and I rise to accompany him. This is enjoyable and perfectly innocent. A lady can get into all kinds of trouble if she looks for it, but I feel freer and more girlish than I have in years. Tessa is right—it's only a dance.

# CHAPTER 11

*Tuesday, October 6, 1931*

Halfway through dinner, the eeriest sound I have ever heard interrupts our conversations—a whirring that changes from a low moan to a higher-pitched screech. If I believed in ghosts, this is what I think they would sound like. We look anxiously at Arthur.

"Little Hawk," he roars, jumping up, "the windows!" The two men run out the back door, the four cowboys following.

"What's happening?" Beatrice asks Ramona, her eyes flashing panic.

"It's a dust storm," Ramona says. "The men will board up the windows so we don't lose them. Please go up to your rooms and shut yours tight. Neppy and I will help you." As she stands, she adds, "And there will be a lot of dust."

We scurry to our rooms and do as Ramona has directed. From my north window, I see a menacing cloud rise from the ground like a geyser and creep eastward. My whole body shudders as I fasten the window locks and draw the curtains. I put on my green sweater to fend off a new chill.

Back at the dinner table, we pick at our cold food in silence. Arthur, perspiration running from his sideburns, tells us the obvious—there will be no rides into town tonight.

The sound of hammering pounds on my nerves. Beatrice, the whites of her eyes as large as moons, wrings her hands.

Arthur glances at Ramona, who remains mute. Gerry, the range rider, comes into the dining room mopping his face with his bandanna. "All boards in place, boss."

"What about Thistlena?" I ask. She had been in town all afternoon.

Just then, Neppy returns to offer seconds of an Apple Brown Betty, and we all accept. I pray that Thistlena will be safe.

While getting ready for bed, the Brown Betty doesn't sit well in my stomach, and I retch into the toilet.

Madeline opens the bathroom door and frowns. "You don't have to do that, you know," she says. "You're very slender."

What does she mean by that?

"It wouldn't stay down." I lower myself to the edge of the tub and hang my head. "I feel so powerless. What's going to happen to us? Will this ranch blow apart?"

Madeline takes a washcloth, runs it under cool water, and presses it to my cheeks and forehead. "I know what it is to be gripped by fear. A little dust is nothing compared to the fists of my husband."

I have difficulty falling asleep—the wind roars for so long. *What am I doing here?* I have traveled so far to this strange place. I haven't even begun my second week of residency in Reno, and here I am, thrown into a dust storm. I have come to Reno with a purpose. Is this God's way of telling me I'm wrong, that I must go back?

The walls shake, and I fear this sturdy house might lift off its foundation. The endless blowing is, at times, interrupted by a crash of metal or a loud thump. A tree branch? Loose boards? I hide under my covers while my teeth chatter like a woodpecker. Exhausted, I finally drift off.

## Wednesday, October 7, 1931

This morning, dust coats my pillow. Still in my bed, I run my tongue over my teeth and taste something gritty. Have I actually swallowed dirt? I hold my breath and listen—not a sound. It seems that the whipping wind has died down at last, and I pray this is so.

As I sit up, I sense a fine coat of soil particles on my arms, on my face. I reach for the water pitcher and fill my glass. Relief, at least in my mouth. I tiptoe to the west window and open the curtains. A cloudless sapphire sky frames the mountains. As if nothing has changed, they appear large, rugged, and mighty. However, the landscape closer to the ranch is altered. Up against the outbuildings, the fence posts, and the cacti are white drifts of many heights, undulating in waves, like dunes at the seashore. The sunlight streaming through my window reveals my footprints in the dust that covers the floor. I reach into the armoire for a sweater set and skirt and shake them vigorously before putting them on.

The smell of frying bacon draws us to the dining room. Henry and Little Hawk have removed the boards from the front windows, and Madeline, Beatrice, and I confront a panorama of destruction. Everyone stares open mouthed at the chaos of tossed fence posts, wagons covered in blankets of sand, and tumbleweeds stacked against the barn. Smoky Joe, Zack, and Gerry are on horseback dragging the larger pieces of debris into a pile. Ramona, seated at the head of the dining table, is silent, her jaw rigid.

Arthur enters. Spurs on his boots jingle with his heavy footfalls. "I rode to the entrance and back, and everything's secure. There are drifts, but a horse can get through." He sinks into his chair at the other end of the table.

Our shoulders relax in unison. We fill our plates and sit down.

"Ramona and I have to drive the buckboard out and check on our herd after breakfast," says Arthur. "Any of you gals want to come along, you're welcome. Pass the potatoes, please." He heaps two spoonfuls onto his plate.

Lost in daydreams of dust, I chew slowly. How often do these storms come? If they are a frequent occurrence, I am going to be too afraid to venture back into town. I might get trapped there like Thistlena.

Helping Neppy clear the dishes, we are distracted by the sputter of a car motor outside. Thistlena and Candace Niven burst into the living room.

"As I live and breathe," says Beatrice coming out of the kitchen.

Thistlena, with nary a hair out of place and looking picture perfect in a taupe two-piece suit—*Is it new? I haven't seen it before*—and a pearl choker, introduces Candace all around. Thistlena could be a model. I'll have to ask her if she's ever walked the runway. Color has returned to her cheeks. Whatever ailed her the other night at the dance hall has passed.

Still in her journalist's uniform of a black jacket and pants, Candace sets down her large camera. She shakes hands like a man. Arthur invites them both to join us for breakfast. He also invites them to accompany us into the hills to check on some cattle.

Thistlena, it turns out, found shelter from the dust in the Grand Café, where she was having tea, as was Candace. They struck up a conversation, Thistlena hired Candace to photograph the hotel and casino project, and Candace offered to share her room at the Colonial Apartments. Those ladies didn't waste any time getting down to business.

"Is everything in town covered with dust too?" asks Madeline.

"Oh yes," says Candace. "Sidewalks are impassable, storefronts obscured. It's like a ghost town."

I feel the hairs on the back of my neck stand at attention, and pull my sweater closed.

"Well, I don't care," says Beatrice. "Dust or no dust, I need a shampoo and set. I feel like the entire Nevada desert has landed in my hair."

"No rides into town till tomorrow morning, ladies," Arthur says. "There will be few if any businesses open today."

Beatrice grimaces and brings one hand to her forehead in her overused gesture.

"The best thing to do after a storm like this is to go outside and brush your hair," says Ramona. "The breeze will carry away most of the dust."

As instructed, we fetch our hairbrushes. Five gals, including Neppy, bend over the front porch railing and brush furiously. Candace clicks her shutter while little puffs of grit float away. I deliberately turn to the side, avoiding her lens.

"C'mon, Evelyn," she barks. "I need all five of your faces."

I turn my back and retreat inside. "Not in this lifetime," I mumble to myself. The last thing I want is to be recognized by anyone anywhere.

The infernal dirt has seeped under doors, around the edges of windows, and through cracks in the walls. Ramona, Neppy, and Little Hawk set about changing our bed linens, dusting, and mopping as if there is nothing out of the ordinary. Arthur announces that we will depart to check the herd at ten o'clock.

As we ride north in a large wagon pulled by four horses, Little Hawk and the cowboys trot ahead of us on their own mounts. Neppy, in her dungarees and a cowgirl hat, sits up front between Arthur and Ramona, while the six-weekers plus Candace commandeer parallel bench seats in the back. I'm the only one still wearing a skirt. All the other women are in pants. I don't own any.

The way is bumpy and slow going, and we are thrown against one another. Arthur guides the horses, zigzagging around the largest drifts. The terrain is how I imagine the surface of the moon—gray white, pockmarked, and completely still. Perhaps not the moon after all—this is how the end of the world will look. Everyone in the wagon stares with their mouths open. We are speechless, and it puts me in mind of my arid and empty marriage. My loneliness was as suffocating as this desert vista.

Giant saguaros have toppled, and a few thorns stick out above their burial mounds. Wherever there are boulders, the sand heaps up against them like snow. Arthur stops for a moment so that Candace can photograph the desolation. Where have the birds gone? I can't even hear the buzzing of a fly, only the click of Candace's shutter.

The wagon continues to climb until we reach a plateau that backs up against steeper hills. Gnarled trees stand off to our left, sheltered from the west wind. Arthur says there is a stream beyond. We climb down, shake our limbs, and admire the cows. As I shed some of my anxiety, I think there is something very soothing about the cattle. They are gentle creatures, and I have seen plenty of them in New Jersey. My family has often enjoyed country drives on Saturdays, savoring the smells of newly mown hay and the freshness of the crisp, clean air.

The cowboys whoop and holler, interrupting my daydreams. Riding in and out of the trees, they slap their hats on their thighs. A few cows begin to emerge in twos and threes. Little Hawk throws down four bales of hay from behind the front seat. The cows trot toward the food.

"I want to check on the calves," Ramona says, jumping down. She walks easily among the livestock. I can't hear her words, but I imagine she is talking to them while she runs her hand down their long backs. Our eyes follow her. What is she searching for? Tall, erect, she peers into the trees, one hand shielding her face from the sun.

Thistlena says, "Doesn't she look as if she is carved from this rugged scenery?"

"I know what you mean," I say. "Neppy tells me she's half–Native American. If ever there was a face fashioned from this landscape, it would be hers."

Does Thistlena admire Ramona? I can't tell. I know I do. "I've never met anyone like her before," I whisper, "but even in the short time I've been here, I've marveled at her majesty. I don't know how else to explain it."

Ramona leaves the feeding cattle and walks into the stand of trees. The cowboys have disappeared, probably gone to water their horses at the stream. Suddenly, Ramona screams, "Arthur! Arthur!"

He runs toward her, followed by Candace and her tripod.

"Two down," shouts Gerry from the edge of the trees.

"Bring 'em out," Arthur calls, still running.

Smoky Joe and Zack emerge from the trees, each with a dead calf draped across his saddle. Candace almost dances as she photographs up close and then backs up for a wider shot. Thistlena shakes her head, her face full of anguish, while Madeline and Beatrice sniff and wipe their tears. Anger simmers at the back of my throat. Candace will make headlines from these poor ranchers' misfortune. I want to slap her. I have always been sympathetic to anyone enduring hardship. I probably learned this from the women in my church. Everything we do benefits those less fortunate. We fold receiving blankets for poor women with newborns, we prepare meals for anyone who is sick at home or just returning from the hospital, and we collect toys for underprivileged children at Christmas. Now, during this depression, we prepare great vats of soup on Fridays for anyone who needs it. No journalists ever write about these efforts. It's what Christians do.

"If we leave the dead calves up here, we'll attract the big cats for sure," Arthur says as he climbs into the driver's seat. Swiping at tears, Ramona joins him, her face blank as stone. Sighing and gazing at Arthur, she asks, "How can we replenish our herd if we keep losing half of our spring calves?"

Candace asks questions about the size of the herd, how many they will take to market for slaughter, and how many they will keep back, while the rest of us bump along in silence. Knowing she wants photos of the ranch that include the six-weekers, I race back to my room as soon as the wagon reaches the house. Reflecting on the morning, I realize I have observed the hardships of ranching life firsthand. To grow their small herd, the Anselms count on those new calves. With the price of beef at a record low this year, can they make ends meet? No wonder they rent out their guest rooms.

# WEEK TWO

# CHAPTER 12

*Friday, October 9, 1931*

Beatrice, Madeline, and I have agreed to visit the development site for Twin Arches. I'm still resistant to the idea, but not wanting to be perceived as a naysayer, I consented to come along for the ride.

Thistlena watches for the men from the bottom of the porch steps while I peer from behind a curtain in the living room. Nat and Ray pull up in their Ford Model T, a large cloud of exhaust in its wake, and jump out. Thistlena greets them both with a handshake and a quick peck on the cheek. Is there a romance with one of these men? Or is it strictly business? Doubts and questions keep tumbling over in my brain. *Evelyn, put a rest to your concerns,* I admonish myself. *You are only going to have a look.*

In her perennial navy-blue sheath and single strand of pearls, Thistlena skips up the steps and calls us to get in the car. Ray drives while Nat describes the fixups they made at the building site after the dust storm. Thistlena sits between the two, her eyelids closed, while Madeline asks questions about their construction timetable. I am worried about Thistlena. Perhaps this business venture is overtaxing her strength. Her clothes hang more loosely than they did when I first met her.

Nat hands us a list of current investors. There are thirty-four account numbers—no names. Anyone can make up a list of numbers.

How do we know they are real? I fold my papers and put them in my bag.

I try to initiate conversation about Nat's and Ray's lives back in New York, but they keep changing the subject to Twin Arches. Unlike the six-weekers on the train, they do not volunteer marriage war stories either. Neither one wears a wedding ring, but then again, hardly anyone does in Reno. Instead, conversation focuses on the many opportunities to make money in Nevada.

They promised a thirty-minute car ride. We have already been bouncing over the desert for an hour, kicking up dust and scaring jack-rabbits, while the Sierra Nevada mountains dominate our view to the west. Who wants to stay in a hotel so far out of town? I tap my fingers on my purse, cross and uncross my legs. Madeline, sitting primly with her hands in her lap, asks, "You're not going to show us some dried-up old gold mine, are you, gentlemen?"

Ray laughs. "Yeah, there's still some gold around here if you want to pan for it."

"All you need is twenty years," Nat adds with a chuckle.

"Actually," I say, "gold's been rather good to my family lately."

From the rearview mirror, I notice Ray's eyes dart to Nat's. Maybe I shouldn't have said that. I don't want these men assuming I'm wealthy. But I also don't want them thinking I'm a pushover. I might be a new-comer to the frontier, but I'm not ignorant about investments. And thanks to my parents' canny buying of mining stocks, my net worth is going up.

After the seemingly endless empty desert, Ray makes a sharp right turn under one of two man-made stone arches and proceeds along a wide paved road with large buildings in various stages of construction on both sides. Ray stops in front of a low, U-shaped building in a courtyard at the end.

Nat hurries to open the rear doors, and we tumble out. I turn in a full circle. Discounting some spiny scrub and dust devils, Twin Arches appears to be a large development, albeit far from complete.

Thistlena takes my and Beatrice's elbows and leads us into the U-shaped building. The others follow. "This used to be the second-largest ranch in Nevada. But a fire destroyed everything. The family resettled in San Francisco and sold the property."

The stucco building is empty, without flooring, but each wing has a tall stone fireplace. They remind me of the one in the Flying N's living room, except these stones are covered with black soot. Large windows in each western wall face the Sierras.

"There's only one way to face in Reno, and that's west toward the mountains," she adds.

Looking west, I see a sliver of moon on the horizon, but I don't see this remote location as a romantic getaway.

Nat and Ray lead us to each building in turn while Madeline plies them with questions about their plans—number of guest rooms, staff quarters, barns for saddle horses, gaming rooms, ballrooms, and more. It's clear that she knows a great deal about real estate development. On the other hand, there are no construction vehicles, no building supplies, and no workmen. Has the project come to a standstill?

"When we have enough investors," Ray explains, "the bank will give us construction loans to finish the job."

Returning outside, I ask, "So there is no construction at the moment?"

"That's correct," says Thistlena. "We will resume when we have our investors. And more are coming on board all the time." She looks to Ray and Nat, who bob their heads like roosters.

"You built it this far and then ran out of funds?" asks Madeline. She isn't wasting any time, our Madeline.

Ray clears his throat. "No," he begins, then coughs again. "The people who bought the property from the original owners built this. They defaulted in '29. We picked it up for a song."

"That's the way it's done," says Madeline.

Beatrice and I look at one another, as if to say, *You may have gotten it for a song, but what did you get?* In front of us is a half-finished hotel.

"Ladies, this is *such* an opportunity," says Thistlena.

Beatrice, much to my surprise, saunters over to Nat, takes his arm, and asks, "Is it an opportunity for me?"

"There is a precedent for this," says Thistlena, "right in town. You've heard of the Deauville Casino and Cabaret?"

We three shake our heads.

"It's set up like a corporation," says Thistlena, "and they're selling shares." Now looking at Nat and Ray, she adds, "We have to take them there."

Nat and Ray nod in agreement. "It's named after the town in northwestern France," Ray says, pushing out his chest.

The mouths of Madeline and Beatrice form perfect O's, so impressed are they by the mention of France. I have traveled there and know of Deauville, but I keep quiet. In fact, my mother took me and June to Europe last summer. We sailed from New York to Southampton, England.

"Anyway," Thistlena presses, "that's the way Twin Arches is organized. Our investors are shareholders."

A breeze comes up, scattering small rocks across the ground. I lift first one foot and then the other to avoid being struck. Suddenly I am doing a little jig. Surely these stones are sending me a message: run—don't walk—from this project. Holding my hat in place, I scurry toward the car, telling Thistlena, "My family doesn't do real estate."

"Oh, Evelyn," Thistlena says, running after me, "you must see the design drawings. They're fantastic. I can envision the hotel filled with tourists—six-weekers as well as many others." She clenches her eyes shut and turns in a circle, arms outstretched like an ebullient child.

I resolve to talk to her privately about why she is so keen on this project.

"And the casino, Thistlena," Nat says, catching up to us. "Don't forget the hotel's casino."

That fact alone confirms my lack of interest. During our jerky ride back to the ranch, Madeline, Thistlena, and I are silent, our eyelids drooping onto our cheeks. My throat is parched, and I am exhausted, grimy, and hungry. I am much more interested in the hot bath and tasty supper waiting for me at the Flying N than the Twin Arches project.

Stepping into the ranch's living room, I always check the desk to see if there is a letter addressed to me. None today, and none on any other day so far. I would so love to hear from Charlie and June.

All of us six-weekers accept Arthur's ride into Reno that evening. As soon as he stops the car on Virginia Street, Beatrice runs to join Ruby in front of the Deauville. Teetering on heels too high, Beatrice glitters from behind many pieces of rhinestone jewelry. Ruby wears a tight red sheath and a hat with a long green feather that winds around the cap, then rises jauntily at the back. As the rest of us approach, Thistlena whispers to me, "When birds spread their feathers like that, isn't it a mating dance?"

Ruby pauses before entering the Deauville and laughs. "I hope so."

Thistlena and I suck in a breath at the same moment and raise our eyebrows. *Oops! She heard us!*

Thistlena, Madeline, and I stroll along First Street wearing coats over our dresses. It is a beautiful evening, though cool, with the indigo sky full of stars and the same crescent moon. My apprehension still clings to me, but like that moon, it is waning. I take comfort in reminding myself that there is safety in numbers and that I will be with my friends. After all, I survived my first night in a dance hall. I hope there will be more harmless fun tonight.

As we return to the Deauville's entrance, the door is opened by a tall, sunbrowned cowboy who looks familiar, but he isn't from the Flying N. On seeing me, he smiles broadly and tips his hat. "Save a dance for me?" he asks.

Have I danced with him before? I guess not, as he is so handsome that I would remember. He certainly missed his chance in Hollywood—a Lew Ayres look-alike with prominent cheekbones—and

I am tickled that he shows interest in me. "I'll try to fit you in," I say, suddenly feeling flirtatious. Inside, the cowboy helps me remove my coat and whistles when he sees my fuchsia shirtwaist with a silver belt and matching shoes.

"Is my face red?" I whisper to Thistlena.

"Like an apple."

Madeline and I head for the ladies' lounge while Thistlena searches for an empty table near the dance floor. As we enter the lounge, Madeline and I shield our eyes against the bright lights surrounding the mirrors. Tall vases hold colorful peacock feathers, and the sofas are covered in red velvet. The air is strongly scented—jasmine, perhaps? I hope it isn't to disguise something unpleasant. Women talk quietly in small groups and eye one another's attire while waiting their turns to use the toilet facilities. Jewels sparkle, cheeks blush, and shimmery fabrics swish against silk stockings. I'm learning that the six-weekers dress to the nines for the dance halls.

As I sit on a chair powdering my nose, another woman chooses the seat next to me. She opens her silver-beaded evening bag and attempts to apply face powder. Her wide-brimmed hat slopes down in front, covering at least half of her face. I can't help but steal looks at her in the mirror.

She heaves a sigh and removes her hat. Viewing her entire face and blond hair, I realize I am sitting next to Mary Pickford. I saw her Academy Award–winning performance in *Coquette* a couple of years earlier, and today her hair is still styled in a 1920s bob. *Is she here with Douglas Fairbanks? I can't believe it—I'm sitting next to Mary Pickford!* Pretending to be busy reapplying my makeup, I try not to stare. I read in some Hollywood magazine that Fairbanks is a womanizer and that they had separated, but I know better than to believe what I read under the hair dryer at the beauty salon. And yet here she is in Reno.

Miss Pickford returns her makeup to her evening bag, and we stand up at the same time. While she replaces her hat, I whisper, "I can't resist telling you how much I admired your role in *Coquette*."

"Oh," she says, surprised, "that's very nice. Thank you." She walks to the door, her blue taffeta dress reflecting the light.

"Imagine," I say to Madeline, "Mary Pickford!"

I can't wait to tell Tessa. When Mary came to Nevada in 1920, the residency requirement to secure a divorce was six months. Reading about Pickford's sojourn to the small town of Minden, Nevada, to divorce her husband first planted in my mind the idea of coming here. Eleven years ago, in 1920—I was only twenty-eight—the thought of escaping my marriage had already crossed my mind. My children were only in grammar school then and so needed my full attention, but Dean was already under a cloud of defeat. I used to look at the classified ads in the back of women's magazines, where Reno stores and other businesses advertised for workers. "Work at Burke and Short while you get your divorce in Reno." Six months was a long time to simply stay in Reno. Many divorce seekers needed to work. I would not have been able to commit to that length of time. Thank goodness the Nevada Legislature reduced the requisite stay to six weeks.

As we turn to make our way to the dance floor, I notice Mary Pickford at the top of the stairs leading to the second floor. Two gentlemen in black suits come forward to escort her into the gaming room. My earlier research taught me that moral crusaders had petitioned the Nevada Legislature in 1903 to confine gambling to the second floor of any establishment. Obviously, this casino is a holdover from that time.

"Evelyn? Evelyn Henderson?" says a woman with brown curls peeking from the bell-shaped crown of her pink hat.

I freeze. My worst nightmare. Gwyneth Armstrong, a notorious gossipmonger from Hackensack, recognizes me. Most women back home avoid speaking to her for fear of vicious defamation. I look toward our table but feel her eyes penetrate me.

"What are *you* doing here?" she asks.

"Gwyneth, allow me to introduce my friend Madeline Abel."

Madeline senses that I need a shield. She stands close to me while she shakes hands.

"I ask you again, Evelyn, what are you doing in Reno?"

"Same errand as you, I imagine." I pull Madeline toward the others.

Gwyneth raises her hand as if interrupted midsentence, but I say, "Toodle-oo," and wiggle my fingers goodbye. I can hear my heart pounding. Now that Gwyneth has seen me, all of Hackensack will soon know that I'm here. Of all my acquaintances back home, her conversation is the most malicious. She will slander us both for certain, and I will be smeared on account of my association with her.

"You look as if you've seen a ghost," says Thistlena.

"Worse."

Tessa, Ray, and Nat join Thistlena, Madeline, and me at a table. While I fan my face with a napkin, they comment on Tessa's new costume, a smashing sky-blue dress with the latest longer skirt and box pleats. Wearing a Garbo-like fedora, she twirls her long, knotted pearls and flutters her freshly manicured hands. This is no longer the colorless woman in gray who sat next to me on the train. Reno is certainly having an effect on Tessa.

The Hollywood-handsome cowboy who greeted us at the door appears at my side. "Sundown Ahrens," he says with a twinkle in his eye. Sundown is accompanied by another man, slightly shorter but also good looking.

I offer my hand. "Evelyn Henderson." In my flustered state, thanks to Gwyneth, I reveal my last name.

"My friend Johnnie Wiggins would like to meet the lady in blue," he says.

Johnnie tips his cowboy hat. I can't get used to men keeping their hats on indoors, but at least this way I can tell the difference between a wrangler and a gambler.

"That can be arranged." I wink, walk around the table to Tessa, and wait while she talks intensely to Nat and Ray. She must be their latest prospect for the casino investment.

I tap Tessa's shoulder. "Excuse me," I whisper. "This is Johnnie. I suspect he'd like to ask you to dance."

Johnnie blushes but steps forward and offers his hand.

"Delighted," Tessa says while lowering her eyelids.

As Johnnie and Sundown pull us onto the dance floor, I observe Thistlena bent toward Nat and Ray. The angle of her frown and creases in her forehead make me think this is not a friendly tête-à-tête. I hear Ray snap, "We don't have a lot of time!"

Sundown is a graceful dancer. He holds me close, and I breathe in his aftershave. As he turns me out under his arm, I giggle despite myself. Everyone seated at the tables is watching us. When the song ends, Sundown dips me low. My eyes must reveal my surprise. On bringing me back up, he kisses me on the mouth. Part of me wants to slap his face, but he flings me out to his right and bows. I take his cue and make an exaggerated curtsy. Everyone applauds, and I overhear whispers.

"From Hollywood?"

"Professional dancers?"

"I'm certain I've seen her in pictures."

I'm getting the sense that everyone in Reno is obsessed with celebrities. Well, I've already spoken to Mary Pickford.

The band starts up again, and another cowboy—tall, slender, dressed in black, with a roguish grin—taps Sundown on the shoulder and says, "May I?" Before I can protest, I am whirled away to the strains of a western song.

"Good evening, ma'am," he says. "Guy Robinson at your service."

Another cowboy cuts in. He is no taller than me, with red hair and a herd of freckles splashed across his sunburned face. The redhead turns out to be only one among a stag line of fellas who are doing their best to keep all the women thirsty. I see Sundown from the corner of my eye and mouth, "Help!" He laughs and thankfully comes to my rescue, then brings me back to our table. I fan my moist face with my gloves, tools completely inadequate for the job.

He laughs again and says, "Don't worry. I've spread the word. You're sitting this one out." He waves over the waiter so that I can order another lemonade, and I wonder what special hand signals these cowboys use to lay claim to six-weekers.

Meanwhile, the band launches into a Charleston rag, and Tessa and Johnnie command everyone's attention as she jiggles her hands and kicks her feet. Even Madeline, off to the side, is giving a lesson to the redheaded cowboy. Her face is flushed as she turns in a circle and taps her heels with her hands like a flapper. Sundown, too, is smiling from ear to ear. Again, Tessa was right—it's only a dance, or two, or three. I haven't felt this gay *ever*.

Could there be people in Hackensack who go out dancing? Certainly not any of the people I know. Certainly not from the Dutch Reformed Church. Maybe I've been confined to a moral straitjacket. One thing I know—I'm breathing new, fresh air tonight, and it's exhilarating.

Tessa interrupts my musings. "C'mon, Evelyn," she says, blotting her face with her hankie. "I need the ladies' lounge."

I follow her, but she chooses to climb the stairs rather than return to the facilities on the first floor. "Why are we going upstairs?" I ask.

"It's much less crowded up here, and it's fun to peek into the different gambling rooms."

Would we find Mary Pickford in one of those rooms with other actors? Why would anyone in their right mind throw money away? Yes, I hear the occasional shout when someone wins their round, but it doesn't happen often. Even I know that all the odds are stacked in favor of the house.

Straight ahead at the top of the stairs is a large room with crystal chandeliers, but all I see are the backs of many men wearing eastern suits. I hear a commotion. Standing on tiptoes, Tessa tries to determine what they are watching. She waves me forward until I stand beside her. The odors of tobacco and liquor assault my nose, and I tug her wrist in a move to leave. She breaks from my grip and leans her ear toward the center of the room. A loud crash shakes the floor. Tessa and I back up flat against the wall. A waiter with a tray of drinks crosses the room's threshold as two of the biggest brutes I've ever seen collide with him while they carry another man by his elbows. The man, whose legs churn as if he is running in the air, shouts, "I rolled it! I rolled it! The pot is mine!"

"Not with those slick dice of yours," shouts one of the men.

The waiter bends to the floor to retrieve the glass pieces while the gamers grouse to one another. I cover my face with my hands and hear what can only be the sounds of fists connecting with faces and the resulting *ugh*s as bodies topple. Wood splinters as a chair comes crashing down over someone's skull. I move left in time to avoid a head of curly black hair charging at me like a bull. He strikes the wall head-on and slumps to the floor.

Panting in terror, I whisper, "Tessa, I'm leaving!" I search for an opening, but the crush of bodies going out the door leaves me no escape.

"Don't you want to see who the players are?"

"Playing at what?"

"I'm pretty sure it was a game of craps—throwing dice—and we can assume the stakes were very high."

I recognize the hat coming toward me. Mary Pickford walks nonchalantly, flanked by two louts in black suits and another woman—this one dressed in sapphire blue with jewels that look like real diamonds around her neck. I can't place her from the silver screen.

"Miss Pickford," I say, surprised by my audacity. "Are you all right? What happened?"

She stops, and then there's a moment of recognition. "Crime doesn't pay, ladies. Crime doesn't pay." The two men hurry Mary and a friend through the door while my heart continues to race. The last of the gamblers trickle out of the room.

"Was that . . . ?" Tessa whispers.

I nod, close my eyes to inhale, and take her by the hand to lead her to the downstairs ladies' lounge.

"Where have you girls been?" asks Sundown, rising from his chair. "We were going to send out a search party."

Sinking into my seat, I say, "I need a drink, a *real* drink." Sundown leaves to get our beverages. While I try to regain my composure, I am forced to conclude that Reno is a violent place. First dust storms, then upturned tables and flying fists. A person can get seriously hurt in a casino. Maybe coming to Reno was a dangerous mistake. From now on, I will have to be extra vigilant. And, furthermore, I will leave the construction of one of these places to Thistlena, Nat, and Ray. It certainly isn't for me.

Back at the Flying N, safe and sound, I review the evening. As shaken as I was by Gwyneth Armstrong's recognizing me, subsequent distractions made me forget her intrusion. But now, in this time of quiet reflection, I realize I have yet another person in Reno to avoid—first Candace and her camera, now Gwyneth.

After my six weeks are done, I will never have to see Candace again, but avoiding Gwyneth in Hackensack will provide another challenge. According to my sister, Marion, I have already sullied my reputation by coming to Reno. What else will Gwyneth do to tarnish my name at home?

I try to recall what I know about Gwyneth, her marriage, her family. Our paths have crossed in meetings of the Ladies' Aid. On those occasions, she appeared friendless. Her reputation as a malicious gossip must be well known.

I vow never to be without my disguise—my sunglasses—either in Reno or in New Jersey.

# CHAPTER 13

*Saturday, October 10, 1931*

This afternoon, I am reading by the fire in the living room. *Shadows on the Rock*, by Willa Cather, falls on my chest as I doze. Someone jiggles my shoulder, and I wake to find Thistlena leaning over me, her face scrunched up in worry. "Evelyn," she whispers, "I need to speak to you."

"Of course." I stand and start to pull over a nearby chair.

She stops me. "No, please come with me to my room."

I have been hoping for an opportunity to bond with Thistlena. Perhaps her need at this moment will hasten an attachment. Thistlena's hands tremble while she twists a handkerchief. I leave my book on the couch and follow her to her bedroom. She offers me the only seat, a squeaky rocker, and sits on the edge of her bed. Wiping her palms on her skirt, she clears her throat.

"I need your help," she says. Her eyes well up, and she swipes them with her hands.

"What's wrong?" I ask.

"I'm pregnant." She covers her face.

My arched eyebrows betray my shock. I think immediately of Ray and Nat. One of them must be the father. "Are you certain?" I ask.

"Very certain," she says, as tears run down her cheeks. "I'm so nauseous I can barely keep any food down." Come to think of it, lately she barely touched Savannah's tasty meals. And there was her nausea at the dance hall on Monday night.

I phrase my next question very carefully. "Have you told the father?"

"Heavens, no." She retrieves a new handkerchief from the top of her bureau and begins to pace as she blows her nose. Her blouse is untucked in back, her stocking seams askew. "My husband is the father. My soon-to-be *ex*-husband."

She must see my stunned face.

"I have no intention of telling Peter. He would insist I stop the divorce. Oh, Evelyn"—she sobs—"I need an abortion."

I gasp. She isn't thinking clearly. This predicament has caused her to become irrational.

"I'm sorry," she says, collapsing again on the edge of her bed. "I have no right to burden you with my troubles."

I want to get to know Thistlena better. I have more in common with her than the others, but she is always away from the ranch with Nat and Ray. Even when we are together in the cafés and dance halls, we are not. She is always talking to possible buyers. I am grateful she has chosen to reveal her secret to me, but an abortion is completely out of the question. I come to her side and put my arm around her, struggling to find the right words. "Tell me what happened," I say.

She and Peter Duncan were unable to have children. Medical tests showed the fault lay with him, not her, but they accepted their fate and became devoted aunt and uncle to many nieces and nephews. The marriage thrived until they lost their entire life savings in the stock market crash. The risky investments Peter had made became worthless. "He became *despicable*," she says.

It suddenly occurs to me why Thistlena is so driven to sell shares of the hotel and casino project. If she is penniless, she no doubt hopes to recoup her losses by attracting investors to the venture.

"Peter handled our investments, and he always assured me everything was fine. His deceit was the last straw," she says.

I take her hands and search her face. "But, Thistlena, a child is something you have always wanted. A child is a blessing. Peter deserves to know. You must reconsider your divorce."

"Never!" she shouts. "He betrayed me, Evelyn. He assured me everything we had was safe. Do you know what it's like to have a federal marshal show up and confiscate your car and furniture, even your fur coat?" Thistlena looks off into the distance as another tear falls from one eye.

"Peter stood on the sidewalk, his hands in his pockets as if he were out for a stroll. The deputies loaded our furnishings into a van while all our neighbors and friends watched. I cried my eyes out. Afterward, no one would speak to us. I have never felt such shame. A curtain of disgrace came down that day, and my heart froze. I took the train to my sister's in New Rochelle and never saw Peter again."

I feel instant recognition. I didn't watch my belongings get carted away to pay my debts, but I did oversee three sweaty, unshaven men empty our home in Lawrenceville and unload our possessions into the basement of my parents' home in Hackensack. Neighbors in both locations observed our humiliation. The hairs on the back of my neck rise up as I feel again the stigma of "fired" and "unemployed."

Thistlena's sister must have helped her financially. Otherwise, she wouldn't have been able to afford the trip to Reno. And Arthur had said she arrived by plane. There are missing pieces in her story—Nat and Ray and Twin Arches. I hope she will continue to confide in me. I will try my best to help her get through this.

*Okay,* I conclude, *Thistlena is going to go ahead with the divorce. So together we must find a solution.* I sit down beside her and rub her back while she weeps. "I'm so sorry," I whisper. "I'm so sorry."

She looks at me, her eyes red, her cheeks haggard and blotchy. "I've learned where to go to get rid of the problem. She's a Native American. And I have the cash."

I stand and back away. "Thistlena," I say in a loud whisper, "you *can't* be serious. Abortion is illegal."

Thistlena feels betrayed by Peter. No, she certainly can't remain married to such a scoundrel. But an abortion? I can't be a part of anything so dangerous. I want to help her. I *will* help her, but Thistlena will have this baby and either keep it or give it up for adoption.

"I have it on good authority that the Native American woman is very capable," Thistlena says, ignoring my reaction. "The women she has helped have been okay. I'm told I'll be uncomfortable for a day or two. But, Evelyn, I can't face this alone. Say you'll come with me."

It is my turn to pace. I am rendered dizzy from what she is asking. I want to comfort her, but accompany her on a devil's errand? Never. I plant my feet in front of her and place my hands on her shoulders. "Thistlena, stop. You must find someone else. I can't be an accessory to this."

She lifts her face to meet my eyes. Her despondency calls to mind a dead tree, gnarled and stripped of hope, but I also glimpse something else—steely rage. At me? At herself? At Peter?

"Who can I ask?" she says. "Madeline? She's more nervous than a bird. Beatrice? She would faint at the mere mention. Neppy? She's a child."

"Perhaps Ramona?" I suggest.

Thistlena straightens her back and sweeps her skirt as if dusting off sand. "Evelyn, I chose you because I can see you're strong, but I can see I've made a mistake. I'll have to find someone else." She walks to the door and opens it.

I follow her and push the door closed. "There's another solution we haven't talked about."

Her mouth twisted with doubt, Thistlena stands mute.

"Carry this baby and deliver it, as God intended. Raise it as your own or give it to a couple who yearn to be parents. My two children mean everything to me, despite their disappointing father. You and Peter must have considered adoption yourselves. Did you?"

"That was so long ago. I'm too old for this now. It's out of the question." She reaches beyond me and forces the bedroom door open. The clanging of the dinner bell ends our conversation.

As I descend the stairs to the living room, I review some of the confessions I heard in Hackensack. My hometown friends had uttered some startling revelations—about their own infidelities, their disappointments in the bedroom, their profound relief upon learning they were not pregnant. So, too, had the women on the train, but no one has ever asked me to attend an abortion. My only exposure to abortions is from the headlines—a doctor arrested for performing them or a woman dying after using a coat hanger. Encounters like the one I just had with Thistlena cause me, once again, to rethink this six-week residency. Perhaps there is a way to manage a divorce in New Jersey. This is all too much.

# CHAPTER 14

***Sunday, October 11, 1931***

After a restless night, I wake early, hungry enough to eat a horse. The weather has turned colder, and I find frost crystals on the inside of my windows. The aroma of strong coffee draws me into my warmest sweater and skirt and downstairs to the kitchen, even though I know it is still an hour before breakfast. Coffee will do the trick until Savannah puts out the eggs and all the rest.

I find Little Hawk adding more logs to the fireplace, the dry wood crackling as the flames leap higher and higher. For a small man, he is exceptionally strong. The muscles of his forearms bulge below his rolled-up denim sleeves. His black hair shines in the firelight, and I think, *Yes, he was born of this place.*

Instead of Savannah, Arthur and Ramona are busy in the kitchen. "Good morning," I say, poking my head in. "I know I'm early. Any chance of a cup of your special Flying N coffee?"

Ramona, her hands covered in flour from rolling biscuits, lifts the large pot from the cast-iron stove and pours me a cup. Arthur, already in his cowboy hat and denim from head to toe, is cracking eggs into a large bowl. "Damn," he says when one falls onto the floor.

He sees my automatic frown. "Excuse me, Miss Evelyn. Savannah is under the weather this morning." I can't read the knowing look he gives Ramona.

"Let me do that," I say, stepping into the kitchen. "I'd like to help."

"Give her an apron," says Ramona.

Tying an oversize white cloth around me, Arthur says, "I'll leave you two gals to it, then." The scrape of his cowboy boots stops abruptly after he steps outside onto the desert ground. The backroom door slams shut.

I resume breaking a dozen eggs into the earthenware bowl and add the freshly chopped thyme and parsley that have been set out. Ramona leans over to place a large tray of biscuits into the oven. She sweeps stray pieces of hair from her face, leaving spots of flour on her cheeks.

"How did you come to employ Savannah?" I take up the grater and a block of white cheese.

Ramona looks off into space. "Arthur found her walking along the train tracks."

"Where had she come from?"

"Don't know."

"I couldn't help noticing that long scar on her left cheek."

Ramona offers no explanation. We work in congenial silence.

"When Arthur found Savannah, she looked hungry and tired," Ramona finally says, "but she asked him if he needed any help at home. We had lost our cook."

I nod, determined not to press her for information, letting her take her time.

"Arthur asked her if she could prepare breakfasts and dinners, and she said she could. And so he brought her home. That was three years ago."

"If Savannah is sick this morning, should I prepare her a breakfast tray?" I ask.

Ramona stares at me as if I'm deranged. After retrieving half-baked potatoes from the oven, she continues. "Every once in a while, Savannah says the demons come and find her. When that happens, she has to lie low for a couple of days."

Arthur's boots sound again on the dining room floor. He pops his head into the kitchen and puts three empty liquor bottles into the trash bin. "Savannah's demons," he says, and then retreats.

"She always comes around again, though," Ramona adds as she brings me a box of fresh oranges and the juice squeezer. "Know how to use one of these?"

"I do indeed," I say as I cut an orange and put a half to the pressing mechanism. Ramona begins slicing bananas. "I'd say there's a special place in heaven for the likes of Arthur and Ramona Anselm. You help people. I bet Little Hawk has a story like Savannah's."

"It's our way of life. Arthur's people were homesteaders. Came out here with nothing and built a successful ranch. Neighbors lean on each other here. We have to."

As I push the squeezer, I recall our neighbors in Hackensack. We always paid attention to our behavior so that they wouldn't think less of us. Growing up, we were drilled in the etiquette of how to address our elders, like through those punch-serving lessons at dancing school. There was a right way, and a wrong way, to do everything.

Are all our motivations in the East superficial? To live in a civilized society requires certain standards of behavior, but I can't help thinking that the western pioneers are to be much admired for the society they have built. They must sacrifice appearances for survival, and so they take care of one another and reserve judgment.

Neppy bursts into the kitchen and grabs her apron from a hook. "Miss Evelyn, that's *my* job," she says, taking the orange from my hand. "So sorry, Ramona. I overslept."

There is so much more I want to ask Ramona. How did she meet Arthur? Do they have any children? What is Little Hawk's story? And how about Neppy?

"No problem," I say. "I enjoyed pitching in." The rest of the stories will have to wait. I return my apron to its hook and take my coffee to the living room, where I sit under the elk's watchful eye.

# CHAPTER 15

*Monday, October 12, 1931*

Tonight, Madeline and I meet Tessa at Belle's Barn, about a mile south of town on the Hall Ranch. The idea of dancing in a "barn" gives me pause—will it be shoddier than the dance halls in town? But the cowboys promise to keep close tabs on us, so I agree to go. And there is Belle, larger than life, adorned in feathers and rhinestones, greeting every patron.

We join Sundown, Johnnie, and Red, the freckled-faced cowboy. The others tease him mercilessly, calling him "Freckles Finch," but we women stick with "Red." Though his name implies a tall, Viking-like bruiser of a guy, Madeline's dancing partner is anything but. He is bashful but has a contagious sense of humor and frequently has our table in stitches when he comments on a six-weeker's appearance. "Look at that poodle mop," he says. "Would look better on a poodle." He and Madeline are quite the pair.

I have never seen an orchestra made up entirely of African American musicians, and I thoroughly admire their Paul Whiteman arrangements and enjoy their Bessie Smith and Louis Armstrong numbers. I always need a dance or two to loosen up. When the band picks up the pace, Sundown's playful moves help me relax and bring out the showgirl in me. I find myself stepping coquettishly, as if I am performing in a musical. I know that everyone is watching Sundown and me, but I reassure myself by thinking, *There's no one from Hackensack here.* Thank heavens I have had no more run-ins with Gwyneth.

As the center of attention, Sundown doesn't allow any cut-ins. He holds me tighter and tighter during the slow numbers. Even though I try to make light conversation, I love having his arms around me. The feel of his muscles under his soft denim shirt thrills me. I tuck my chin into the crook of his shoulder. It has been forever since I've been held closely like this.

When we return to the ranch, my feet ache, and my emotions are all in a spin. Later, as I lie in bed, I keep thinking about being swept around the dance floor by Sundown. I can smell him, feel him. I change my position, feel too warm, and throw off a blanket. Then chilly, I cover up again. In the distance, I hear muffled sobs. Despairing of ever falling asleep, I put on my robe and follow the sound downstairs. I pause on the bottom step and listen.

"I can't be alone," says a voice. "I can't. I'm not going to make it these six weeks. Frank, please come and take me home. I need you. I need *someone.*"

As I enter the room, Beatrice sits weeping on the sofa before the dying embers of the fireplace. Her black hair hangs loose and wild; her robe is untied.

"Beatrice," I say, my voice soft so as not to startle her, "I couldn't get to sleep and couldn't help hearing you crying."

"Sorry . . . sorry," she sputters. "I came downstairs so I wouldn't wake Thistlena. Sorry to disturb you." She clasps her head in her hands and moans. If I didn't know better, I'd swear she is Mrs. Rochester from *Jane Eyre.*

"No, it's all right," I say, coming closer. "I'm wide awake, and you're upset."

Like a phantom, Little Hawk emerges from the shadows carrying a tray upon which two small glasses sit. "Brandy for tears, Ramona always says." As quickly as he comes, he disappears.

Beatrice stares into the smoldering ashes and takes a sip of her brandy. I sit down next to her on the sofa.

"I'm so lonely," she begins. "I can't bear it. When I think about how my life will be when I return to Philadelphia, I can't breathe. What will I do without Frank? I don't want to live." She leans back and closes her eyes. Her face is etched with anguish. "Do you know, when Madeline's husband boarded the train to kidnap her, I was *jealous*? I want Frank to come out West, abduct me, and take me home."

Beatrice isn't thinking clearly, that is certain. Madeline's husband is a wife beater and has put her in the hospital in the past. Beatrice's husband, Frank, played around every chance he got. Dean never sought the company of other women that I know of. Both of their experiences cause me to feel grateful.

I remember on the train when Beatrice confessed her fear of being alone. I couldn't empathize at that time, so desperate was I to live independently, to be rid of my depressed, incompetent husband. Now I need to muster some sympathy for her.

"I don't want to be here," she says. "I want to go home. I want Frank." She hugs herself and falls forward over her knees, sobbing.

"You've made it this far," I say. "You can't turn back." Gently, I rub her back. "Next week, we will be at the halfway point. Only three more weeks to go, and then we will all have our divorces. I want mine more than anything."

"My father, my stepmother, and my sister all *made* me come," Beatrice wails. "They gave me the money and put me on the train."

I identify with her powerlessness. My mother made me marry Dean and then forced me to remain in a loveless marriage. I remember feeling as if I carried a mountain of disappointment on my back—a bulk so huge that my spine rounded from its weight. My friends commented on my slumped shoulders.

Beatrice stops weeping, sighs deeply, and sits up again. I take advantage of her calm to remind her of the second fact she confessed in the dining car when I first met her—the humiliation she had suffered because of Frank's infidelities.

"Oh yes," she murmurs. "The gossip, and then the conversations behind my back when they thought I wasn't looking. I saw them. The shame was unbearable. After a while, I stayed indoors, as if I were contagious."

I don't have a womanizing husband, but I have known profound shame. I still bear the stigma of being married to the only man in my circle who, after 1916, couldn't find work and forced us to accept the support of my parents.

A new tack is needed here. "Don't you realize that your friends will be impressed by your courage?" I ask. "By ending your marriage to Frank, you will regain your self-respect, as well as theirs. Instead of your neighbors' contempt, you will feel their admiration."

"I suppose so," she says without conviction.

Some admiration from my friends? I wouldn't object to a bit of that too. Betsy and Sally were always solicitous of my feelings, but when I shared the truth—that Dean's job-searching efforts had yet to bear fruit, all they could offer was pity. And they quickly changed the subject.

If I press on, perhaps I can help turn Beatrice's thinking around. "We women who come to Reno are the strong ones. The weak ones— just as unhappy but lacking in courage—stay back and continue their lives of misery."

"*You're* strong, Evelyn."

"And so are *you*. I see you back in Merion, standing tall, shoulders back, with a new confidence in your smile . . ."

Beatrice blinks her wet eyes and nods.

"But we will wear the stigma of 'divorcée.' Outside of Hollywood, there aren't many women who, like Hester Prynne and her scarlet *A*, are branded with a scarlet *D*. I fear that gossip too. Maybe I'll just hide in my house."

The fear of this ostracization has also crossed my mind. Will my close friends abandon me? For my sake, as well as for Beatrice's, I continue. "Nonsense. I see you having lunch with your friends, shopping at Wanamaker's, and volunteering at the museum."

She nods again.

"Think how you will hold your head high, and they will say, 'Look at that Beatrice Winters. She got rid of that philandering Frank. How beautiful she looks.'"

"I suppose so," she repeats, this time with a little more assurance.

"I *know* so," I say firmly. I stand, face Beatrice, and pull her up. "I'm going to take you to your room. We should try to get some sleep, but this conversation is not over."

After I tuck Beatrice in, smoothing her hair as though she is a child, I tiptoe back to the living room. The embers in the fireplace throw off the faintest light, and I can see through the windows that another day is dawning. I resolve to keep a close eye on Beatrice.

# WEEK THREE

# CHAPTER 16

*Thursday, October 15, 1931*

After breakfast, I set off on my daily walk north behind the ranch house. It seldom rains in Reno, but today clouds are trapped over the Truckee Meadows. Some relief from the intense sunlight is welcome, even if rain never comes. For a few hours, I feel blanketed—protected—and the air is still. The birds sleep, enjoying the coolness, and I can't even hear an insect. The quiet of the landscape brings serenity. I inhale with a smile and drift toward the horse barn.

I make my way down the aisle between the stalls, pausing to greet each horse by the name that is burned into the plank above its stall. The horses doze while swishing their long tails, shifting from one foot to the other, expelling their breath in a gentle flutter. For once, I can't feel the hammering of my heart. I, too, am relaxed and free in this old barn.

At the end of the aisle, I hear weeping. I stop and hold my breath. Having comforted Beatrice a few nights before, I wonder if it's her or another guest who has private grief.

Tiptoeing forward, I discover Thistlena. In between wrenching sobs, she makes great sweeps with a grooming brush on the back of a horse called Babe. I stand off to the side of the open end of the stall and watch her, brushing with one hand and swiping away tears with the other. She does not fill out her clothes, and I fear she has lost more weight. She was already so slender.

I clear my throat, and Thistlena jumps, dropping her brush. "I'm sorry," I say. "I didn't mean to startle you."

"I didn't see you there," she says as she wipes her palms on her riding pants. She takes a shuddery breath, then retrieves her brush and resumes her grooming. "Brushing a horse calms me—most of the time."

"The horses are like a sedative for me too. I visit them every day on my walks."

Thistlena drops her brush again, curses, and collapses onto her haunches, her face in her hands. I have never seen such misery on a face. I bend to touch her shoulder as I search for words to comfort her.

"Tomorrow, Evelyn," she says, looking up at me with red, watery eyes. "Tomorrow's the day."

"What's tomorrow?"

"My abortion," she whispers.

I can't believe my ears. She intends to go through with it. We haven't spoken of her pregnancy since that time in her bedroom. In fact, we have scarcely talked at all. She is always occupied with Nat and Ray and showing the casino site.

"I am so frightened," she continues. "I can't eat. I can't sleep. Some days I think I'm going to die."

When she dissolves into yet another fit of weeping, I begin to tremble, and my mouth is dry. I have to do something.

I crouch down beside her. "I'll come with you and hold your hand," I say, my compassion sweeping aside my concerns.

"From what little you have shared with me," I continue, "I believe we have come to Reno for similar reasons. We don't have ex-husbands who drank too much, who beat us, or who, like Beatrice's Frank, were continually unfaithful. No, you and I have experienced a different kind of betrayal. Yours invested foolishly, and mine couldn't find work, becoming so discouraged that he couldn't act. I, on the other hand, decided I was not going to hide behind his resignation. I am entitled to my independence. So here I am." Will I admit the rest? Not at this moment.

She turns to look at me, tears still falling. "Exactly so," she says. "I will never forgive Peter for his stupidity and the resulting scandal."

As Thistlena pushes herself to a stand, she whispers, "And thank you for agreeing to accompany me. I will *never* forget this."

And may God forgive us both. In her overwrought condition, I doubt she is strong enough to carry and deliver a child. She will have to live with her decision, and so will I.

As I return to the ranch house, I tell myself I have agreed to help a desperate friend. What might happen if I do *not* stand beside her? I will never know.

# CHAPTER 17

**Friday, October 16, 1931**

After breakfast, Little Hawk drives the Anselms' Ford west toward the mountains. Thistlena and I sit in the back seat, our eyes fixed on the austere desert but no doubt both consumed by our private fears. There is no road that I can discern, only rocks, cacti, and sagebrush. The car leans to the right as it follows a streambed, making me queasy. I thank God that Thistlena's errand is not mine. I pray that the Native American woman, whoever she is, knows what she is doing and that Thistlena will survive.

I know she is less than three months along in her pregnancy. Her suit jackets and skirts hang loosely on her frame because of the relentless nausea. She has dark circles under her eyes due to not sleeping well.

Despite her obvious frailty, Thistlena joins Ray and Nat in their car every morning, and they do not return until right before supper. We six-weekers gather in the living room to await the dinner bell. We always hear Thistlena's quick steps on the front porch as she bursts through the door, shoulders squared, and exclaims, "Three more investors today," or similar good news.

I have to admit that she has amazing stamina. Madeline has accompanied her to the site on two more occasions. And even Beatrice proclaims her enthusiasm for the project. "I'm very interested in this hotel," she says as she squeezes Nat's elbow every chance she gets.

∽

Little Hawk stops the car in the middle of nowhere to blindfold us. He ties a coarse black sash around Thistlena's eyes and then around mine.

"Ouch!" I say when he pulls the knot at the back of my head. "Is this really necessary?"

"Yes, necessary," he says, then restarts the car.

Thistlena reaches for my hand. I feel like I am going to faint. Why did I ever agree to come? Maybe Thistlena and I will be kidnapped, or worse. How can we be sure that we will be returned to the ranch? The only sounds are the car's motor and the occasional crunch of a rock. It isn't too late to turn back.

I lean over and whisper, "Are you sure you want to go through with this?"

"I have to," says Thistlena.

After a while, I hear the sounds of children playing. Little Hawk stops the car and opens our doors. He brings Thistlena around to me and then leads us into some kind of shelter. The air is cool and smells of herbs.

A woman's voice says, "Thank you, Little Hawk. I will take them from here."

Take us where? "May we remove our blindfolds?" I ask. I fully expect her to say no, but to our relief, we are permitted to take them off. The speaker, a Native American woman, is about forty, I would guess, and has glasses. A barrette keeps her straight black hair gathered at the back of her neck, and she wears a medical-looking white coat.

"You have brought the cash?" asks the Indian woman.

"Here," says Thistlena, handing her a bulging brown paper bag.

"Who is the patient?"

"I am," says Thistlena. "This is my friend. I want her to stay with me."

The woman nods. She leads us into a second adobe-walled room with small windows near the ceiling. There is a long, raised table covered with sheets and a wooden chair to one side. The space is well lit, much to my surprise, by many kerosene lamps. I need to sit down in that chair, or I will pass out.

"This is my daughter," the woman announces.

The girl, about ten, also with long, black hair, steps forward and hands Thistlena a mug of hot liquid. "Drink, please."

I am alarmed that a girl so young will be a part of this procedure.

Thistlena takes the mug while I sit down.

"What is it?" I ask.

"Something to help her relax," the woman says. Her brown eyes pierce me with their intensity. She places a mask over her nose and mouth, then hands Thistlena a folded sheet. "Take off your clothes from the waist down, and cover yourself with this."

The setup is clean and tidy, and the sterile appearance is reassuring, but I can't quiet the shouting in my head. *It's not too late, Thistlena. We can leave. You can be a mother or let someone else be one. I'm frightened by how God will punish you for this. And punish me!*

Thistlena lies on her back with her knees up and her feet placed on short metal bars at the foot of the table. She grips my hand, and I feel her trembling. I should have said no. I should have insisted.

As much as the surroundings are foreign to me, I can't help but remember my two visits to Hackensack Hospital to give birth to my children. I recall the buzzing of the lights above, the cold slab I lay on, and the indescribable pain of the contractions. I had competent obstetric care but was told that I almost died from loss of blood during Charlie's delivery. When June came eighteen months later, she was easier.

As uncomfortable as I was during both deliveries, I held, at the end, a beautiful newborn, a miracle created by Dean and me. I remember counting Charlie's fingers and toes. Then he opened his big blue eyes and looked right at me. June, just like a doll, was such a quiet, good baby. It was a joy for me to have them both.

I will never reconcile myself to Thistlena's decision. She created something but would destroy it. Then again, when my children were born, I was married, we had a home, and my husband had a job. How would I feel if I became pregnant today? Perish the thought!

Leaning close to Thistlena's face, I try to smile. The girl, padding around silently in moccasins, brings me a small cloth and a basin of warm water. "You may sponge her face," she says. I am grateful to be given a task.

I am aware of the clattering of metal instruments, the smell of alcohol, and the strong scent of herbs. The girl hums an unknown melody as she walks back and forth doing the woman's bidding. I watch Thistlena's anguished face—she bites her lower lip and scrunches up all her features like a dried prune, then exhales slowly while tears escape the corners of her eyes. I press the facecloth to her forehead and cheeks while I match my breathing to the rise and fall of her chest.

Minutes later, the woman carries a small basin covered with a towel into another room, separated from us by a beaded curtain. A new life gone. My chin drops to my chest. I feel like dying.

The girl removes Thistlena's feet from the bars so that she can extend her legs, then brings another mug of liquid. I help Thistlena rise onto her elbows. "This will help stop the bleeding," the girl says.

"Is it finished?" Thistlena asks.

"All finished," says the woman, emerging through the curtain, still wearing a surgical mask.

It is over quickly. Thistlena has felt pain today, surely, but maybe the medicinal herbs have minimized her discomfort. I bring her skirt and other items of clothing to the table, where she sits dangling her feet.

"Where did you learn your . . . your trade?" Thistlena asks.

"I helped the doctors deliver babies at Fort Collins for ten years," she replies.

"And my procedure?"

"Was always performed after a woman miscarried," she says.

This small room is nothing compared to the facilities and care I experienced at Hackensack Hospital, but I had expected much worse. I had imagined Thistlena on a dirt floor, perhaps, subjected to unsterile instruments. While I want to locate Little Hawk and return to the ranch as soon as possible, I am grateful that Thistlena has avoided a back-alley abortion and all of its attendant horrors.

"You will have some cramping and bleed for several days," the woman says, removing her mask. "Get plenty of rest. Make a tea of this, and drink it every morning for five days." She hands Thistlena a clear packet of dried herbs. "If you develop a fever, you must consult a physician."

The shadows under Thistlena's eyes appear grayer, deeper. I put my arm around her waist and start to lead her to the door. Though I feel racked by guilt for being part of a devil's errand, I admit the Native American is a remarkable woman. I ask if she helps the women on the reservation deliver their babies.

"All the time," she replies, "and I'm teaching some of them the skills that I learned.

"There is no medical training for Paiute people," she adds.

*And that is too bad,* I think.

"I must put your blindfolds back on," she says. "Sorry."

"I understand," Thistlena says.

"Must we?" I ask as she ties the sash behind my head.

"Evelyn," Thistlena whispers, "no one must know how to find her."

"But how *do* women . . . white women . . . find you?" I ask.

"Miss Helen usually makes the arrangements."

Before we arrive back at the Flying N, Little Hawk stops the car and removes our blindfolds. Color has returned to Thistlena's cheeks, and her facial muscles have relaxed. She is no longer pregnant. I try to read her thoughts. I have never known a woman who made this choice. Does she feel only relief? Not an ounce of regret? She must sense my misgivings.

"I have no words strong enough to thank you," she says to me. "I have never been so frightened. And you held on to me. You gave me the strength to go through with it."

I nod but also feel speechless. While I pray that I will be able to calm my conscience, I think, *Today, Evelyn, you helped a friend.* And maybe, for anyone who sits in judgment of me, that is commendable.

# CHAPTER 18

Today Arthur drives the four of us into Reno before supper. Madeline and I have late-afternoon hair appointments. Thistlena, carrying reams of papers, heads for the hotel, and Beatrice goes off shopping.

Madeline and I are keeping a close eye on Beatrice. She has lost a lot of her spunk lately. She mopes around the ranch—slumping in chairs, kicking stones in the yard—and stays back at the Flying N more than she goes into Reno. I also overheard Little Hawk tell Ramona that the level of brandy is markedly lower in its bottle.

The beauty salon is quiet for once but, as always, as spotless as an operating room. Violet is busy tallying the day's receipts, and the only sounds are the click-click of her long fingernails on the calculator keys and the crunching of the hand crank.

"Looks like you're having a good day," I say.

"Oh, Evelyn, Madeline," Violet says, looking up, "we're all ready for you."

Violet gets to know the six-weekers quickly and calls us by our first names. Back East, I am "Mrs. Henderson," but, well, I am learning that things are less formal in the West.

As she ushers us back to the waiting sinks and the beauticians, I say, "I admire a woman in business."

Violet sighs. "Thank God for the six-weekers. I'm saving up to open another salon."

"I'm impressed."

"I came out here for the same reason all of you come. Only I stayed," she says with a grin.

"What an inspiration it is to meet a woman who plans to expand her business in this depression."

Violet cocks her head and winks. "You know what they say about beauty and hard times."

I give her a quizzical look.

"A woman will spend her last dime on a hairdo or her lipstick." Then she becomes serious. "The banks won't lend me a dime; I run a successful, in-the-black business, but I'm a woman. If I want to expand—open another shop—everything has to be cash."

As I recline in my chair and feel the warm water soak my scalp, I am certain Violet will have a string of salons in no time. And if what she says about beauty in hard times is true, there will be modeling work for me on the runway when I return East. I will cling to that thought.

After basking in the new sense of well-being that only a shampoo and set can deliver, Madeline and I enjoy dinner at the Grand Café. Later we will move to the Silver Slipper. Of course I say nothing about my earlier errand with Thistlena. We talk about Beatrice's continued depression.

"She's worried about being alone," Madeline says. "Me? I can't wait to live by myself."

"Same for me."

"Good evening, ladies." Gwyneth Armstrong, wearing an absurd royal-blue hat whose tassel falls on her forehead, attaches herself to one side of our table, sucking in her girth so that others can pass. "Having the spring chicken, I see. Isn't it divine?"

Leaning in my direction, Gwyneth whispers, "I still can't get over finding you here."

I put down my fork and take a deep breath. "Gwyneth, like every six-weeker in this town, I am entitled to my independence."

Thank goodness the other three gals from her table urge her along toward the exit. Gwyneth turns around as if to say something, but

I smile at Madeline and ask that she tell me more about the Twin Arches development. I believe that from the heat of my embarrassed face, Madeline can tell I need a distraction.

Her knowledge of real estate dealings is, by now, awe inspiring, and it appears to me that she is going to buy in. Evidently, Thistlena's salesmanship is reaping shareholders, and Madeline says she has every confidence that the project will be completed. "I've been back to the site, Evelyn. What's more, I've met other investors. Like me, they have experience with real estate and seem very knowledgeable. Is it simply all the room to expand out there? I don't know. But I can easily envision what they have in mind, and I can imagine vacationing at Twin Arches."

After dinner, we walk north on Virginia Street, under the arch to the Silver Slipper on East Fourth Street. The cool evening air helps to diminish the stubborn perspiration and flush emanating from my face. Alas, I can't get Gwyneth out of my head. *That woman!* I scream inside, my teeth clenched. I can't wait to lose myself on the dance floor.

Sundown, Johnnie, and Red have already grabbed a table for us, and they stand promptly as we approach. I observe Red clutch Madeline's hand when she sits down, her cheeks blushing the color of her pink silk dress. Tessa, adorned in a new mauve sheath and matching pumps, finds us and sits next to Johnnie. By this time, we have learned which bands are playing where, and we follow our favorites. The Buckaroos replay the same standards, but Sundown and I don't care. I pretend I am Adele Astaire dancing with her brother, Fred, in *Funny Face*, the Gershwin musical I saw on Broadway, and everyone claps for us at the end of each number.

Escaping into my onstage fantasies, I can release the clench of my teeth against Gwyneth and give in to the growing attraction I feel for Sundown. His holding me, leading me, is becoming so familiar that it's as if we have been partners for years. But something else is bubbling up deep in my gut, something new and frightening, like an electric current. *Easy, Evelyn. Keep it light. Keep it fun.* I want nothing to come between me and that final decree.

The cowboys are doing their best, but Madeline and I catch all three of them stifling yawns. Sundown stands and tips his hat. "Ladies," he begins, "I must apologize. We have long days on the range. Our foreman has us up at four a.m. to ride into the hills for fall roundup. I promise we'll make it up to you, but this time we must bid you good night."

For the first time, I have sympathy for these men. They turn up shaved and scrubbed night after night to show the six-weekers a fun time in exchange for a few measly drinks. I forget that they ride horses all day. No wonder they have dark shadows under their eyes. We wave goodbye to the cowboys and to Tessa, who skips along holding fast to Johnnie.

Madeline and I need to stop in the ladies' room. The boys say they will walk Tessa to the post office so that she can catch a ride with her ranch mates.

When we step out of the Silver Slipper, a full moon lights up the town like a lighthouse beacon. We cross the railroad at Center Street, choosing to avoid the hordes clogging Virginia Street.

"Let's take the alley," I suggest, turning west in front of the Bank Club casino.

"I don't know . . . ," says Madeline, who has stopped at the corner.

"It's as bright as day out here, and the alley is wide. If we take the shortcut, we'll arrive at the post office with the rest of them. I don't want to miss the car going back to the Flying N."

Madeline toddles after me obediently.

When we both stop to gaze at the moon, two loud blasts split the air. I clap my hands over my ears and catch my amethyst ring in my hair. Good Lord, has someone been shot? Am I next? From a doorway, a man's body falls with a thud at my feet, his eyes open, his white shirt punctured and soaked with blood. I'm confused. What should I do? I turn in time to see Madeline slide into the dust. Someone shouts in Spanish. A door slams. I try to take a breath and pray for the strength to scream.

Before I can open my mouth, Little Hawk is by my side. Bending low, he heaves Madeline over his shoulders while I grab her purse. Head down and running toward the other end of the alley, he pulls me with his free hand. My alligator bag and Madeline's bang against my hip, and sand clogs my open-toed shoes. *Please, God,* I pray, *let me live!*

Before Second Street, Little Hawk knocks on a wooden door, which opens promptly, and brings us inside. A woman dressed in royal-blue satin stands there. I don't remember meeting her, but she looks familiar.

My head is spinning. The woman in blue leads me to a burgundy velvet chaise where I willingly recline and try to slow my racing heart. Madeline lies on another chaise, her eyes closed and her mouth open as if she is dead. Maybe she has been shot like the man. My whole body quivers.

My eyes take in the room. Everywhere, candlelight reflects off crystal pendants. A fireplace with a carved mantel is off to one side, and drapes that appear to be silk frame the small windows. Little Hawk must have brought us into an elegant Reno home.

The woman assumes a seat beside me and offers a small glass of brandy on a silver tray. My eyes fix on the elegant sapphire-and-diamond brooch at her neck. I try to form the words, but I can't get my lips to say "Thank you." I catch the scent of Chanel No. 5.

Madeline is still slumped against the back of her chaise, all color drained from her face. A striking young woman touches Madeline's forehead with a moist cloth. The girl, for she is no more than fifteen, wears a red gown and teeters on silver slippers. Her blond hair is held in place with rhinestone combs.

"She's fine," says the woman in blue. "She hasn't come to yet, but she will."

The brown liquid warms my throat. At the same time, I shiver when it reaches my belly.

"You've had a shock," the woman says. "Little Hawk told us you witnessed a shooting. We like to think Reno has become a safer place in recent times, but wherever you have gambling . . . well, things happen sometimes."

Did I really witness a shooting? I remember the shattering blasts of gunfire, and I can still see the bloodied man at my feet. His face was distorted—grotesque—as was the blood soaking his shirt. I will never forget that image.

Tonight's events are causing fear to take over my every breath. Reno is, indeed, a dangerous city. Perhaps I should return to Hackensack and hire Al Gardner to guide me through a divorce in New Jersey. At least I could live at home.

Tasting bile, I sip more brandy.

The woman offers a refill.

I manage to croak, "No, thank you. Water?"

Little Hawk comes over carrying a glass and two blankets. I nod, and he spreads one over me, the other over Madeline.

Someone knocks at the door, and the woman opens it to two gentlemen, both impeccably dressed in crisp suits and highly polished shoes. They remove their hats and speak in low voices while the woman tilts her head in our direction. The men move to the stairs leading to the second floor, but not before accepting cocktail glasses from Little Hawk's tray and stopping to kiss the cheek of the young miss still pressing a cloth to Madeline's face.

"I fear we are imposing on you," I manage to whisper.

"No, you are not," says the woman, returning to the chair beside me.

"I think she's coming around," the girl in silver shoes says.

Madeline tosses her head back and forth, moaning, but I can't make out her words. She fainted in the alley, but was she also injured? It all happened so fast. I didn't see her bleeding from anywhere, but she was unconscious.

"Little Hawk," says the girl, "may we have some water?"

He fetches another glass while the woman takes a seat on Madeline's chaise and massages her hands.

"Evelyn? Evelyn?" Madeline whispers. She remembers we were together in the alley. She sips her water and stares vacantly into the room. The blond girl sets down her cloth and bowl of water to answer the door. Two more gentlemen, older and with identical protruding bellies, kiss the blonde affectionately, then bow to the woman.

The men are obviously familiar with this house, as they walk straight to the stairway leading up. I observe one of them cup his hand around the blonde's bottom and squeeze. I look away. How inappropriate. What a rogue!

Madeline is alert by this time and accepts a glass of brandy. The woman stands and opens the door to two more guests, both men laughing loudly at a private joke. Again, she jerks her head in our direction, and they both harrumph into whispers.

"Ladies," says the woman, "will you excuse me a moment?" She follows her guests to the second floor, leaving Little Hawk in charge of our care.

"Where are we?" Madeline asks me.

"Little Hawk rescued us from the alley and brought us to this house."

While Madeline assesses her surroundings, I relate the events that transpired after we left the dance hall. "And this is the lady in blue's home?"

"I assume so," I reply. "Isn't it grand?"

"Evelyn," she says, "we could have been killed!"

"I know." All the energy drains out of me, and my head lolls back. I want to sleep for a hundred years. I want to disappear into a cave and never come out.

"Little Hawk," Madeline says, "I'll take some more of that brandy." She downs her glass's contents in one gulp.

"I don't know where he came from, but Little Hawk got us out of harm's way."

Muffled laughter sounds from the party upstairs.

"Evelyn," Madeline whispers, "you realize we're in a whor . . . a brothel. Miss Helen is the local madam."

I had assumed that we were in an elegant Reno home and that our arrival had interrupted the hostess's party. And she had dropped everything to see to our needs. But the fancy clothes, the lush furnishings—Madeline's account is making sense. How would she know about these places? True, Madeline had lived in New York City, where even I knew speakeasies and houses of sin thrived, even in this depression. Swallowing hard, I remember the beauty parlor, the glamorous woman having her hair brushed and styled, and Violet describing Miss Helen as wealthy and very philanthropic. Imagine! I'm in a . . . It's too unimaginable.

"Why did you turn down that alley?" Madeline asks.

I squirm in discomfort. "You saw the moonlight. That alley was as illuminated as a Broadway stage. If we cut through, we could get to our ride much sooner."

"But, Evelyn," says Madeline sitting up, "I'll say it again. We could have been killed!"

"I know, Madeline," I say. "I'm sorry."

Miss Helen descends into her parlor with a loud, proclamatory step. "Do you feel up to returning to your ranch? Little Hawk can drive you."

Madeline sticks her chin in the air and looks away.

I clear my throat. "I can't thank you enough for your hospitality. May I reimburse you for your trouble and our brandy?"

"Of course not," she says. "I'm in the business of rescuing women." Her face is stern.

I look at her with curiosity as she continues. "No woman ever sets out to work in an establishment like mine, but my girls are well cared for, clean, and in good health. In most cases, they've run away from abusive homes or relationships, the horrors of which you have never known. And if anyone lifts a hand to one of my girls, they go to jail for a long, long time, or worse."

Miss Helen gives her skirt a defiant swish and steps to a bar shelf to fill a tray with new glasses. I have to hand it to her. Anyone can think what they want to about Miss Helen's "business," but she runs a tight ship.

"Madeline," I whisper, "do you think you can stand?"

Little Hawk reappears to assist her.

I walk to Miss Helen's side. "We are indebted to you."

"There is no debt," she says sharply. She lifts her skirt to ascend the staircase with her tray. "But don't be too quick to judge me."

⁓

During the ride back to the ranch, Madeline, Little Hawk, and I are silent, lost in our own thoughts. I am numb—semiconscious. In my mind's eye, I see the dead man in the alley and grip my seat cushion. But the stronger impressions are those of Miss Helen—her tender ministrations to our shock. She placed us comfortably on her best furniture, offered fine brandy, and knew what we needed.

And what about Little Hawk? He works at the Flying N, but it appears that he is also employed by Miss Helen. I wonder when he sleeps. His eyes flit everywhere like a nervous bird. I don't know what to make of this miniature man—he is always lurking in the shadows. He appears from around a corner and makes me jump. But I am sure glad he arrived in that alley tonight.

"Little Hawk," I say, retrieving some courage, "what can you tell us about Miss Helen?"

"She runs a gentlemen's club," he says. "The best in town."

"And who belongs to this club?"

"Rich businessmen, some gamblers, some actors from Hollywood. Everyone is well dressed and well mannered. To join, you must be recommended."

Interesting. Miss Helen had created a rich man's club.

"Miss Helen makes a lot of money," Little Hawk adds, "but she gives a lot away to charity."

"But isn't it illegal," I ask, "to have her kind of club?"

"In this county, yes, and in many others, but Reno is safer because of places like Miss Helen's. The sheriff looks the other way."

And probably gets paid off, I assume. I take a shuddery breath while trying to absorb all that has happened. I have certainly never been near such a house before, and I should feel not only shocked but also appalled. I still feel the trauma of the shooting, but as for Miss Helen, I am mostly fascinated and impressed by her kindness, by her business acumen, and by her success. I'd love to know her story—how she ended up in Reno and how young girls find her.

Suddenly, the happenings of today—an abortion and a shooting—come crashing down on me like an avalanche. "I'll never survive six weeks in this town," I mutter as my head swoons against my seat.

Back in my room at the ranch, my suitcase lies open on my bed. Tonight's events may send me back to Hackensack ahead of schedule.

☙

### Saturday, October 17, 1931

I have never been so terrified in all my life and have scarcely slept a wink. I stay in bed through breakfast but manage to get dressed in the late morning, and after a few bites of bread and cheese, I return to my room. I'm so exhausted that I feel like a lead weight, but if I close my eyes, I will relive the terror in the alley.

I cut this from the next day's *Nevada State Journal*:

> Sunday, October 18, 1931, Reno, Nevada—Roberto Gonzalez of Mexico City was found shot to death in

the alley behind the Bank Club shortly after 11:00 p.m. Friday. No witnesses have come forward. Gonzalez appears to have died from a single gunshot to the chest. Shortly before, he had left the Owl Club on Commercial Row after a large win at the blackjack table. Anyone with information is urged to contact the Reno Police Department.

Madeline and I stay at the ranch for the rest of the day and the next to recover from Friday night's ordeal. The quiet and peacefulness here assuage my jitters and reduce my constant revisiting of the look on Mr. Gonzalez's face. For the time being, I restow my suitcases under my bed, resolving to stay out of Reno alleys. On Thursday, I will reach the halfway mark of my stay, and please, God, may I retain my determination to stay my course.

# CHAPTER 19

*Tuesday, October 20, 1931*

By Tuesday, it is time for manicures, after which Madeline, Beatrice, and I will meet Tessa for lunch. Thistlena has been unavailable these past few days. If her abortion tugs at her conscience, she shows no sign of it. Every morning she flies down the porch steps and into Nat's car. They must be busy luring investors.

Arthur has been in the barn all morning. Ramona says he won't be driving into Reno for at least an hour, so I set off for a walk in the desert. Madeline declines to come, but I coax Beatrice into joining me, and together we laugh at our feet. The walking shoes we have bought in Reno are so homely we can't look down without wincing. However, given the risk of ruining every pair of chic pumps we packed, we realize buckskin tie shoes will serve our purpose.

The sun from the east is slightly obscured by high clouds, the air cool and dry. I fill my lungs with deep breaths, relishing how clean and pure they feel, like clear water from a mountain stream. These almost-daily walks have become a source of peace for my soul. They are perfect antidotes to the roller coaster of emotions that swoop me up, then plunge me down and make me dizzy.

Beatrice trudges along beside me, her head down, lost in her own thoughts. I fear that she conjures up old memories, old hurts.

I admire the Native Americans and the early settlers, the pioneers who tried to carve a living out of this barren land. A jackrabbit jumps out in front of us. Beatrice starts, but I am accustomed to their sudden appearances. His speckled brown fur is a perfect camouflage, and he has the biggest ears I've ever seen. I encounter coyotes slinking through tall grasses, lots of mule deer, and desert tortoises when they pop out of their burrows. I stay out in the open, preferring not to come across any snakes among the sagebrush. As long as I keep the roof of the ranch house in my sights, I do not lose my way.

Looking ahead, I recognize Neppy sitting atop a large boulder, her booted feet crossed and her denim pants dappled with colors, the source of which I can't make out. She sees us approaching and waves. On close inspection, I realize her pants are smeared with blotches of colored pastels, which also cover her fingers. In her lap, she holds a large pad on which she has drawn a view of the Sierra Nevada. I am stunned by her talent—so accurately has she captured the earthy brown tones of the West. Beatrice ogles the drawing too.

"You're a real artist. Isn't she, Beatrice?"

"Nah," says Neppy, scratching her nose and leaving behind a spot of green. "It's only a hobby." She continues with her chalk pastels.

Beatrice stands behind her other shoulder, mute, inspecting the drawing.

"I see a lot of talent on that page. Have you had any training?" I ask.

"Actually, I started art school," she says. "Philadelphia."

"Are you from Philadelphia? I live near there. And Beatrice here, she's from Merion."

"Farmland west," says Neppy.

"You mean West Chester?"

"Farther out than that."

"I'm sorry. I don't mean to pry. You've told me you're a six-weeker too, and I feel like I haven't had a chance to get to know you."

Neppy blows chalk dust from her pad. "I got pregnant and had to drop out of art school. My dad's laid up due to a farm accident, so

Mom has to do everything. After my six weeks are up, I'll go back home to help. Oh, and my soon-to-be ex-husband is in jail for a long time. That's my story."

I am about to launch into a speech about the importance of going back to school, but in this depression, perhaps that's unrealistic. All of a sudden, we are startled by shouting from the barn. Arthur stands outside the entrance, waving both arms over his head and calling for Neppy. She throws down her pad and takes off at a run.

Beatrice looks at me, the corners of her mouth turned down.

"I think we'd better go too. They might need our help." Head down, elbows pumping, I head for the barn at my fastest walk.

Even before I go inside, I hear the wails of a horse in distress. The brown mare lies on her side and thrashes violently. Neppy clings to the mare's neck, trying to keep the horse steady and on her side. "Easy, Cocoa, easy," she says, but Cocoa jerks her head up, as if trying to stand.

Neppy has her hands full—that is certain—but she seems to know what she's doing. I don't know the first thing about calming a hysterical horse.

Beatrice creeps into the stall, her back flat against the wall, her eyes lit with terror. Arthur has his arms around the head and front hooves of a foal in its birthing sac that is half in and half out of the mare.

"What can I do?" I ask.

"Arthur, you have to trade places with me," says Neppy, perspiration shining on her face. "It's going to take both of us to get this foal out."

"Evelyn, hold Cocoa's head," says Arthur.

I sink to my knees and hang on to the horse's neck. Golly, she's strong. Those muscles could fling me against the wall. In the split second when Cocoa lies back down, I climb on her neck and sit astride.

Cocoa is hurting, panic in her eyes. I lean forward and stroke her muzzle while I say into her ear, "There, there, Cocoa. There, there."

"Pull *down*, Arthur," Neppy says. "*Down*, not out." She has heaved her torso over Cocoa's rump. "I've seen this before. Cocoa's birth canal is abnormal."

"This foal won't budge," Arthur shouts, breathless. "We're going to lose them both."

*Oh God,* I pray, *don't let this horse die.* Cocoa's neck is wet where my tears have fallen.

"Switch places with me," Neppy commands. "Let me have the foal."

Arthur dives across Cocoa's hind end and strokes her belly while Neppy moves to the foal.

"Beatrice, get me that towel," Neppy says, pointing with one arm.

Beatrice grabs the towel flung over the stall wall and, hand trembling, gives it to Neppy.

"Cocoa's going to stroke out," Arthur cries. "Damn this foal." His eyes are clenched tight, and veins bulge from his forehead.

Neppy wraps a towel around the foal's sac and front hooves and pulls down toward Cocoa's rear hooves.

Up at my end, the horse has stopped thrashing. The hairs on the back of my neck stand straight up, and my mouth is parched. She can't be dead, she can't. Her eyes have rolled back into her head, but her chest still heaves. Her breathing reminds me of the steam engines from the train. I continue to massage her neck and speak my mantra into her ear: "You can do this, Cocoa. You can do this."

Where is the veterinarian? It will be tragic if Arthur suffers yet another loss of livestock—this mare *and* her foal. I pray again: *Please, God, let Cocoa release her foal.*

"Come hold her feet," Neppy says. "I'm going to have to put my boots against her belly so I can pull."

Arthur lies on his side and locks his arms around Cocoa's rear legs. Neppy grunts as she pulls and releases, pulls and releases, on the half-born foal in its mucus-y sac. Arthur wheezes and exhales expletives. Suddenly, Neppy howls as the foal's sac bursts, and out the filly slides. All three of us cry tears of joy, and Beatrice slides down in the hay beneath her feet while she fans her flushed face.

Neppy scrambles to pull the filly out of the way and uses the towel to wipe her down. I don't know anything about birthing horses, but she is an expert and has proven it this morning. She should become a vet. I resolve to encourage her every chance I get.

"Look out, Evelyn," Arthur says as he lifts me off Cocoa's neck seconds before the horse stands.

I back up against the wall while Arthur holds Cocoa's head by her halter. She still wheezes as she gulps air in and expels huge blasts of congestion.

"Is she sick?" asks Beatrice.

"She's going to be fine," Arthur says, stroking the animal. "A horse is meant to stand, not lie down. Her lungs will clear on their own."

Cocoa's gasping subsides, as Arthur had predicted. We tiptoe to the front of the stall. Cocoa begins to lick her baby, who is trying to stand.

"Filly looks good," says Neppy, drying her hands on her jeans. "Not quite ready to stand yet, but I predict she will within the hour."

"You were *amazing*," I say, smiling at Neppy.

"Amazing," Beatrice echoes.

"Any farm girl knows birthing." Hands in her pockets, Neppy looks down at her boots.

We tiptoe into the next stall. Beatrice and I collapse against the wall and shed new tears of relief.

"Isn't she a beauty?" Arthur says from next door.

"Sure is," says Neppy.

"Couldn't have done it without you."

"You needed a little help, didn't you, girl?"

"More than a little."

"I'm obliged to you too, Evelyn and Beatrice," Arthur says over the stall walls. "This required a team."

◦◦

Beatrice and I walk slowly back to the ranch house, each lost in our own thoughts. "Boy, that Neppy," I say aloud.

"She is a wonder," says Beatrice. "Wish I was good for something."

I look at her sharply, but she doesn't notice. "Arthur said we were a team. That included *you*."

Eyes downcast, she plods toward the house, kicking up desert grit.

What could have been a disaster for Arthur and Ramona—losing a mare and her foal—turned into a triumph, thanks to Neppy, to her knowledge and her strength. I feel proud to think I have been a part of something . . . something *lifesaving*. So much of western life teeters on the edge of a cliff: rain waters the crops, or the crops die; cattle live, but calves die; mares carry foals in their bellies, but sometimes they don't survive the delivery. People help one another, as I have already observed, but life is hard, and there aren't a lot of doctors or veterinarians. Maybe life is hard everywhere, and people withstand the storms with perseverance and a big dose of luck. An ounce of courage doesn't hurt either.

# WEEK FOUR

# CHAPTER 20

*Thursday, October 22, 1931*

I come downstairs to the living room with my book, intending to read by the fire. I have awakened from a long sleep, and at the risk of not being able to fall asleep tonight, I figure I had better stand up and move my limbs. However, a walk outdoors is not an option, as the wind is howling, and there are predictions of another dust storm.

I admit, I feel refreshed—having had my first sound sleep without a recurring nightmare since the shooting. Maybe I am going to get past this after all. I haven't been to Reno for days. Madeline seems completely recovered and tells me repeatedly that Sundown is asking for me. Most days, my nerves feel like a barrel of snakes.

The quiet I seek is not to be, as I come upon Madeline and Beatrice sitting at the dining room table with Ray, Nat, and Thistlena, examining architectural plans and talking like excited children at a birthday party. Nevertheless, I sit on the sofa in the living room and open my book.

"You're saying we will be shareholders?" says Beatrice. "We will own a piece of this hotel?" She could keep flies away with the continuous flickering of her eyelashes. I can't help but wonder what Nat is thinking of her blatant flirtations.

"That's exactly what we're saying," he says, his shoulder touching hers as he lifts his eyebrows and grins. He points the tip of his pencil at official-looking papers while she twirls her café-length strand of pearls.

"But when will our shares increase in value?" Beatrice asks. "What if I want to sell them in a couple of years?"

"Then you sell them," says Ray.

"What if they've gone down in value?" Beatrice asks.

Even though she appears to be purring, she is asking pointed questions.

"Not possible," Nat says. "Have you seen the activity in town? In the casinos?"

Madeline has been studying the architectural drawings, moving her index finger over the page. She looks up. "It looks to me as if all the tourists in Reno are six-weekers—here today, gone tomorrow."

"And there are trainloads more arriving every day," says Thistlena. Ray nods to her.

"But the six-weekers stay at the ranches," says Madeline.

Beatrice's eyes follow each speaker as if watching a tennis match, but they always come back to rest on Nat. She feigns a demure countenance, but I suspect there is a femme fatale underneath.

Ray unbuttons his jacket and rests his forearms on the table. "That's what's available these days. We're betting that many of the ladies would like more glamorous quarters. And the Hollywood types—don't forget the actors and entertainers."

"He's right," says Beatrice, leaning coquettishly toward Nat. "Evelyn talked to Mary Pickford in the ladies' room of the Deauville. Tessa told me all about it. Isn't that right, Evelyn?"

Not lifting my eyes from my book, I nod.

"And there are many visitors from Hollywood that we don't recognize," Nat adds. "I've talked to a lot of them."

"How many of them have invested?" Madeline asks.

*Good for you.* Leave it to Madeline to get straight to the point.

"I have the list right here," Ray says. He glances at Thistlena. "Let me count."

"I think I'm going to buy in," says Madeline. "I've been to the site four times. I've seen the plans, and I've spoken to some of the other investors."

I tiptoe to the kitchen, where Savannah and Ramona work in silence. Savannah looks at me and rolls her eyes, while Ramona's detached expression speaks volumes. I pour tea into a cup, add sugar, and stir.

"Oh, I'm so confused," Beatrice says with a dramatic whine. "It seems like a smart move, and Lord knows I could use the money. But I don't know. What do you think, Evelyn?"

She had seen me go into the kitchen. I move to the opening to the dining room. "I've seen the site and the plans too, but I'm very conservative where money is concerned."

Thistlena moves to stand behind Beatrice's chair and puts her hands on Beatrice's shoulders. "If it has ever crossed your mind, now is the time to dig in. We are going to close our deal as soon as we get thirteen more shareholders. We need two hundred, and we are this close." She holds up her forefinger and thumb, which are almost touching.

I am confident that Madeline knows something about real estate—she has been fixated on this development ever since she first heard about it. Yesterday, while I was reading the latest book by Fannie Hurst, I came upon Madeline poring over Twin Arches contracts. But I am worried about Beatrice's naivete. A lot of six-weekers can be fooled if they aren't careful. I carry my cup and saucer to the table. All eyes are on me.

"I'll grant you," I say, "the three of you have worked tirelessly on your project. Your list of buyers is very impressive. Before I can consider it, I must have my attorney back East examine all your materials."

Ray frowns while loosening his necktie. He sighs as if gearing up for a hard pull. I don't want to anger them, but Madeline isn't the only one who can ask the smart questions. I am certain my lawyer can come up with a couple.

Ray clears his throat. "Let's review. The property is forty acres. Phase one of the hotel will have a hundred and eighty rooms, a restaurant, and a ballroom. Imagine wearing your most glamorous gown and dancing under crystal chandeliers to Benny Goodman and His Boys."

I admit that sounds very inviting. And I keep bumping into Boyd Whitaker on the streets of Reno. He's very insistent that I let him take me to the Willows.

"You ladies cut such fine figures. You will want to swim in the Olympic-size swimming pool and go on trail rides. The casino, in a separate building, will have its own bar. God knows Prohibition can't last much longer."

Beatrice fans her face with copies of the financial papers. "I never imagined returning to Reno after my divorce, but you make it sound like a very desirable vacation spot."

"One thing is certain, ladies," says Thistlena. "Reno will continue to serve as the divorce capital, with more and more unhappy folks coming here to dissolve their troubled unions so they can begin again."

Speak for yourself, Miss Duncan. Another marriage is the furthest thing from my mind.

"This is your opportunity to get in on the ground floor," Ray says, looking over at Nat and Thistlena, who both nod in agreement.

I concede that Ray makes a compelling argument. I will call Al Gardner back in Hackensack. There is no doubt I can use the proceeds from an investment like this. I plan on returning to modeling and saving for a place of my own, but perhaps in this depression, I will not find work. If I invest in Twin Arches, I can sell my shares after a few years and perhaps afford my own home. "I'll pour myself another cup of tea," I say as I return to the kitchen.

"Madeline, are you ready?" asks Nat.

"I am."

"And Beatrice, what about you?"

"I think I'm ready too."

I stick my head in the doorframe and add, "And I promise to give it serious consideration."

# CHAPTER 21

*Friday, October 23, 1931*

I tear open an envelope addressed to me from Charlie. Finally, a letter from my son.

> Dear Mother,
> First, I received your letter about your trip to Reno, and then I got a letter and a book of checks from Aloysius Gardner instructing me to send support checks to Father at his new residence in Brooklyn, New York. I want no part of this. It's none of my business. I have returned the package to Mr. Gardner. If you choose to send money to Father, it's your affair.
> Charlie

Tears collect in my eyes. He didn't even write "Love, Charlie." He didn't say anything about the divorce, but I feel as if I've been slapped. Is he angry at me? At his father? At Aloysius? He's probably furious with all of us.

Blotting my tears, I remember when, soon after we had moved from Lawrenceville back to my parents' home in Hackensack, Charlie would look up at me with such earnestness and ask, "Did Papa get a job today?" I would shake my head, then whisper in his ear, "He will find one soon."

I made this arrangement with Al Gardner in the hope that Charlie would write to his father when he sent a check. Obviously, he is refusing to be a part of his father's financial support, but I pray he will keep in touch and, yes, even visit Dean in Brooklyn. Charlie and Dean had a strong rapport, especially where sports were concerned. They listened to baseball games on the radio, and when Charlie went away to Exeter to finish high school, they talked often about crew. This letter, however, makes it very clear that Charlie wants nothing to do with the divorce.

I had tried to delegate this chore to Charlie to distance myself from its necessity, but I have failed. How shall I respond? I should apologize for putting Charlie in the middle of all this. I guess the support check will have to come from me after all. I'm also inferring that Charlie is furious with me for abandoning his father. I don't know when, or if, I'll hear from June, but she would never write to me as bluntly.

◦⑨

"Did you love being married?" Beatrice asks.

"Hmm?"

Beatrice interrupts my brooding about Charlie's letter. We sit in the Grand Café, having a bite of lunch while Tessa and Madeline finish their hair appointments. As we observe the fashion parade out the window, today's temperature is cooler, and many six-weekers are draped in stone marten furs. In fact, the dining room looks like a convention of furriers. Across the room, one woman draped in a silver fox stole looks like Norma Shearer. Maybe it *is* Norma.

"Did you love being married?" Beatrice asks again.

"Yes . . . I guess I did . . . in the beginning."

"I *adored* it." She rests her chin on her white-gloved hand and gazes into the distance. This is not what I care to talk about.

"Did you work before you were married?" I ask.

She looks at me in surprise. "Are you kidding?" she says. "The girls in my family are brought up to be wives and mothers, period. The husband is the provider."

He is supposed to be. My lips form a grim line.

Beatrice recounts the homemaking lessons she learned from her grandmother after her mother died—cooking, sewing, nursing the sick, doing the laundry. While I feign rapt attention, I am flooded with memories of Marion and me learning the same skills at our mother's side. As soon as we could hold a needle and thread, we practiced our stitches. We mastered how to bleach out stains with lemon juice and sunshine, how to disinfect our skinned knees when we tumbled in our roller skates, and how to prepare and roll out a pie crust.

Beatrice lost her mother and then her oldest sister. I know the emotional canyon that grief can carve, and wince at the memories of my two dead brothers.

"Evelyn? Evelyn?" says Beatrice, interrupting my daydreams. "I don't know what I will do, how I will spend my time. You have modeling to return to. Without a husband to take care of, I have *nothing*."

"Where will you live?" I ask gently.

"With my sister, of course."

"Then you will help your sister take care of her house and children."

"It's not a large house," she says, "and Abigail has her own ways of doing things."

I know what she means. Marion has her set ways too. As Beatrice explains her situation, I realize that I commanded Dean to find an apartment of his own, but how Marion and I will get along after I return is unknown. She has always been difficult, and I have practiced how to stay out of her way. If I continue to model, perhaps I can afford to buy my own house and be free of my sister's constant criticism. Then there is the possibility of earning a profit by investing in Twin Arches. *That* possibility is a strong temptation.

"Now let's think about this," I say. "You have other options."

"Options?"

I tell her to take a careful look around Reno after our lunch. From my observations, there is not only an abundance of six-weekers but also a myriad of working women—shop clerks, café hostesses, beauticians, and more. Years ago, when the residency requirement to get a divorce was six months, many more of the divorce seekers had jobs here. The women's magazines advertised these opportunities. "Get a Job While You Get Your Divorce" read the classified ads.

"I've watched you at the ranch," I say. "You do beautiful needlework."

"Oh, *that*. It's only a hobby."

I enumerate how her "hobby" could bring her income—by teaching it, designing the screens, or selling the finished products.

"You think I can?"

"I *know* you can."

"With every passing day, I think of ending my life," Beatrice says. "What do I have to live for?"

Nearby patrons are watching us. I try to swallow the huge lump in my throat. "Don't talk that way," I whisper. "It takes *courage* to come all the way out here. *You* have courage. You are a brave woman. If I've observed one thing since I've been here, it's that we six-weekers are loaded with bravery. The world is full of wives who remain in loveless and sometimes abusive marriages. We're the ones who have said, 'Enough!' And do you know what it really means? We've decided that we deserve *better*."

"If only I could marry again," Beatrice says dreamily.

Does she hear anything I'm saying? I chew my sandwich and search for encouraging words. While Beatrice continues to stare into the distance, the corners of her mouth drooping, I hear happy giggles and exclamations of joy around me. "He has the bluest eyes I've ever seen," one says. "We danced until morning," says another. The four diners at the next table burst into convulsions of laughter.

"What do you think of Nat?" asks Beatrice. "He's kind of cute. A perfect gentleman. Maybe he'd like to marry me."

"Maybe you'll want to give marriage a rest," I say. "Take some time to regain your footing. I have no idea if I'll ever marry again. It's the furthest thing from my mind. I have two grown children who will soon embark on their own lives, I have a few devoted friends, and I have my faith.

"I *hope* I can continue to model. I made it a point to keep up with my agent, but we're in the middle of a depression. Who knows if there will be work for me when I return? But no matter what happens, I will be *free*—free from my parents' expectations and free from the choke hold of a depressed husband. And with this investment of time and money, I will have earned back my self-respect. You, too, will go home with yours."

"I will go home with nothing," she says.

"Beatrice!" I whisper. How can I shake some sense into her?

"Don't forget," she says, opening her compact to inspect her lipstick, "*you* wanted to come out here. I was pushed."

We pay our bill and walk along the Truckee River in silence. In my head, I dispute Beatrice's easy assumption that I wanted to come to Reno. I want a divorce, and this expedition is a means of securing it. I know fear, and I know despair and perhaps a small amount of guilt, but my heavier burden is shame. I have been living a lie, pretending that Dean and I were happy.

As Beatrice said, her family forced her onto the train. I know what it feels like to be compelled, under duress, to give in to a stronger authority. My mother gave Dean a lovely diamond, which he paid to have set. Then came the engagement announcement in the papers, followed by endless bridal showers—kitchen, linen, and "personal." Then shopping for a wedding dress. Looking back all these years later, I realize that I didn't want to marry Dean Henderson in the first place. At only nineteen, I would have given anything to get off the marriage train, but I lacked the courage to hold my ground. Since Beatrice has also been pushed against her will, I worry that she, too, lacks the necessary fortitude to rid herself of her philandering husband. Maybe she needs more time. And yet she declares that living with gossip and shame is unbearable. Poor Beatrice.

When I tried to break off my engagement to Dean, I remember my mother saying, "This wedding will proceed, and you will be happy." In 1912, just like Beatrice, I did as I was told.

∞

My memories are interrupted when my shoulder is jostled by Boyd Whitaker.

"Miss Evelyn," he says, stepping back, "I apologize for crashing into you." He tips his hat.

"Mr. Whitaker, permit me to introduce my ranch mate Beatrice Winters."

"Good afternoon," he says quickly while his stare is locked on my face. "I didn't mean to bang into you, Miss Evelyn, but this encounter is fortuitous. Please agree to accompany me to the Willows this evening. I've just had word of an award-winning orchestra appearing there tonight. Pick you up at eight?"

I grab Beatrice's hand and start marching toward the post office. "Thanks, Mr. Whitaker," I call behind us. "We're both spoken for tonight."

"Who is that, Evelyn?" Beatrice asks, running to keep up with me.

"Mr. Whitaker is my Reno attorney."

"He wants to take you to the Willows. I would *kill* to get invited there."

I stop in my tracks and ask, "Why?"

Beatrice lifts her eyebrows. "It's Reno's most exclusive resort."

"So?"

"It's elegant and famous, but a lady must have a male escort. And it's full of Hollywood actors."

When I return home, will it be important to say I went to the Willows? I'd rather be in Sundown's arms on the dance floor.

# CHAPTER 22

*Saturday, October 24, 1931*

Madeline, Beatrice, and I meet our group back at Belle's Barn. Tessa phoned to tell us that the Buckaroos would be supplying the music for dancing. At this news, even Beatrice had seemed to bounce back from her despondency. Her face had lit up even brighter when, peering into the dark interior, she'd spotted Thistlena, Nat, and Ray holding a large table beside the dance floor. She'd waved, then bounced up and down like a schoolgirl seeing her best friend and shouted, "Yoo-hoo!" Poor Nat doesn't stand a chance with any of the other six-weekers tonight.

"You seem distracted," says Sundown, holding me close on the dance floor.

"I apologize," I say, smiling up at him. "I'm keeping an eye on Beatrice."

"Some of the boys have commented . . . She's got a thing for Nat, doesn't she?"

"I believe you're right. I fear she's determined to return to Pennsylvania with a new husband."

"She won't be the first," he says, whereupon he twirls me out and then brings me back closer than before. As the night wears on, Sundown and I become breathless after many up-tempo dances. Thank goodness the band takes a break. Dry mouthed, I point to our table and mime taking a drink. We find Beatrice leaning her head on Nat's shoulder, showing every sign of too many cocktails.

She stands, saying she is headed to the ladies' lounge. Walking like a sailor in rough seas, Beatrice bumps into two couples leaving the dance floor. Nat catches my attention with his eyes, pleading that I follow her. Madeline joins me.

We open the door to the lounge—well appointed, if not as elegant as the Deauville's—but we don't see Beatrice. Madeline knocks on the stall doors, each occupant replying, "Busy," except the last, which offers no reply.

Madeline puts one eye to the vertical gap where the hinges are fastened and waves me over. By now, several six-weekers are asking, "Is she sick?" and "Should we call Belle?" I peek through the slit and observe Beatrice astride the seat but leaning left and snoring. Meanwhile, Madeline has retrieved a small footstool, which she places in front of the door.

"I'm not willing to slide under at the risk of cleaning the floor with my dress," she says. "You're taller, Evelyn. You stand on the stool and wake her up!"

"Beatrice," I call. "Beatrice, wake up." And soon we have a chorus of other ladies calling and banging on the stall door.

Beatrice pops her eyes open and waves to me with a smile. I step down from the stool, which Madeline quickly returns to its corner. As Beatrice comes out of her stall, appearing not the least bit fazed, Thistlena comes in with Candace Niven.

Gasping at the sight of Candace, I take both Madeline and Beatrice by the hand and pull them out. Candace has missed a photographic moment, thank goodness. Running to catch up to us, Thistlena whispers, "Everything all right?"

I give her a thumbs-up, but I am very worried about Beatrice.

∾

Every day there are more letters for my ranch mates waiting on Ramona's desk, but today I see that there is one for me from June. After the sting of Charlie's words, I can't help but fear what she has to say.

Dear Mother,

As soon as I read your letter, I tried to telephone Father at his new residence, but he does not have a phone in his room, so I had to leave a message. Eventually, we connected. I met him at Penn Station, and he escorted me to the YMCA on Ninth Street in Brooklyn. What a dreary place! As I sit here at my desk at school, I feel sick to my stomach and sick at heart. How could you abandon our father like this? He has lost weight, and his face is etched with deep lines of sorrow. We took a walk in Prospect Park, and he tried to feign cheerfulness and ask about my classes, but we were so often interrupted by skid row bums begging for coins that we hurried back to the YMCA.

For meals, he takes a very long walk to the Horn & Hardart automat. He has no friends. I have decided to leave college, return to Hackensack, and take care of Father. I simply can't stand by and watch him fade away.

Your daughter,
June

No sooner have I read June's letter than Ramona calls me to the telephone on the wall beside her desk. "Your sister, Marion, for you," she says.

We had all gathered in the living room for our ride into Reno. Madeline and Beatrice wait by the dining table, whispering to one another. I'm sure they're wondering who has died, so infrequently do the six-weekers get telephone calls.

My sister, Marion, tells me what I already know—that June has left college and returned to Hackensack. I glance at the postmark on June's envelope and see that she mailed her letter more than a week ago.

"May I speak to June?" I ask.

Marion tells me that June, crying in her room, is far too upset to come to the phone. "Do you know that she has been to Brooklyn to see her father?"

"She wrote me about her visit," I reply. And my heart sank when I read of her despair. I realize that June holds me responsible for her father's living conditions.

"Did she also tell you that she is devastated to see her father in such reduced circumstances?"

I assure Marion that June had written this to me.

"Do you see what you have done?" Marion asks. "Your daughter is falling apart."

I imagine Marion sharpening a sword. June's sadness has given her plenty of ammunition to attack me. Of course I must shoulder some guilt for June's distress. She has always been my sensitive child. But is everything my fault? Not hardly.

"I believe Dean bears some responsibility for his meager accommodations."

"Evelyn, you are *heartless*. How can you subject your children to your selfish whims?"

"Whims, Marion? Divorcing Dean is not a whim but a decision I wrestled with for many years. I send him money every month. He will survive."

"But will your daughter survive?"

I tell Marion I must conclude our call. Others are waiting to use the telephone. My palms are slick with perspiration, and I lurch to the kitchen for a glass of water. That sister of mine, I'd like to ring her neck!

Blasting out the front door, I head for a fast walk around the ranch house. Am I liable for everyone's misery? Dean's? Charlie's? June's? I feel that they're trying to drown me in a sea of remorse, that they want me to just set everything back the way it was.

I can imagine June feels like she's in a cage of anger and sadness. Isn't that ironic? I wonder if she can sympathize with me, a woman who was enclosed in a loveless marriage. June is younger and inexperienced. I used to feel just as she does.

During our ride into Reno with Arthur, I wonder if I can persuade Charlie to reason with his sister, get her to stay in school. Philadelphia is just a train ride from Swarthmore, where her school is located. But he's furious with me, as he expressed in his letter. How will he react to June's actions? I feel completely helpless.

# CHAPTER 23

*Tuesday, October 27, 1931*

Madeline, Beatrice, and I amble along Virginia Street, stopping to examine what the merchants are offering outside their front doors. I am momentarily distracted by the gloves on sale outside Burke and Short, loose tea with exotic aromas inside bins in front of Hilp's Drug Store, and Native American jewelry—turquoise and silver—across the street in front of the Waldorf. The sellers, all women, wear buckskin dresses trimmed with elaborate beadwork along with fine moccasins. Their brown hands turn over the pieces we admire, but they give no verbal sales pitch. At one end, a young mother with an infant strapped to her back accepts cash and places our purchases into plain brown sacks.

The temperature has turned cooler, but the afternoon sun warms the earth and those of us walking on it. Again, the sky is cloudless and so penetratingly blue I shield my eyes, even with sunglasses. The Native American jewelry is especially fine, and I ponder buying pins for myself and June and possibly a belt buckle for Charlie. While I examine the different pieces, turning them over to check their fastenings, Madeline stands aside, her knuckles white from clutching her bag. She has been fidgety ever since we arrived at the post office.

"What is it, dear?" I ask.

She turns away and squints in the direction from which we came. A black Ford near us honks loudly, and she yelps, drops her bag, and covers her ears.

"Madeline, what's wrong?" I plead. "It's broad daylight. I don't think we're going to witness any more shootings."

Her lower lip trembles. "I have a feeling," she stammers. "He's here. Owen's here in Reno."

I put down a silver pin and take Madeline by the elbow. As we walk, I try to distract her with my observations of the six-weekers' outfits. "Look at that suit with the mink trim. It looks expensive," I say. "Oh, see that smart cloche with the feathers. Isn't it stunning?"

We plan to have afternoon tea at the Silver Slipper—I want to divert her from her fears—since East Fourth Street is away from the bustle of Virginia Street. Madeline continues to babble. "He's sent me letters. He's sent me telegrams. He says he's changed. He needs me."

I try a rational approach. Has she seen Owen in town? At the ranch? In a dance hall?

She shakes her head. "It's just a feeling I get whenever he's close. I felt it when he came for me on the train. The hair on my arms is standing on end. Look." She pushes up her sleeves so that I can see.

I try to reassure her, saying that sometimes my fears get the better of me too, and I imagine evil portents that never happen. "When my crazy imaginings don't come true, I realize they're just that—crazy." I say this for Madeline and also for myself. June's letter lurks in the back of my mind. I believe June wants to help her father, but I question Marion's assessment that she's "falling apart."

When we reach the Silver Slipper, we secure a table by the window and order a pot of tea. Madeline stares out the window, wringing her hands, while we wait. "Unfortunately, my antennae are usually accurate."

"Then let's tell the sheriff," I say.

"I already have. I showed him my threatening letters. He and his deputies promised they'd keep their eyes open, but I don't know.

The two deputies had their feet up on their desks and were reading magazines."

"What can I do?" I ask while secretly wondering if all the Flying N girls are crumbling—first Thistlena and her unwanted pregnancy, then Beatrice's depression and too much alcohol, and now, Madeline is crippled by fear.

"There isn't anything you can do," she says, covering her eyes with her napkin. After she stops crying, Madeline continues. "People said, 'Leave him,' and I did. Several times. But he always found me and vowed to change."

I don't know what to say. Sometimes I hear stories like hers at church. They're not about anyone I know well but usually include a runaway husband or a family that moves abruptly and without good-byes. The truth is seldom known, only guessed at through gossip—often spurred by Gwyneth Armstrong, in fact—and always swept under the rug.

"When did you decide to come to Reno?" I ask Madeline.

She, like me, came into a small inheritance after her mother died, and that allowed her to make a break for it. She intends to get her divorce, move to San Francisco, and change her name. Imagine! Feeling so frightened that she will assume a new identity.

"He knows where I am," she says. "He learned it on the train."

I try to divert her attention, commenting on the ladies' hairstyles around us. Like the flapper dress, gone are the straight-haired bobs of the 1920s. Today the girls sport side parts with straight hair at the top and curls at the ends. Barbara Stanwyck wears her hair that way.

I also tease her gently about Red's attention in the dance halls. Nothing works. She picks at her tea biscuit. I keep up a one-way conversation, occasionally interspersed with a monosyllable from Madeline. Mostly, she scans the windows that face the street, clasps her arms, and looks away when a gentleman walks past. We pay our check and walk to the post office for a taxi back to the ranch. Madeline is too frightened to think of dancing tonight.

Much to my surprise, a telegram waits for me when we return.

NO CAUSE FOR CONCERN. STOP. I WILL BRING JUNE BACK TO
COLLEGE. STOP. SHE MUST COMPLETE HER EDUCATION. STOP.
DEAN.

Madeline has taken refuge in her own room. Clutching the telegram, I collapse onto the couch in the living room. No one is around to
witness my tears. God bless Dean for taking charge. All of a sudden, his
virtues as a father drench me like a cold wave. He may have abandoned
me and ruptured our marriage, but he was always attentive to Charlie
and June. He was involved with their schoolwork, with their athletics,
and with their friendships. When Charlie was discovered to be exceptionally bright, it was Dean who telephoned Phillips Exeter Academy
and arranged for him to attend. He praised June's efforts on the piano,
as well as her writing. He wrote to them at summer camp and then at
college, enclosing newspaper clippings he thought would interest them.
I climb the stairs to my room, longing for the oblivion of sleep.

From a deep sleep, a man's loud voice rouses me. When I open my
bedroom door, I hear harsh words. "Can't do this to me. I forbid it.
I've come to get you."

I creep down the steps in my bare feet. There is no light except
for the dying embers of the fireplace. Madeline is crumpled on the
sofa, sobbing. A dark figure paces in front of her, punching out
phrases: ". . . have always cared about you . . . mustn't desert me . . .
can't live without you."

With a burst of bravado I didn't know I possessed, I shout, "Who
are you? What do you want with Madeline?"

A man turns to reveal a bouquet of roses held in one hand. He
is movie-star handsome, but his fiendish eyes cause me to step back.

"Good evening, madam. Owen Abel at your service." He gives a deep bow before he turns, goes down on one knee, and places the roses on Madeline's lap.

"I've come to fetch my wife," he says to me though he looks at Madeline. "I have missed you so much," he says to Madeline, his voice smooth. "You must set aside this divorce foolishness. I've changed, and I want to prove it to you."

Madeline sweeps the bouquet onto the floor and shakes her head. "No. Never again."

"I hear the lady," I say, marching right up to him. "She says no."

Owen stands abruptly and, bowing again, extends his hand to me. "Excuse me," he says. "I didn't catch your name." Despite his syrupy charm, this man is dangerous.

I shake his hand, so conditioned am I to do so. I also understand how easy it would be to fall prey to his charms. He wears an expensive worsted suit, and his black shoes shine to a fare-thee-well. I inhale slowly and wonder, *How do we get rid of him?*

"You may call me Miss Evelyn."

"Pleasure," he says.

I can see through his forced smile and maniacal eyes that he is rethinking his strategy. He sweeps his arm out in a grand gesture. "Please join us, Miss Evelyn. Perhaps you can help me convince Madeline that I am devoted to her and only want what's best for her. I have missed her dreadfully and want to bring her back home."

He sounds crazed, and I don't have to remind myself that this is the same man who has put Madeline in the hospital. "I heard what she said, Mr. Abel. She said no. Did you not hear her?"

Owen's eyes narrow to slits. "You are Madeline's friend?"

"I am indeed."

"Then surely you, too, must want her to be happy."

"I do."

"We've all had our upsets," he says, pacing. "That's the God's truth. But I'm a new man." He turns in a circle as if he is modeling. "I have a new job and a swell apartment to bring Madeline home to. And you believe in second chances, don't you, Miss Evelyn?"

"Second chances, Mr. Abel? I do. But I don't believe in third, fourth, and fifth chances."

His eyes again narrow into devilish slits. "Can you lend me a hand?" he asks.

"Why?"

"We need to go to her room to gather her belongings." Owen grabs Madeline's arm. She jerks it away. I am not sure I'm strong enough to stop him. What should I do? As he is about to scoop her into his arms, the front door opens and in stomp Arthur and the sheriff.

"You say this man is attempting to abduct one of your guests?"

"He is," replies Arthur, moving between Owen and Madeline.

Owen shouts, "This is none of your business—it's between my wife and me!"

Arthur and the sheriff each grab Owen by an elbow and lead him to the patrol car outside. The sounds of their strong footfalls drown out Owen's protests. I immediately go to Madeline's side, gather her into my arms, and rock her as her shoulders shake in convulsing sobs. That was a close call. Thank God Arthur and the sheriff arrived when they did. Ramona appears, her long gray hair falling loose over her nightdress, to dab Madeline's face with a cool cloth.

By now, all the commotion has awoken Thistlena, Beatrice, and Neppy. Together we help Madeline back to her bed, and they all stand guard. Though Madeline is whiter than a ghost, she is able to sip some brandy brought by Little Hawk.

I return to the living room and sit on the couch with Ramona. She assures me that this is not the first attempted kidnapping at the Flying N and won't be the last. I close my eyes, lay my hand over my heart, and wonder what else could possibly threaten us.

Arthur returns after circling the ranch and reveals that the cowboys had been on alert since a man in town—Owen—was asking too many questions about the ranch in general and about Madeline in particular.

He tilts his head toward his and Ramona's bedroom, but Ramona says, "I'll be along."

"That's it, then," Arthur says. "He's not coming back here. Thanks for your help, Miss Evelyn."

I turn to Ramona. "Not only do you give us six-weekers food and shelter, but you get all our problems in the bargain."

She sighs. "Don't these kinds of things happen back East?" she asks. "You've got bigger cities with lots more people."

"Of course they do, but they're much more removed, or at least they are from me. I read about them in the papers. With this depression, there are horrible tales—fathers jumping off buildings, children starving. The longer I live, the more I realize how sheltered I've been."

"You have many blessings to count," says Ramona.

We both sit quietly, lost in our own thoughts. As the light from the fireplace wanes, fatigue creeps in behind my eyes. I have suffered disappointment, shame, and profound loneliness, but I have never been threatened with, or received, *physical* harm. For this, I am grateful.

"And Little Hawk," I say, lifting my brandy glass, "he always seems to show up when we need him."

Ramona's mouth forms a knowing smile.

"How did he come to be at the ranch . . . if you don't mind my asking?"

"Little Hawk was abandoned at birth," says Ramona. "The Native Americans do that sometimes when a baby is born prematurely or in some way deformed. They believe the spirit mother calls back the baby's soul. Arthur and I were not blessed with children. When we heard about the cowboys who had discovered a crying newborn, we investigated.

"When the tribal elders heard about our interest, they said we could raise Little Hawk, but we couldn't adopt him. He didn't belong to our people.

"So that's what we did. Little Hawk, whom the elders named, is small in stature—I've heard some call him a dwarf—but he has the strength of two men. Arthur and I would not have been able to hold on to the ranch without him. And he is, in every sense of the word, our son."

"Does he visit his people on the reservation?" I ask, remembering my blindfolded trip with Thistlena.

"Yes. And he's welcome there."

"Does he know which ones are his parents?"

"No, but they tell him they are all his parents."

"But what about you and Arthur?"

"He calls us his 'feet pointers.' I think some would say 'footstep guides.'"

I clear my throat. "When he rescued Madeline and me after the shooting in the alley, I realized that Little Hawk also works for Miss Helen."

Ramona smiles again and stands to return to her bedroom. "Little Hawk may be small, but he's a full-grown man, and . . ."

I raise my hand. "I understand."

The next morning, Madeline tells me how impressed she is that I stood up to Owen. I don't tell her I think he's more than a little crazy.

"I'm so grateful to you. I will never forget it."

"Truthfully," I tell her, "I have no idea where my courage came from, but I was not going to let any harm come to you."

Soon the sheriff arrives to personally assure Madeline that Owen is in prison and will remain there while awaiting trial for trespassing, breaking and entering, and—most serious—attempted kidnapping. Unfortunately, Beatrice's distorted thinking reveals that she envies Madeline because her husband wants her so much.

As Neppy is clearing our dishes, Arthur announces that the Flying N and several other ranches are joining forces to give the six-weekers a barbecue and a square dance Friday night. This news sparks considerable enthusiasm, and we line up at the phone to schedule hair and nail appointments in town.

Beatrice wants to know how we are to dress for the dance and if there will be enough cowboys so that she won't feel like a wallflower. Arthur assures us that the cowboys will come from miles around. Ramona even offers to loan some full skirts and crinolines, which she says are perfect for western dancing. I am a little anxious about western square dancing with a professional caller, but Ramona persuades me—all of us—that there is nothing to fear. Everyone is a beginner.

Beatrice continues her barrage of questions about what we will eat and drink and how we will get there and home. Ramona patiently answers.

"Is Neppy invited?" I ask.

"We're all invited," says Arthur.

# WEEK FIVE

# CHAPTER 24

*Thursday, October 29, 1931*

Our happiness is contagious tonight at the Deauville. Even Madeline, loosened with a little gin, beams at Red without restraint. Tessa, decked out in yet another frock of autumn red, and Johnnie win the Charleston contest. Beatrice resorts to pulling Nat onto the dance floor and appears to be leading him, but I notice she is sticking to plain lemonade—a good sign. She talks nonstop and lifts his arm to duck under it when she needs to take a breath. Poor Nat's face seems like a plaster mold with a toothy grin. But Ray and Thistlena dance as if they are enjoying themselves.

Sundown holds me tight while I fill him in on the week's events, as well as on our anticipation for tomorrow's square dance. He assures me that the call has gone out to all the bunkhouses. "These dances happen every six weeks," he explains, "and we look forward to them."

"I can follow you in most any step," I say, "but I'm not sure about this 'swing your partner' or 'allemande left.'"

The song ends with a cacophonous drumroll, and Sundown swoops me down into a low dip. My eyes must reveal my surprise—and fear of falling—but he lifts me up into his agile arms and kisses me hard. I wonder if he's being fresh, but at the same time, I want more. When we stop, the dancers are clapping for us. "A breath of fresh air?" he asks.

"Definitely." Anything to mask the bloom on my cheeks.

Sundown leads me by the hand. This is a new sensation—being ushered by a strong man—and I like it. After Dean lost his job and failed at securing a new one, he surrendered his ability to lead, and I resented it. And my resentment grew like a cancer. How divine it feels to be escorted by a partner in charge.

We inch our way around the tables and out the front door. I shiver against the night's chill, and Sundown gives me his worn leather jacket.

"It's not nice enough for a refined lady like you," he says, pulling the front lapels close to my chin.

"Oh, but it's warm indeed," I say. "Aren't you cold?"

"Not one bit." Sundown mops his brow with his bandanna.

I am touched that he refers to me as a "refined lady." Although Sundown is employed as a ranch hand—a wrangler—I have the highest regard for his gentlemanly manners. I don't know anything about where he comes from or his upbringing, but someone has taught him the finer points of how to treat a lady and how to dance.

We continue to chat about my myriad adventures in Reno— horse deliveries, Beatrice falling asleep in the loo, and Owen trying to abduct Madeline—but I decline to mention the shooting in the alley or Thistlena's abortion. Sundown doesn't have to know that I almost abandoned my mission after the shooting. I also avoid telling Sundown about the dramas back in Hackensack.

More than hiding my exploits, I am distracted by the delicious scent drifting up from Sundown's coat to my nostrils. It is the most delightful smell—a combination of hay, aftershave, and manly perspiration. Several times during our conversation, I say, "I forgot what I was going to say," so seduced am I by the jacket's warmth and aromas.

When I see Sundown's shoulders quiver from the cold, I say, "Let's join the others for a few more dances."

Back at the ranch, I fall asleep with Sundown's contagious smile as the last image on the backs of my eyes. And I thank God that our paths have crossed.

# CHAPTER 25

*Friday, October 30, 1931*

As the six-weekers and everyone else gather on the front steps to go to the square dance, we resemble the cast of a Tom Mix movie. Ramona draws whistles from the cowboys as she comes out the door wearing silver-and-turquoise jewelry in her hair, on her neck, and in her ears. Arthur swings her out from one arm and then the next, his freshly pressed, light-blue shirt closed at his neck with a silver-and-turquoise bolo tie.

Next comes Little Hawk in a starched white shirt and red bandanna holding Savannah's hand. She is all decked out in a yellow calico skirt with crinolines and a white blouse with white embroidery. Savannah is round in the middle but surprisingly light on her feet as she skips down the steps in little flat shoes. The cowboys applaud, and I know Savannah is blushing.

Beatrice, Madeline, Thistlena, and Neppy come down the steps two by two. In a fuchsia shirtwaist, Neppy is the beauty among them. Someone helped her apply makeup, and she has changed into a head-turner. The cowboys are speechless. The little dimple in her right cheek blooms like the pink of her dress.

We raided Ramona's costume box to find full skirts and petticoats and then bought blouses in town at Montgomery Ward. I purchased an embroidered white shirt very much like Savannah's; I have no idea where I will wear it again—perhaps to the seashore—but it complements my blue gingham skirt. Beatrice's top is too low cut, as usual, and Thistlena reminds me of Mary Pickford in *Rebecca of Sunnybrook Farm*. Over her teal shirtwaist—one of the few dresses she wears so often—she has tied a starched white apron with ruffles.

Even though spirits are high, I am anxious about this new experience. I don't know the first thing about square dancing. The moon is almost full, and it lights up the panorama as we pile into cars for the drive to Three Peaks Ranch. The sun always sets early in Reno, the Sierra Nevada pushing it down behind the lonely pinnacles, but the pink-and-purple hues that hover over them render us speechless as we bump along the desert floor. Tiny stars float in the azure dome above us, gradually growing brighter. I wonder, *Is it possible I will miss this severe but breathtaking landscape when I return East?*

We pull up beside a line of cars against a split-rail fence. "Meet the Martins," Arthur says. The family members—all eight of them—run to open our doors. John Martin and his four boys of ascending heights, each wearing string ties over white shirts, offer their arms to us, while two little girls in full skirts clamp their arms around Savannah and Ramona.

"How's my favorite sugar, Caroline?" Savannah asks. Little Hawk picks up Caroline's sister and swings her around while she squeals. Arthur, Ramona, Neppy, and Olivia Martin hug each other and laugh in unison. Ramona's face shines as if she is center stage under a spotlight.

We walk toward the music and come upon an amphitheater that is set between three buildings and strung with paper lanterns. Between the almost-full moon and the lanterns, the area looks like a party at noon. A large wooden dance floor has been placed in front of the musicians, and many tables stand on three sides. The musicians—three men and a woman with a tambourine—are tuning up, but a Victrola plays a familiar tune. Tessa and all four of her ranch mates come running up to us.

"Evelyn, we've staked out a table," she says, her cheeks in high color.

Nat and Ray are absent, I notice, as is Candace. Johnnie arrives, his hair freshly cut and groomed. He is carrying a tray of glasses. "Ladies, I have here Methodist punch or Lutheran punch," he says, pointing to the two offerings. "What'll it be?"

I know enough to begin with the alcohol-free Methodist variety, as do Thistlena and Madeline, but Beatrice chooses a glass of Lutheran. So much for sobriety.

Tessa, who has gone completely native in a white dress trimmed with gold, curtsies and flutters her eyelids. We learn that the so-called squaw dresses aren't worn by Native American women at all—only by tourists and six-weekers—but they have the advantage of full skirts. Laughing, she twirls around to demonstrate.

I look around for Sundown. He is trapped by a large group of cowboys who refuse to let him pass with his tray of corn bread.

"Sundown is smitten. Sundown is smitten," one of them jeers, and others join in.

"We're supposed to show up at the dance halls for free drinks," another adds. "No fallin' for 'em."

"No lovin' with these highfalutin rich ladies from the East. Just dancin'," a third says.

Poor Sundown. He winks at me, his face apple red. I can't rescue him, so I follow Tessa and her ranch mates to our table.

First, the locals demonstrate square dancing. The caller, Tex, has an infectious sense of humor, admonishing us all to "watch how it's done." Arthur, Ramona, Savannah, and Little Hawk are first up, along with Zack and Smoky Joe and two of the Three Peaks Ranch girls. Three other groups of eight come to the floor.

We watch in awe as each couple performs the moves in unison. Savannah and Little Hawk steal the show; she lifts her crinolines high, and when told to "swing your partner," Little Hawk, with a dreamy smile, nestles his face right under Savannah's bosom. These dancers are good enough to join the Ziegfeld Follies, but mixed-race couples would never be tolerated back East. Of course, there is Josephine Baker, the

African American dancer who moved to Paris since she wanted to live where legal segregation did not exist. *Where is the harm?* I ask myself. *Where is the harm?*

Next up are the six-weekers, each on the arm of a seasoned square dancer. Sundown races to my side and leads me to the floor. "Free at last," he whispers in my ear. I let out an audible sigh, but my heart is racing.

Tex teaches us our steps, which we practice without the music. Then the instrumentalists join in, and we're off. Of course, having a partner who knows all the moves doesn't hurt, and Sundown holds me in a vise grip every time we turn.

The ranchers have this party down to a science. After one group of six-weekers has two square dances, they head for the chow line, and the next group takes the floor. And as Beatrice has noted, there are no wallflowers. Dancers and audience members alike clap after every number, and smiles are wide.

It's our table's turn to go back to the dance floor. We learn some new steps and then repeat a dance from our first round. I find myself stomping my feet and clapping my hands like a schoolgirl. While I try to focus on Tex's calls, my mind keeps wandering back to the dances I attended in high school. Soft music, white gloves, parent chaperones. The gentlemen bowed, the ladies curtsied, and couples, though touching, were very separated in their dance postures. Customs had relaxed considerably during the Roaring Twenties, but I never danced a Charleston. I was too busy raising children and doing church work—anything to keep my mind off my failing marriage.

Sundown takes me back to our table and brings us fresh glasses of punch. He blots his brow with his bandanna. I am square dancing's newest fan, but there is no doubt that a good deal of perspiration comes along with the high stepping. And along with this perspiration comes a serious thirst. Bursts of laughter ring out, and I catch Beatrice's unmistakable shrieks; she sounds too loud and too sloppy. Madeline catches my eye and raises an eyebrow.

I turn to Sundown. "You are such a fine dancer. I can't help thinking you belong in Hollywood."

"Oh, Miss Evelyn, I've heard that before, but the life of a range rider . . . it suits me," he says. "I grew up on a ranch—didn't even finish the eighth grade—and took to the saddle as soon as I could."

"Haven't you thought of settling down, finding a pretty wife, and having a bunch of kids?"

Sundown laughs and tweaks my nose. "You've seen too many Tom Mix movies. Life is hard out here. Have you heard of ghost ranches? I've seen a lot of them in this depression—a lot of dust and some fallen-down barns, everything dead. But Reno's doing all right now—thanks to you six-weekers and the gambling. And may I add, if anyone belongs in Hollywood, it's you. You're the prettiest gal here tonight."

I look down at my hands.

Sundown stands. "Let's take a stroll," he says. "I'm cooling off, but I could use a break from the noise."

We walk hand in hand, swinging them like a couple of kids. I chuckle. "I bet there have been plenty of six-weekers who wanted to march you right into that chapel across the street from the Washoe County Courthouse."

"Well, there have been a few," he says, his eyes merry, "but if a woman is too eager . . ."

"I know. Takes all the fun out of it."

"A new crowd of six-weekers arrives at the train depot every week. I love dancing and befriending them, and yes, I've given my heart away a couple of times, but they all get back on that train going East."

I had never thought of things from the cowboy's point of view.

"Don't misunderstand me," he continues. "A long night in the bunkhouse is a lonely night. I'd much rather wash off the dust, have a few drinks, and entertain the ladies."

So he is working from his strengths. He is handsome and a good dancer, but deep down, I suspect he thinks that he doesn't have much to offer.

Reading my mind, Sundown says, "I've had a few offers to go back East as a kept husband, to live in the lap of luxury, but I can never give up the freedom of the range."

We stop and gaze at the sky. Sundown steps in front of me and takes my shoulders. I close my eyes at the soft brush of his lips. Every nerve ending in my body has come alive as we kiss gently and then passionately. I hold my breath. Finally, I arch my head back. "I need to breathe," I whisper. We sway in each other's arms to a nameless tune. Confused by what I am feeling, I say, "I need to find the ladies' room."

"Right behind the chuck wagon," he says.

I hold his cheek and give the other a peck. "Meet you back at our table," I say, and take off at a trot.

One end of the food wagon is very crowded—they are serving bowls of ice cream—so I head for the other end. As I round the rear wheels, I come face-to-face with a wall. I have no choice but to move to the end of it, where, hopefully, I will find the bathrooms.

"Who do you think you are?" a woman shouts like a drill sergeant. "How dare you hurt my friend!"

As I turn the corner, I see Beatrice lying on the ground, her skirts pushed up to her waist. Madeline stands with her hands on her hips, looking up at a cowboy standing over Beatrice, his legs on either side of her. A second cowboy is unfastening his belt.

A head shorter than the cowboy who straddles Beatrice, Madeline steps closer, tilts her chin up, and roars into his face: "I said, get *off* of my friend!"

I remain behind the corner. I'm ready to rush in if needed, but Madeline appears to be taking charge. The cowboy backs off, his palms up in surrender. Madeline goes up close to the second man. "What are *you* waiting for?" The man runs after his friend while struggling with his belt.

Beatrice rolls onto her side, moaning. I run to her and pull her skirts down.

Little Hawk appears and helps us lift Beatrice to a sit. I hold her up from behind as she collapses against my knees. Her head hangs down, her mouth drooling.

"Let me have your kerchief," Madeline says to Little Hawk. She blots Beatrice's face while I remain frozen in place.

"I'll get help," says Little Hawk, and he runs off toward the amphitheater.

"Can she walk?" I ask.

"I don't think so," says Madeline.

Little Hawk returns with Arthur and Gerry. Without a word, Gerry bends down and hoists Beatrice across the back of his shoulders in a fireman's carry.

"This way," Arthur whispers as he points away from the crowd at the chuck wagon.

"Lutheran punch," says Little Hawk, as he shakes out his bandanna and reties it.

I clasp Madeline's hand, and we stand there as if in a trance. I have never seen anything so abhorrent—a woman incapacitated by alcohol about to be violated, and the nasty men getting ready to molest her. I have read about these things, to be sure, but seeing cowboys about to abuse Beatrice? Deplorable.

"Madeline," I say, "you were extraordinary. You stood up to those men and prevented them from raping Beatrice."

"I guess I did, didn't I? Well, I learned it from you. I'm worried about Beatrice," Madeline says. "I'm afraid tonight's events are going to add to her depression."

Madeline's compassionate words shake me. We have all been watching out for Beatrice, but I had thought she'd perked up lately, in anticipation of this party. Now I agree with Madeline—Beatrice is headed for more melancholy. I suddenly remember I need to find the bathroom. "Meet you back at our table."

Those two cowboys almost raped Beatrice. Are we all vulnerable to these attacks? I'm so frightened that my teeth are chattering.

I concentrate on slowing my breathing. Maybe I'll stay behind at the Flying N for the rest of my residency.

⁀୭

"You look like you've been spooked by a banshee," says Sundown.

I force a smile and pinch my cheeks, then cover my face with my hands.

"Evelyn, what's the matter?" he asks.

Between convulsive sobs, I tell him about the attempted rape of Beatrice that Madeline interrupted.

"Which cowboys?" Sundown demands.

"Oh, Sundown, I have no idea. Arthur and Little Hawk took Beatrice back to the ranch. It was horrible."

He blots my tears with his bandanna.

"That was the most frightful thing I've ever seen. I suspect Beatrice had a little too much Lutheran punch, but now I'm fearful for the safety of all the six-weekers."

⁀୭

The musicians are taking a break, but someone has put on a recording of *Show Boat*. I had been lucky enough to see it when it opened on Broadway in 1927.

"I love this music," I say, needing a distraction. Should Madeline and I return to the ranch with Beatrice? I want to trust that she will be safe with Arthur and Little Hawk.

"Then let's enjoy some of your eastern tunes," he says as he leads me back to the dance floor. We move quickly to the number, and like in the dance halls, everyone claps when we finish. Sundown moves right into a vigorous waltz.

"Where did you learn to do this?" I whisper in his ear.

"We didn't have much, but my mother had a Victrola that she had brought out West, along with a few grainy recordings. Mama taught her sons—all four of us—to dance. Most evenings after supper were devoted to it."

"Your father?"

"He watched."

I try to picture it—two parents and four sons in a snug cabin with a wood floor, mother winding up the Victrola and waltzing with each son in turn. "Are your parents still alive?"

"All gone. Ranching killed 'em."

"And your brothers?"

"Scattered to the winds."

The final chord sounds, and Sundown dips me low, brings me up, and kisses me soundly on the mouth. The crowd erupts into applause. I recall the shock of my first kiss from Sundown at the end of a dance. Now I hope there will be many more. What is happening to me? I wonder. I feel conflicted by the strict standards of behavior imposed on me by my family, but inside, I feel myself becoming more malleable. Do I want to give in to this strong attraction I feel? I'm beginning to think I do.

"Now that's what I call a fine waltz followed by an even finer kiss," says Tex, who has returned to his place. "Now that you have all enjoyed your ice cream, it's time for more square dancing."

Couples race for a spot on the dance floor while Sundown takes me to the chuck wagon in hopes of finding some cooling dessert. With heaping bowls of hand-churned strawberry ice cream, we find two empty seats at a new table.

Sundown and I sit quietly, relishing each mouthful and taking in the scene. It is impossible to describe the smiles on everyone's faces, and I wonder if I have ever been to a party as delightful as this one. Smoky Joe lifts Neppy high into the air, her crinolines flying, and everyone applauds. And then I am diverted by the memory of Beatrice on the ground with her skirts up to her waist.

"Last dance," Tex announces, and couples scramble for a place to dance to a medley from *Lady, Be Good.* Those who can't fit on the wood floor dance on the ground.

Sundown is quiet, although he holds me close, and with the press of bodies near us, we can't do much besides sway back and forth. I lift my head off his warm shoulder and ask, "How many of these barbecues have you been to?"

"Oh, a fair number," he says, "but this one will stand out—like that bright moon up there—in my collection of memories." He kisses me softly on the lips, then lowers his cheek next to mine and continues to sway. After the final chord, everyone claps for the musicians, but it is a half-hearted applause because it signals that the party is over. I know that the joy of tonight's dance will provide sweet dreams for many a six-weeker tonight. It will take a huge force of will to recall the good times rather than Beatrice's ordeal.

Guests begin to search out their rides home while ranch hands set about breaking down the floor, tables, and lanterns.

We are all admonished to tiptoe back to our rooms so as not to wake Beatrice, who was tucked in hours earlier. I wonder how much of tonight she will remember. I worry that I'll have a devil of a time falling asleep once I climb into my bed—I keep seeing Beatrice lying on her back with her skirts pushed up. As an antidote, I will try to conjure up Sundown's rugged, handsome face.

# CHAPTER 26

*Saturday, October 31, 1931*

My brain has been itching with the idea of investing in Twin Arches. It isn't the kind of thing I am used to. My family has never gone in for buying real estate, but I know that a lot of people have gotten rich by doing it. Whether or not I choose to buy shares, it won't hurt me to explore the option. Furthermore, Madeline has been enthusiastic about the project from the beginning, and her family knows about this kind of thing. I must pay attention to that, and perhaps I can learn something.

I airmail one set of documents to my attorney in Hackensack and keep the other for myself. The papers don't make for entertaining reading, but I go over everything line by line. Al Gardner has promised to send me a telegram after he has checked everything.

I don't know how I feel about Thistlena, Nat, and Ray these days. I recall my first impressions of Thistlena—how I hoped that she shared my eastern sensibilities and that we would become fast friends—but she became so busy attracting investors, there was never time to relate to her, woman to woman. And yet she came to me in her hour of greatest need, afraid and desperate. And now that the deed is done, it's as if it never happened. She's a hard one to figure out.

I want to at least investigate this opportunity, but not out of any desire to help Thistlena.

The more I contemplate my life after Reno, the more I realize I prefer to live *away* from my sister. Yes, I hope to return to modeling, but in this economy, that may be a pipe dream. I am not wealthy, but I can probably spare enough to buy a few shares. And who knows? I may make some money.

# CHAPTER 27

*Monday, November 2, 1931*

Ever since the attempted rape, Beatrice has been profoundly sad, dragging herself through her days, eating little. She refuses to go into Reno during the day or evening and spends long stretches of time alone in her room. Even Neppy, Madeline, and I, from our side of the house, can hear her weeping. Little Hawk and Neppy bring her cold water or afternoon tea, but those trays return to the kitchen untouched. Ramona and Savannah glance at one another, but I can't read their thoughts.

When we do see Beatrice, she is unkempt—her hair in wild disarray, her sweaters buttoned out of line, her stockings sagging around her ankles. I try to engage her in cheerful conversation, but she seldom answers.

"Beatrice," says Arthur, "I think you left this on the dining table this morning." He hands her a small medicine bottle.

"Tummy trouble," she mumbles as she heads back to her room.

Madeline stays back at the ranch to keep Beatrice company. It is a big sacrifice for her to miss time with Red on the dance floor.

I meet Tessa and the cowboys in town, and we are soon joined by Thistlena, Nat, and Ray. Early in the afternoon, Tessa and I shop for new dresses—an indulgence, to be sure, but we decide to celebrate having made it to week five. The first dress I choose has broad shoulders and leg-o'-mutton sleeves in a deep-rose silk.

The flapper look is fading, and my new dress has a longer skirt and a wide belt. I still can't get used to the new man-made textiles. Tessa selects a shirtwaist dress in deep purple, which makes her green eyes sparkle. Later, at the Silver Slipper, Thistlena compliments our new costumes, and I feel a twinge of regret that she is forced to alternate between her three dresses. Sundown, Johnnie, and Red whistle and hoot when we approach our table. Embarrassed, I cover my mouth with a gloved hand, but deep down, I am pleased. Poor Red retreats into the background when he learns that Madeline did not come into town with us.

The dance band is especially upbeat, with a cowboy crooner named Bill Bradbury, who can yodel like Gene Autry and makes me laugh, which lets me shed some of my sadness over Beatrice's depression. Swaying in Sundown's arms and then kicking up my heels, I come alive again.

# CHAPTER 28

*Tuesday, November 3, 1931*

Arthur drops me off at Reno City Hall. I carry all my documents regarding the Twin Arches project and have a list of questions that my attorney told me to ask.

A long line of six-weekers extends out the door and snakes around the corner. Everyone seems full of gaiety, dressed in a rainbow of costumes. A few hold hands with a man. *What party is this?* I wonder. Then I recognize several ranch owners, hosts from the square-dancing event, interspersed among the ladies. I realize the ranchers have come in to witness their six-weekers' residencies so that the soon-to-be divorcées can get their divorce papers from the court. Thistlena, Madeline, Beatrice, Neppy, and I, God willing, will be doing this with Ramona or Arthur in less than two weeks.

I am about to push my way past the crowd, since I'm headed to the registrar of deeds, when a group of women come bursting out, shouting, "Yippee! Yahoo! Free at last!" One gal in a coral suit, laughing and holding on to her matching hat with one hand and to another woman with the other, yells, "Everyone to the bridge!" The ladies in line and I turn our heads in unison.

The celebrating six-weekers stand four abreast across the arch of the Virginia Street Bridge. The one in coral counts to three, and they all fling something—I can't see what—into the water.

"What are they doing?" I ask aloud.

"Throwing their wedding rings into the river," a tall woman standing near me says. "It's a tradition."

The women in line wave to the ring throwers and clap for them. The next row of four steps forward, and on the count of three, they also toss their rings. The happiness of the newly divorced is contagious, each one smiling and jumping up and down. They look as if they have each shed a huge burden—they appear lighter than air, like balloons let loose in the sky. I hope I will feel that freedom too. I left my wedding ring at home, so I will have nothing to throw. Leaving my ring behind was deliberate, a symbol of my desire for independence.

I push my way into the building and stand staring at three hallways of mottled-glass doors, each identified with faded lettering. The cacophony of chatter, interspersed with booming directions from a sheriff wearing a tall Stetson hat, causes me to freeze in confusion. Shifting my papers to the crook of my other arm, I inch closer to the deputy and ask, "Which way for the registrar of deeds?"

"Speak up, lady," he says, cupping one ear with his hand.

I stand on tiptoe closer to his face, where I can see the stubble of a day-old beard and smell the stench of someone who has skipped his bath. "Registrar of deeds?"

He jerks his thumb over his shoulder. "Third door on the left."

I open the door to a small office crammed with black metal desks, all unoccupied. A string bean of a man stands, then wipes his eyes with his handkerchief. He wears a crooked name tag that says Mr. Blum.

"Allergies," he says, coming forward.

There is one open window that lets in plumes of desert dust, planting a thin film across every surface.

"I close the window and die of heat, or I open it and tear up all day," he says, swiping his red eyes again.

"I need to check a deed," I say, pinching my nose in anticipation of a sneeze.

Mr. Blum takes the papers I hand him and walks to a metal file cabinet in the corner while humming a cowboy song. "There used to be people at all these desks, but the depression killed that," he says. He peers at me down his beak nose and over his glasses.

"But everyone tells me Reno is coming back," I say, "and there are many investment opportunities."

"So I'm told," he mumbles. The file drawer screeches as he opens it.

"I'm considering an investment."

Mr. Blum shuffles forward. "Everything's in order here, ma'am," he says. "You're not the first person to come in here about this project. Property title, registered deed, in the names of Duncan, Sessions, and Harrison. They purchased the foreclosed property from the bank." He hands me my copies and stares at me with his rheumy eyes, as if to say, "Anything else?"

"Thank you, Mr. Blum." I turn to leave.

Once again, I am sandwiched between a herd of bodies in the hallway. The sheriff in the Stetson hat continues to shout his directions. "Next four to the court! Next four to the court!"

I hoist my papers in both arms like a shield and press toward the exit. The logjam of six-weekers looks impenetrable at the moment, so I take refuge inside the Bureau of Water Restriction. Again, the office is crowded with empty desks, and one man, whose badge reads Mr. Anderson, yells into his telephone. I concentrate on breathing in and out.

"The state of Nevada has taken them over," he says into his phone, his Adam's apple bouncing. "All water rights have been canceled. Open lands for all eternity. By order of President Herbert Hoover."

I inhale, then exhale. The noise in the hall is louder. A woman screams.

"One at a time," says the sheriff. "One at a time."

I look behind me for an opening to escape. Seeing none, I sit down in a chair and close my eyes.

"That's what I'm telling you," says Mr. Anderson. "No water rights. Can't develop land without water. All deeds have been revoked for non-payment of taxes. Fourteen properties in all." He loosens his necktie and unbuttons the top button of his shirt.

I am feeling lightheaded from the close air and all the noise. I desperately want to get outside.

"Plan four-fifty, plan four-fifty-one, and plan four-fifty-two—all rights revoked," he says.

I sit up straighter, straining to hear over the noise from the hall. Did he say plan 452? The Twin Arches Hotel and Casino is plan 452.

"Excuse me, sir," I stammer.

He puts his hand over the mouthpiece, his lips pursed in annoyance, and says, "Close the door, lady. I can't hear myself think in here."

I shut the door, and the noise level diminishes, but my heart beats like a jackhammer. Mr. Anderson slams down the receiver and comes forward.

"Ma'am?" he says.

Gathering my wits as I stand, I ask about what I overheard him say.

"You're investing in the Twin Arches Hotel and Casino?" he asks.

"I'm thinking about . . ."

"All you six-weekers are blind fools," he says. He pulls something brown from his pocket, takes a bite, and starts chewing. Tobacco?

My throat is so dry I can't talk; I pass him the copies of the title and deed. He turns to pace, pulling his tie off completely while chomping.

"This project began in 1928," he says, "but the developers had to forfeit, like all the other stupid speculators out here. They ran out of money and didn't pay their taxes. The state has reclaimed these lands and canceled all water rights. They gave it back to the tortoises and the jackrabbits."

"But I have copies of the title and the deed for the land," I say, blinking back tears. How can this be? What does he mean the state has reclaimed it? "My attorney in Hackensack told me to check everything at city hall to make sure everything is in order. And I followed his instructions."

"Lady, they aren't worth the paper they're printed on," he says as he spits into a spittoon on the floor and swipes his mouth with his hand. "You see those file drawers over there?"

I note three four-drawer cabinets against the back wall.

"They're full of revoked deeds and canceled titles for all the fools who ran out of money. There must be more than two hundred deals that fell through."

"But . . ."

"There *was* a plan four-fifty-two," he says. "I'll give you a copy of the revocation of water rights. Can't have hotels without water." He spits again and returns to the file drawers.

Do Thistlena, Nat, and Ray know about this? There has to be a simple explanation. Canceled this, voided that. Water rights can be reinstated, can't they?

I think of how tirelessly they worked. Endless visits to the building site, poring over architectural drawings with potential investors, providing copies of budgets, timetables, and deeds. There must be a logical answer. Or could this be a new development that Thistlena and the others know nothing about? A new possibility comes into my head: they have known of this certainty all along but have not revealed it to the investors.

Mr. Anderson comes forward, waving a piece of paper as if he is claiming a victory. I accept it with a quivering hand and leave. Seeing a clear path through the front door, I hurry outside into the glaring sunshine.

"Evelyn!" Tessa cries, waving from across the street. "Over here."

When I reach her and Flo Van Dyke, they both notice my watery eyes, but I dismiss their concerns, insist it's the noon brightness, and reset my sunglasses. "I've been in city hall, and it is hot and dusty in there." I blot my face with my hankie.

"Are you sure you're all right?" Tessa asks.

"Fine," I profess as I march toward the Riverside Hotel for lunch. I resolve to say nothing of my findings until I have a chance to talk to Thistlena. It's taken me so long to even consider this investment; I want to give her the benefit of the doubt.

# CHAPTER 29

*Wednesday, November 4, 1931*

Two thoughts whirl around in my head: tomorrow I will commence my final week in Reno, and like an adolescent consumed by first love, I'm distracted by my dizzying feelings for Sundown. My insides feel like a spinning top. When I try to read by the fireplace, I catch myself smiling wistfully as I stare at the elk's head. I can't concentrate on the words across the page. I keep reliving swaying in his arms—the feel of Sundown's skin on mine, the heat of his body against me.

When I'm not daydreaming of Sundown, I recall my findings from Mr. Anderson at the Bureau of Water Restriction. I know I have to tell someone, but who? Should I share my findings with the other investors? That feels very disloyal to Thistlena, Nat, and Ray. I shudder and feel the hairs on the back of my neck stand erect. I resolve to speak to Thistlena today. She is going for a horseback ride. Perhaps I can speak to her before she takes off. With the on-paper revocation of water rights in my hand, I set off to share this new information.

The horse barn is quiet, save for the swishing of horse tails and the sound of someone humming. I find Thistlena with a grooming brush making great sweeps on the back of Babe, who has become her favorite mount at the Flying N. I stand off to the side of the open end of the stall and watch her follow the brush with her other hand, as if to soothe the horse, bending low to groom Babe's legs and then reaching on tiptoe to comb her mane. Her clothes still hang on her. Has she lost even more weight? She is already so slender.

I clear my throat, and Thistlena jumps, dropping her brush. "I'm sorry," I say. "I didn't mean to startle you."

"I didn't see you there," she says as she wipes her palms on her pants. "Want to come out with Babe and me? Great day for it."

"No, thanks. I'm going to catch a ride into Reno after lunch. Time for another shampoo and set."

"I love riding, but nothing calms me down like grooming a horse." Retrieving her brush, she sweeps it in a long arc across Babe's back, then down the horse's flank.

I chuckle. "Babe is certainly enjoying it. Her eyes are closed."

"That's my girl."

I clear my throat again and thrust out my hand with the water-rights paper. "Wanted to show you this. On the instructions of my attorney, I went to city hall yesterday. It was so crowded I was literally pushed into the Bureau of Water Restriction. I happened to hear a Mr. Anderson speak on the telephone about land developments that have been turned back over to the state and had their water rights revoked. And he specifically mentioned plan four-fifty-two."

"Well, that's ridiculous," she says, placing the brush on the floor and taking the paper. "The water and sewer lines are already in, at least the first phase of them."

"I'm certain there's been a mistake, or something." I step forward and point. "But, Thistlena, see what the paper says." I move my finger over the exact words. "All water rights have been canceled. Open lands for all eternity. By order of President Hoover."

Thistlena removes her cowgirl hat and swipes her forehead with her arm. "We go to the site every day. We drink the water from faucets that are attached to the wells." Staring at the paper, she shakes her head and wets her lips.

"I believe you, Thistlena. Honest. But what if this comes to the attention of your investors?"

She lowers her chin and appears to swallow with difficulty. "Why did you go to city hall anyway?" she asks.

"Well, truthfully, I was seriously considering becoming an investor in your project. At least, I was following the instructions of my attorney back East, checking the deed, the title, and so on. But as of this moment, I'm backing off completely."

Thistlena's eyes widen. "I had no idea you were even considering . . . well, we had kind of crossed you off the list . . . after you said your family preferred other investments. Tha-thanks for this paper," she stutters, pushing it into her pocket. "I'll get Nat and Ray on it right away."

Backing up to take my leave, I say, "Please tell them I'm certain there's a perfectly logical explanation, but I thought you should know."

Thistlena lifts Babe's saddle from the stall divider, swings it over the horse, and sets about fastening the cinch with shaking hands. "We'll get to the bottom of it, and I'll get right back to you."

Walking back to the ranch house, I'm guessing my investment is completely off the table.

# WEEK SIX

# CHAPTER 30

*Thursday, November 5, 1931*

Today is the beginning of my final week in Reno, my last seven days of this fascinating odyssey. While Madeline and I enjoy our hot breakfast, Thistlena is long gone—I assume with Nat and Ray—and Beatrice is still asleep. Arthur surprises us by announcing that we will attend a rodeo later. We are delighted by this new diversion, and Madeline goes upstairs to inform Beatrice.

I know that western-themed shows sometimes come through New York City and play at Madison Square Garden—I read about them in the newspaper—but they are nothing anyone in my family cares to see. Since the Crash, very few entertainments have filled that arena. Who can afford to attend them anyway?

Sitting in the stands at the fairgrounds, I realize that photos in eastern newspapers have not prepared me for what my eyes behold this morning at Reno's twelfth annual autumn rodeo. Six-weekers, ranchers, families, cowboys of every shape and size, and even several handfuls of Native Americans fill the wooden bleachers of this outdoor arena. In either direction, I see a rainbow of colors—nationalities as well as costumes—while a man at the loudspeaker tells the contestants to mount up for the opening parade.

Ramona has passed out sombreros to the Flying N women, thank goodness. The sun beats down like a branding iron, and the dust whips across the corrals and then subsides as quickly as it rose. Where is a proper parasol when I need one?

Several six-weekers aim their Brownie cameras up into the stands, and I pray I am unrecognizable in my ridiculous hat and sunglasses. I pull down the sleeves of my sweater to cover the backs of my hands. An eastern lady of good breeding does not expose her skin to the sun. It makes one old before her time, my mother always insisted.

The parade music comes from a Victrola, and the horses step lively, tossing their manes. The sun reflects off the ornaments on their bridles and saddles while their riders wave to the spectators. I'm shocked, and pleased, to see cow*girls* as well as cowboys. And, oh, they are young and pretty in their hand-sewn boots and fringed jackets. Do they grow up on horseback? I imagine they do.

Thistlena enjoys the occasional ride with Gerry. I should have paid more attention to my riding lessons at finishing school. And then I wonder, *What am I good at? What are my skills?* Yes, I can turn heads on a fashion runway, but what else? I definitely admire these multitalented women of the West.

Arthur and Little Hawk sit down beside me, pointing and waving to their favorite riders. Arthur explains that in years past, anyone could be called a "world-champion cowboy." In 1929, however, the Rodeo Association of America standardized the rules and established a point system to determine the champions. "Some of the cowboys don't like it," he says with a wink. "Not everyone can say he, or she, is a *world* champion."

No sooner has the last parade horse and rider left the ring than a wild stallion bursts out of his stall, arches his back, and tries to throw off the cowboy riding bareback. His lean torso, one arm in the air, thrashes back and forth like the snap of a whip. The audience screams its support, and I find myself standing, clapping, and cheering for the rider, who, the announcer says, has made a record time. A bell clangs, the cowboy slides off his mount, and two dusty clowns in baggy clothes shoo the horse into his stall.

After bareback bronc riding comes saddle bronc riding. Some riders hold their mounts while others fly off, landing on their backsides. "Ouch!" I can't help saying, and cover my eyes until the horses are back in their chutes. One cowgirl, an audience favorite, whoops and hollers, her hat in her free hand, her dark braids flying.

"She's been at it for more than twenty years," Arthur says.

I'm incredulous. I've read about the legendary Barbara "Tad" Lucas, but I know she lives in Texas. This gal doesn't look a day over thirty. I'm meeting a new kind of western hero—rodeo *girls*. How different their lives are from mine. And yet I wonder if they really are all that different. Do they go to school, marry, and raise children? They seem so free and independent, competing for prize money by repeatedly putting themselves in harm's way. Even when a cowgirl falls, she is all smiles, waving to the crowd while she slaps her pants with her hat.

While daydreaming, I don't realize that the bull-riding contest has begun.

"The most dangerous eight seconds in a rodeo," Arthur says, pointing to a chute.

"What if a rider is gored by one of the horns?" I ask.

"It happens," says Arthur.

"Next rider up, Sundown Ahrens," says the announcer.

"Sundown?" I cover my mouth and glance both ways.

Is that *my* Sundown? Why is he not on the range? I look hard at a rider with the number 14 pinned to the back of his vest. Hat pulled low over his forehead, he has nothing to hold on to—no saddle horn or stirrups for his feet—save a braided-rope flank strap. The bull's eyes squint against the sun as his nostrils flare.

The bull bucks, rears, kicks, spins, twists, and bucks some more. It is as if the earth shakes when his hind legs crash down. This looks so dangerous. Sundown could be killed! A loud buzzer announces the completion of the eight-second ride.

The crowd leaps to its feet and cheers. Sundown slides off the bull while the clowns corner it and open the gate for its capture. Sundown stands in the center and bows. Now with his hat off, he smiles and waves, his deep blue eyes and finely chiseled cheekbones catching the light.

"Attaboy, Sundown!"

"Another record!"

"No one can beatcha, Sundown!"

"Another record-breaking score—ninety-four—for Sundown Ahrens," the announcer says.

I clap and cheer in spite of myself. To hell with society's rules for a lady. I wave and jump up and down.

Repositioning his hat, Sundown scans the audience. Will he recognize me in this ridiculous getup? I wave again and feel certain he sees me. He winks, and one side of his mouth curls up in a quick smile that I hope is for me.

The contests continue for the next hour—calf roping, steer wrestling, and barrel riding—but I can't think of anything except Sundown's performance, how he appeared glued to the back of the bull, how tall he sat in spite of the bull's attempts to throw him. I take my cues from the audience—standing when they stand, clapping when they clap—but inside I am back on the dance floor with Sundown, held tight in his arms.

I think back to all the nights we spent in the dance halls and realize that's what we did—danced. We didn't talk much at all. Always attentive, Sundown sensed when I needed to sit down for a bit or drink another lemonade, but he didn't ask me about where I came from, or about my family, or about what I did back East. Maybe that's how the cowboys conduct themselves—dance with the girls in exchange for free drinks, keep their distance, don't get involved. After all, there is a new bunch of gals arriving every week down at the depot.

All I know is that he's a range rider, living a life he enjoys because of its freedom and independence. Does he care that I, too, came to Reno so that I can be free and independent?

Sundown could be so much more than a cowboy. Despite a limited education, he is Hollywood handsome and could succeed as a photographic model. What about all those men in cigarette advertisements? What ever happened to Buffalo Bill's Wild West Show? Sundown could be a headliner as a bull rider. I know William Cody died, but his show toured all over the world. Who took his place?

Maybe Sundown wants nothing more than what he has. Still, I wonder: When he's alone on the range, stoking the embers of his campfire with only the moon and its shadows for company, is there an empty place inside him that he longs to fill? Imagining myself held tight in his arms, swaying in time to a slow, sad tune, I realize this champion cowboy stirs feelings within me that I haven't felt for a long time. Indeed, have I ever felt them? One thing I know for certain—he arouses in me a deep hunger that is growing and demanding to be fed.

～☺～

The Flying N girls tease me endlessly as Arthur drives us into Reno after supper.

"You can't stop smiling," says Madeline, giving me a nudge with her elbow.

"See how she blushes," says Thistlena.

I suck in my cheeks and try to hide my giddiness, but it's no use— I'm so eager to see Sundown and tell him how impressed I am by his performance at the rodeo.

～☺～

When we find our tables beside the dance floor at the Deauville, Tessa is part of the crowd surrounding Sundown. While Beatrice grabs on to Nat's arm, the other cowboys shake Sundown's hand, pretending to knock off his hat and slap his back.

"Guess you showed that bull who was boss," says Red.

"A new record for you today, Sundown," Johnnie adds.

Sundown sees me, reaches out for my hand, and pulls me to his side.

"I had no idea you're part of the rodeo." Suddenly tongue tied, I can't think of anything else to say. I pray that no one can see the flush on my face.

Tessa steps up and plants a kiss on Sundown's cheek. "C'mon, girls," she says. "Let's show Sundown how proud we are to know him." One by one, at least a dozen gals kiss his cheek. I pretend not to care and hope I won't lose him to one of his new admirers. *What's this new feeling?* I wonder. Feeling a little possessive? Oh yes, I am, and a little jealous too.

Sundown laughs good-naturedly, then pushes out his palms, as if to say, "Enough." He grabs my hand again and leads me to where Tessa, Red, Johnnie, and Madeline are seated.

"Whew!" he says, blotting his face with his bandanna.

"I wasn't sure you'd be here tonight," I say, "after all your work at the arena today."

"And miss a chance to dance with my favorite partner?"

Now I know my cheeks are reddening. The band starts up, and all three couples take to the dance floor. By now, many of the tunes are familiar, and we perform the routines we have perfected. Sundown dips me low at the end of the song, and huddled observers clap their approval. Do I feel like Ginger Rogers? Definitely.

As the evening wears on, several ladies try to cut in, but Sundown tips his hat and mouths, "No, thank you." Of course I'm pleased. I also find myself consumed by an overwhelming desire for this man. Ever since the rodeo this morning, I have felt on fire. I can't push it away any longer. When Sundown puts his arm around my waist, I move in closer to him, and my breasts feel the heat of him. When he places his cheek against my forehead, I stand on tiptoe so that I can press my nose and mouth into the crook of his neck. When I inhale, I am drunk from the smell of him. My ardor has taken over every inch of my body.

"Shall we get some fresh air?" Sundown asks as the musicians set down their instruments for a break. He leads me outside, and we sit on a bench across the street from the dance hall.

I can't think of anything to say, and thankfully, Sundown holds my hand and looks toward the tiny splinter of a moon. I match my inhales and exhales to his as our body temperatures cool in the crisp night air. The dance hall doors are closed tight, and I hear only the faintest noise from inside, as if it were miles away. The desert stillness should be like a sedative, but my heart rate doesn't slow. How long has it been since I have felt such yearning? Sundown puts one arm around me and then turns me toward him with the other. His eyes lock on mine, and we kiss, softly at first, then with increasing fervor. His kisses, his breathing, and his caressing reach something buried deep inside me, and I want more. The earlier effects of the cool air are defeated by my arousal.

The dance hall's doors open, and laughter spills out as our friends make their way down the steps. Like a couple of young people caught in the rumble seat of a car, we sit up straight and press our backs against the bench. We both giggle as we try to assume straight faces. Thistlena and Madeline motion me to join them as they make their way toward the post office and our lift back to the ranch.

We stand, and Sundown takes both my hands in his. "Tomorrow's my day off," he says. "What would you say to a horseback ride and a picnic lunch?"

"I'm nowhere near the rider you are," I say, remembering the bull-riding skills he demonstrated earlier that day.

Sundown smiles so handsomely that I fear I will melt into a puddle. "Oh, we'll take it easy. I promise."

❧

Later at the ranch, I listen to the silence. The desert is hushed; the only light comes from the small lamp on my desk and the feather moon outside my window. I look back at my rumpled bedclothes, where I tried in vain to find rest. This is week six of my required stay in Reno. Next Thursday, I will go to the courthouse, then board the train for New York. And all I can think of is how much I want to feel Sundown's skin against every inch of mine.

From our very first dance, Sundown always treated me as a lady, showing manners as refined as any eastern gentleman I know. And he's so good looking that I know he can have any woman he wants. Lord knows many a six-weeker would bed him in a heartbeat. I've seen the flirtatious smiles cast in his direction by the other women. But he doesn't seem to be that kind of man. He attaches himself to me every night when he could have so many others.

Now he appears as smitten with me as I am with him, but I'm no fool. There is no future for me with Sundown. He's a range rider and a bull rider, and whatever else I may think him capable of, he has made it very clear how much he values his independence. And isn't it my desire for freedom that brought me to Reno in the first place? He already has what I want.

Much to my surprise, I'm feeling incredible passion for this man, a reawakening of a hunger long buried. On the one hand, my cravings reassure me that I can still have these feelings—that I can desire and be desired. On the other hand, at thirty-nine years old, I can still get pregnant, and I certainly don't want to go through what happened to Thistlena. And heaven knows having another child is out of the question.

I feel as if I am teetering on a precipice. I can hold back, keep my desires in check, and return to my eastern roots with my respectability intact. Or I can give in to these hidden hungers and return home a liberated woman. I feel like a small boat being tossed in a storm. When I reach dry land, I pray I can live with my choice.

# CHAPTER 31

*Friday, November 6, 1931*

I find Sundown in the kitchen with Savannah, filling an extra set of saddlebags with a picnic lunch. I know Sundown doesn't work at the Flying N, at least not regularly, but all the ranch hands know all the other cowboys, and they all know Savannah.

Glancing out the front window, I can see that Sundown has ridden to the Flying N with a second horse. The two mares are tied to the front rail, making white puffs of air with their nostrils and pawing the dirt. *Is the horse going to run away with me? Where are we riding to? What in heaven's name am I doing?*

I borrowed my riding costume from Neppy. "You look like a Reno cowgirl," she had said as she tied a red bandanna around my neck. She placed her western hat on my head and stood back, arms crossed. "Turn around." Smiling with satisfaction, she said, "Miss Evelyn, you're ready for the movies."

When I come into the dining room, Sundown says I resemble Annie Oakley.

"But, Sundown, she was a riflewoman," Savannah teases.

"Oh, but she rode a horse while she was firing that gun of hers."

"Miss Evelyn's much prettier than ol' Miss Oakley."

My face blushes, which is getting to be a regular habit with me. What do I know? I've never seen one of those Wild West shows.

"I'll grant you that," Sundown says, and plants a kiss on Savannah's cheek as he hoists the bags over his shoulder. "Ready, cowgirl?"

"As ready as I'll ever be." Sundown takes me by the hand, and I look back at Savannah. She is smiling from ear to ear.

The day is unseasonably warm for early November. The bright sun climbs higher into the azure sky, but for once, no wind disturbs the sagebrush. As the horses walk out, the air holds a softness that I haven't felt before. On this still morning, my face doesn't feel as if it's going to flake off from the constant dryness. I sigh. I want to always remember this arid beauty that I've come to love.

My horse, called Old Blue, begins a slow trot, but I pull her in. "Sundown," I say, "you spend every day, six days a week, on the back of a horse. On your day off, are you sure this is what you want to be doing?"

"Oh, I'm sure," he says. He winks, and one corner of his mouth turns up in his quirky half smile. Is that a reddening I see coming over his face? He sucks in his cheeks as if to resume a straight face. His horse, Belle, starts to trot, and Old Blue follows.

Oh Lord, I can't bounce here for long, the way one is supposed to on a western saddle. My horse has a gentle gait, but old habits die hard, and I rise to post each time her right shoulder goes up. Sundown and I ride companionably, side by side, not needing conversation. Old Blue and I soon find a natural rhythm, and for a moment, I close my eyes. There are no sounds but the horses' hooves thumping across the desert sand. What do I smell? No specific odor of tree or flower or animal but an all-encompassing purity—almost an innocence—in the air. Having learned to live in the East with automobile exhaust, coal dust, and before that the endless droppings from horses pulling carriages, I find this western air to indeed be a gift.

Sundown must be reading my mind. When I exhale deeply, he says, "Pretty swell, huh?"

"You can say that again." Looking ahead, I realize the area appears familiar. "I've been here before." I point to a stand of trees in the distance, at the foot of the hills. "After the dust storm, Arthur and Ramona brought us here in the wagon to check on the livestock. They found two dead calves over there."

"I heard about that," he says. "Happens a lot, I'm afraid."

We slow to a walk and enter the stand of trees. The water of the stream within is low but flows gently over rocks that reflect many colors in the sun.

"It's so beautiful," I whisper.

"That it is," he replies.

We turn north and follow a narrow trail alongside the stream, Sundown leading the way. He swivels around in his saddle and asks, "What's beautiful about where you come from?"

"Well," I begin, "lots of things."

"For instance?"

Wrenched from my current surroundings, I need a moment to gather my thoughts. I haven't visualized my Hackensack environment in weeks. Gradually, I recall the green cathedral created in summer by hundred-year-old elms that line both sides of Union Street; the first flakes of wet, heavy snow icing the green leaves and red berries of holly bushes; and then the tiny heads of blue squills and crocuses that emerge from the dark ground in early spring. I tell him about going to Atlantic City in the summertime to see and smell the Atlantic Ocean, to admire the rainbow of ladies' parasols on the boardwalk, and to eat saltwater taffy.

"Sounds nice," he says. "I've never seen the ocean."

I swallow a big lump of regret and stop talking. I want to remember *this* ride, *this* day, not dwell on Hackensack.

A large clearing opens on both sides of the stream. Sundown's horse, Belle, and my Old Blue strain at their bits. "They want to drink," Sundown says. We dismount and hold the reins while the horses step into the shallows and quench their thirst. Then we tie them to a couple of saplings in the shade.

Sundown retrieves a colorful Native American blanket and spreads it next to a sturdy tree trunk. I sit down, take off my hat, and lean against the tree. As if reading my mind, Sundown sits beside me with two plain bottles and a couple of tin cups. I am, indeed, thirsty, but what is in those bottles? I wonder. He sees me look askance and chuckles. "No gin in the bottle, Evelyn. Not to worry. I've brought plain water and a little bit of local cider."

He removes his Stetson and bandanna and loosens the bandanna around my neck. The touch of his fingers on my face is enough to send me into more spasms of blushing. I hold my breath while I shake my hair loose and pull off my neckerchief. He pours two full cups of water, and we clink our cups. "To my favorite dancing partner," he says.

I don't know how to reply. The cool water is a gift to my throat and to my nerves. "Thank you for this, Sundown." I inhale deeply for courage, then blurt out, "I feel blessed to have met you." I sweep my arm in an arc across the view. "And I will always remember this place, this day."

Sundown's eyes search my face. He sighs, then touches me, as soft as a whisper, under my chin. We kiss gently at first, then deeply. We pause and part. He holds my face in his hands. I am relieved that I have a chance to catch my breath and, at the same time, long to resume our kissing.

"This calls for a drink of cider," he says, reaching for the second bottle. "See if you like it."

I try the apple-scented liquid and find it sweet and quenching.

"Who makes this brew?" I ask, pretending to spurn it.

"Recipe of an old medicine man."

"Promises to cure what ails me?"

"Yes, ma'am. This will cure all your ills."

We laugh, toast again, and lean back against the tree trunk. I let my head drop onto his shoulder.

"I'm not accustomed to taking a lady on a trail ride," he says. "It's something I usually do by myself."

I lift my head. "Then to what do I owe this pleasure?"

"Don't you know how special you are?" He caresses my hand. "Not only are you beautiful and a good dancer, but there's something much more . . . more than pretty . . . I guess I'd call it 'class.'"

"That might be the nicest compliment I've ever received. You're a good man, Sundown. I sensed that the moment I met you."

I'm getting nervous. Time to lighten the mood. "It's obvious how much you enjoy dancing at the dance halls," I say with a teasing grin.

"And the free drinks don't hurt either." He chuckles. "Some cowboys really like to take advantage of the six-weekers, the ones who act desperate. Some women are frantic to find their next husband. They're the ones who head back on the train in worse shape than when they arrived. I don't ever want that on my conscience. That's not to say I don't enjoy some huggin' and kissin', Miss Evelyn."

He gathers me into a long, steamy kiss. The hairs on my arms rise. Heat rushes through my body, weakens my muscles, and leaves me limp. All of a sudden, as a breeze blows by, I am aware that we are outside, able to be observed by anyone.

While covering my face with kisses, he loosens my clothing. He takes his time and seems to enjoy exploring every inch of me. He runs his tongue over my nipples while I struggle with the buttons of his shirt. His skin is soft to my touch in spite of the taut muscles underneath. I follow the scent of him and taste the silky skin of his neck and shoulders. Yes, we are outside, but we are sheltered by a dense thicket of cottonwoods.

He helps me remove my pants and fumbles with a latex sheath. I kiss him on his shoulder and pull him on top of me. "Not to worry. I've taken precautions."

Thank goodness I had an enlightened mother. As I began packing in Hackensack for this trip, something caused me to throw in the pessary that I had used to prevent further pregnancies after June was born. Having sex while in Reno was the furthest thing from my mind, so what caused me to pack it? A minuscule hope for new love?

Sundown braces himself on both hands and closes his eyes as he penetrates and gasps, "I've never wanted anything so much."

I feel the heat of his longing, but even after he drives into me, he slows his thrusting and searches my face. While every fiber of my being is on fire, I sense a new freedom—a weightlessness but not a helplessness. I feel lighter than air, but I am the pilot of my course. I am directing this powerful attraction between two equals. Not only has my clothing been cast aside, but so have the barriers of "respectability." Sundown told me I have class, and yet I feel as if all my class restrictions have been stripped away.

"Is this all right?" he asks.

I have no answer except to arch my hips and cry out as I pull his mouth to mine.

⌒꙳

I don't remember too much of the rest of the afternoon. I know we napped awhile, legs entwined. I shiver, and Sundown fetches my blouse, pants, and jacket.

"Can I interest you in a cheese sandwich?" he asks, his eyes smiling. He brings the saddlebags to the blanket while I struggle to reassemble my clothing. Before putting on my socks and boots, I wade into the stream and splash cold water on my face and neck.

My body feels more alive than I ever remember, but I hear my sister's voice. I'm an adulterer. I have just had intercourse with a man to whom I'm not married. Indeed, I'm still married to Dean!

However, something in me changed under those trees and changed for the better. Like a fledgling leaving her nest, I chose to fly with an exceptional man who wanted me for the woman I am. Sundown likes me for *me*. And in so doing, he has made me feel every bit like the woman I know I am. Natural. Sensuous. A woman who is beginning to believe she can soar. No matter what occurs when I return East, I know in my heart that the memory of this day will never disappear. I will cherish it like a precious stone.

# CHAPTER 32

*Saturday, November 7, 1931*

Madeline and I want to do something nice for Neppy to thank her for taking such good care of our rooms and meals. I ask Ramona if we can take her to lunch in Reno.

"It's her day off," she replies. "Ask her."

Neppy beams when we speak to her after breakfast. "Lunch? In Reno?"

"Our favorite is the Grand Café," Madeline adds. "We think you'll like it too."

"What should I wear?" she asks, tucking loose strands of hair behind her ear.

"Whatever you like," I say, "but make it special."

"Is Thistlena sleeping in?" Madeline asks. "We could ask her to join us."

Neppy sets down a plate of hot biscuits. "She left real early this morning. Nat and Ray came and got her."

I watch butter melt on my open biscuit while I take another sip of coffee. I haven't said anything to Madeline about the water rights. I feel I owe Thistlena some time to clear this up, or else I have exposed a very sophisticated con job. I want to believe in Twin Arches, but time will tell.

Neppy, Madeline, and I wave goodbye to Arthur, who has dropped us off at the Reno post office. We are headed to Montgomery Ward, where they are having a sale on silk stockings. Out of the corner of my eye, I see Nat and Ray on either side of Thistlena, hurrying up the steps to city hall. Good. They're wasting no time in setting things straight, I hope.

Neppy has dressed in a ruffled ivory blouse and a full denim skirt over which she wears a teal-colored poncho that complements her hazel eyes. I watch her finger the stockings, first one shade, then another.

"These would be good for your skin tone," I say, gathering up three pairs and handing them, along with three pairs for me, to the salesgirl. Neppy's mouth opens as if to protest.

"My treat," I say, patting her arm.

We snake our way along the wooden sidewalk in the direction of the Grand Café, bumping into other six-weekers, who are by now familiar faces and greet us with bright smiles and courteous nods. I know that many of the ladies recognize me from the dance halls. Several turn to follow us with their gaze. I catch my reflection in a store window—strawberry blond, youthful complexion, slender figure. I know I have a new spring in my step—I'll have to call it "Sundown"— and I struggle to wipe the grin off my face. Does anyone suspect the reason for my ebullience?

We settle in at our table at the Grand Café. Neppy touches her starched white napkin and the chrysanthemum blossoms in the small vase and exclaims over the tiny salt-and-pepper shakers at each person's place. Madeline asks her what she is looking forward to when she returns home.

"Giving my boy Davy a big bear hug," she says, her eyes as big as saucers. She tells us about her older sister, Cassie Jo; her brother-in-law, Eric; and their four kids. "They're farmers too. Dairy. And Davy loves visiting his cousins, 'cept Cassie Jo's latest letter said Davy's been down in the dumps lately." She looks down at her lap.

"Six weeks is a long time to be away from your momma," I say. "Have you ever seen any of Neppy's artwork?" I ask Madeline, changing the subject.

"Artwork?"

"She's a gifted artist. I discovered her on one of my walks. I thought her picture was exceptional. She told me she's been to art school."

"Well, I hope you're going to continue when you get back to Pennsylvania," Madeline says.

"Not likely," Neppy mumbles. "I have a boy to raise and a farm to run."

I reach out and give Neppy's hand a pat. "Her father can't work anymore, so it's all up to Neppy and her mother."

"I see," Madeline says. "I still hope you'll find a way to keep drawing."

Our lunch arrives, and again Neppy marvels over the delicate sandwiches, their crusts removed and their tops adorned with parsley leaves. A dollop of sour cream floats atop each bowl of mushroom soup. She waits until we begin to eat, watching our movements, and mimics us as we dip our soup spoons from front to back. Madeline smiles at me. Yes, we are glad we invited Neppy.

"What are your plans, Miss Madeline?" she asks.

"Well, Neppy, unlike Evelyn, I'm continuing west to San Francisco. I have a cousin with whom I will live for a while. I plan to open a shop."

"What kind?" asks Neppy.

"I'm not sure." Madeline dries the corners of her mouth. "I'll have a look around first."

Neppy looks at me as she leans toward her next mouthful of soup. "And you, Miss Evelyn?"

In fact, I have been thinking about my plans quite a bit in the last couple of days as my six weeks in Reno inch toward their close. Just this morning, I imagined telephoning my friends at the modeling office. The staff at the Powers Agency has shrunk since the depression began, but Colin and Frances are still there, arranging photo shoots for the few ad agencies that have managed to hang on. Colin always welcomed me enthusiastically when I visited the offices on Market Street, and Frances came flying out of the back rooms, wisps of unruly gray hair escaping from the bun at the back of her neck, to take my coat and insist I stay for tea.

"Can you come back to modeling?" Colin had asked during my last visit in September. "We'd have to update your portfolio a bit, but both Macy's and Gimbels would choose you, I'm certain."

Am I too old at thirty-nine? Is my waistline too thick despite my cinched corset? Will the new lines around my eyes diminish my chances? I'm counting on Colin's certainty. I know I can do what's required, but I pray there will be work for me.

I shake myself from my doubts. "I will live in Hackensack with my sister in the home we inherited from our parents, and I will return to modeling in Philadelphia and New York." I stretch my back flat against my chair. It feels good to speak of modeling with certainty. I only hope I'm not being overly optimistic. I also will have some fence-mending to do with my children. That's for certain.

"You'll be sensational," says Neppy. "*McCall's, Good Housekeeping*—I can see you in all of them."

Now I'm embarrassed. "I'll write to each of you when it comes to pass."

"And we can show our friends and say we know you," Madeline says.

We complete our lunch with dishes of ice cream, the best part of any meal, according to Madeline. After settling our bill, we join the throngs on Virginia Street and head back, single file, to the post office. Out of nowhere, Nat and Ray appear, one on each side of me.

"A moment, Miss Evelyn?" says Nat. His forehead is moist, and he has unfastened his top shirt button. He's also short of breath.

What do they want? I tell Madeline and Neppy to go ahead, that I will be right along. Nat, Ray, and I step off the sidewalk into the street so that others can pass.

"Gentlemen," I say, shielding my eyes from the sun, "how can I help you?"

Ray moves in front of me, his piercing blue eyes uncomfortably close to my face. "We want to thank you."

"Thank me?" I say, backing up.

Nat comes beside Ray while blotting his forehead with a handkerchief. "Thank you for telling Thistlena about the problem with the water. At Twin Arches."

Ray smiles and swipes at his mustache with both forefingers. "We've been to city hall to secure proof of our complete entitlement to use of water."

"That's wonderful." My stomach has been churning, but now it is soothed. I exhale in relief. "What happened?" I ask. "How did the water rights get revoked?" We begin to walk back toward the post office where Arthur is waiting.

"Oh, it's a long story," Nat says, "but we got everything straightened out. The Bureau of Water Restriction is preparing an affidavit, and we'll have a copy for each of our investors."

"I can't wait to see it," I say. "If everything is on the up-and-up, I want to be one of your investors."

They both halt, then tip their hats in unison, appearing at a loss for words.

"Thistlena said . . ." Ray begins.

"We had come to the conclusion . . . ," says Nat.

"I know. You had crossed me off your list."

"This is very exciting news." Ray can't contain his smile. He leans back and laughs at the heavens. "We will bring copies of the affidavit out to the ranch as soon as it is ready."

"I look forward to it."

Nat opens the front passenger door for Neppy. Madeline and I stand aside.

"You all look very happy," Arthur says, leaning on his elbows on the roof of the car. "Did someone win a prize?"

Nat says, "We *are* happy. Evelyn has told us she's going to invest in our hotel and casino project."

Arthur climbs in the front seat and starts the car while Madeline and I make ourselves comfortable in the back seat. Eyeing us in the rear-view mirror, he says, "Sounds like another case of 'Reno fever.' Looks like our town is coming back."

# CHAPTER 33

*Sunday, November 8, 1931*

After dinner, Arthur drives Madeline, Beatrice, and me into town. Knowing our Reno nights are waning, we are quiet in the car. The moon is a thin crescent, but the stars light up the Milky Way. I feel torn between nervous anticipation over seeing Sundown again and a growing sadness that this life-changing sojourn is ending.

We find the whole gang—Tessa and Johnnie, Sundown and Red, Thistlena, Nat, and Ray—waiting for us at a huge table inside the Deauville. Wearing an emerald-green dress with a full pleated skirt and a smart hat with a rhinestone pin fastening emerald feathers at the back, Tessa clutches Johnnie's hand. She is bouncing on the balls of her feet like a child who has a secret she is bursting to tell.

"I can't keep it in any longer," she says, her eyebrows arched high. "Johnnie and I are getting married." She thrusts out her left hand to show a tiny diamond on a slim band.

Dumbstruck, we gape at one another. Someone has to break the ice, so I embrace Tessa and Johnnie, feigning enthusiasm. Madeline takes my cue and gives hugs too. Sundown says, "Well, we all have something to celebrate tonight." The band begins to play, so he pulls me to my feet. Fixing on my eyes, he mouths, "What?"

I shrug my shoulders while Sundown fans himself with his hat. "You look beautiful tonight," he whispers in my ear.

A thousand thoughts are spinning around in my head: What is she thinking? Tessa is a girl with eastern sensibilities; Johnnie is a range rider. But stronger sensations fill my body. All I need is a whiff of Sundown's cologne and I want to tear my clothes off. I try to slow my breathing as he holds me close, and we make like Adele and Fred Astaire. At the end of a slow number, we stand there, holding on to each other, not moving. I close my eyes and sigh.

The band begins a peppy tune. Sundown grimaces, then grabs both of our drinking glasses and pulls me by the hand to the stairway off the front lobby. Crowds of people mount the stairs, but we manage to slide along the bronze railing and keep our footing. He leads me down a long hallway, a worn paisley runner on the floor, occasionally lit by a single sconce that does little to lift the dreariness. He hands me our drinks and opens a door. Before I can take in the surroundings of the small bedroom, he sets our glasses on a table, scoops me into his arms, and clamps his mouth on mine. I can't help myself—I whimper. We draw apart from our kiss, and he sits me down gently on the bed.

The nubs of a coarse bedspread press on the backs of my arms and neck, but against Sundown's chest and groin, I feel radiant heat. He stands up quickly, his back to me, and unfastens his shirt and trousers. I raise myself on one elbow and begin to unbutton my dress.

"Allow me," he whispers, and proceeds to undress me slowly, gently, with constant kisses. "Oh my," he exclaims after pulling my shirtwaist over my head, revealing my foundation garment. "I'm going to need your help with this."

I stand and hold on to his shoulders while he unties my laces. I search every inch of his face—the fine lines that sweep up the outside corners of his eyes; his soft, velvet mouth; his perfectly carved nose. "You are the handsomest man I've ever known," I say. "You are also a *good* man." My corset falls to the floor.

He throws off the bedspread and climbs in first. He lifts the light blanket like a tent and smooths the sheet beneath, inviting me in. I lie down and stretch the full length of him. Every one of my pores contains a live electric current, so consumed with longing am I. What is he feeling? Judging from his breathing and grasping, he, too, is on fire.

∾

As we lie entangled and exhausted, the last person I want to think about is Dean Henderson—or, more precisely, sex with Dean, which has never been anything like my encounters with Sundown. Dean relished my body, I remember, but the whole act was finished in moments, and well, after he lost his job and retreated into himself, I lost interest.

I shake myself to empty my mind of those recollections and push up on one elbow. Sundown seems to be dozing, and I watch him breathe, his gentle puffs of air touching my breast like a feather. He opens one eye and smiles. "What?"

"Nothing." I nestle back into the cave of his chest, inhaling the scent of him. "I hate to say this, but do you think we need to get back to the dance floor?"

"Hmm."

"Whose room is this, by the way?"

"You worry too much," he says as he kisses me soundly. Once again, our heat rises up, and we caress and fondle and kiss and give in to exclamations of pleasure. *Thank you, God,* I think in the middle of it all. *Thank you for this man who has taught me that I am a sexual being.*

∾

"Where have you been?" Tessa asks when we return to the table after sneaking back onto the dance floor. "The bandleader announced our engagement, we danced, and everyone cut in."

"We went outside to count the stars, and we lost track of time," Sundown says. Red lifts an eyebrow high, gives Sundown an elbow to his ribs, and takes a draft of his beer. Sundown quickly orders two more drinks and returns me to the dance floor. We move naturally into our favorite steps to the Paul Whiteman tune.

"She's glowing," I hear Tessa say to the table. "Positively *glowing*."

When Sundown and I part tonight, he tells me he will not be in town tomorrow night. The day is to be a last roundup from the high country, and the boys will camp out overnight. To be sure, I am disappointed. Now I need some time to recover from all that has happened.

On the ride back to the ranch, Madeline, Beatrice, and I jabber nonstop about Tessa and Johnnie's decision to marry. "I still can't believe it," Madeline says. "She's such an eastern girl. I thought she would surely return to her old neighborhood in New York City. I mean, I'm very fond of Red, and I know you care about Sundown, but marriage?"

"I'm so jealous I can't see straight," cries Beatrice. "I want someone to marry *me*!"

"I know someone will come along," says Madeline, patting Beatrice's knee.

I think, *You have no idea how much I care about Sundown.* Ignoring Beatrice, I say, "I agree. East is East, and West is West. But, ladies, haven't you noticed the change in Tessa? She was very chatty on the train but also very plain. But during her time here, she has blossomed—new dresses, new hairstyle, new shoes, and always the first one to kick up her heels to the Charleston on the dance floor." I clear my throat. "I have felt some of that rebirth myself." Thank the Lord it is nighttime, as I sense my face burning scarlet.

After we arrive at the ranch, Madeline and I sit up in front of the fire, talking for a long time. For the most part, we continue to air our shock over Tessa's announcement. We both agree that while we have enjoyed—indeed, reveled in—the attentions of Red and Sundown during our time here, we are both levelheaded by nature. We know the cowboys will catch the next batch of six-weekers when they emerge, timid and disoriented, from the train depot. Madeline will seek her fortune in San Francisco, and I will resume life in Hackensack.

"But would you marry Sundown, Evelyn?"

I'm still tingly all over from our lovemaking, but I say, "In the next life, my friend. There are practicalities. Can you see me as a rancher's wife? I can't see Sundown as an eastern businessman." But what I don't admit is that the thought has certainly crossed my mind. Move to Reno. Take up modeling work here. Continue my deep connection to Sundown. Funny, I don't think of marriage.

A cinder snaps as the firelight fades.

⌒⑨

### *Monday, November 9, 1931*

In the morning, I find Thistlena sitting alone in the living room, a book in her lap. Not a usual sighting. Her legs are crossed, serious scuff marks reflecting from her navy pumps. Her single strand of pearls lies against her concave chest, and the sun casts a sheen onto her worn-out navy sheath.

Thistlena stands, book in hand. "Evelyn, may I have a word?"

"I'm going to check on Beatrice," Madeline says.

Arriving at my room, I turn around the desk chair and invite Thistlena to sit. She holds herself plank straight, her hands clasped at her crossed knees. I fling my new aqua silk shirtwaist onto the bed and retrieve a shawl and crystal choker I've purchased in Reno.

"What do you think?" I ask, standing away from my arrangement. "I hope all my new finery will fit in my cases going East."

Thistlena says nothing, and I feel self-conscious and frivolous. There have been no additions to Thistlena's wardrobe during our time here—at least, none that I have seen. And yet she always appears the perfect lady—tastefully dressed, fine featured, with an erect posture that gets noticed. I haven't dwelled on it lately, but in the beginning, I questioned her alliances with Nat and Ray. They seemed beneath her.

Now I understand they are business partners. I sit on the bed and wait for her to speak.

"I want to talk to you about the hotel and casino project."

I fetch a large envelope from the top of my bureau. "I have everything right here. The Hackensack Trust Company is ready to transfer the money. I assume you brought the papers confirming the water rights."

"I have them," she says, standing, "but the thing is, Evelyn, I believe ours is not the right investment for you." She walks in a small circle, leans one hand on my desk, and stares out the window.

"Listen," I say, "I've *never* done anything like this before. 'Taking a flier' is what my father would have called it. But I have the funds and, well, taking this risk is part of the new me."

"New you?"

"I've never made an investment decision on my own before. I was schooled by my parents, and I knew their biases. I feel I've done my due diligence, and so has my lawyer, and most importantly, I agree with you."

"Agree?"

"Reno is growing, and more and more tourists will come. I've decided I want to be a part of that."

"But, Evelyn, I think it's not for you." Her eyes narrowed, Thistlena holds her jaw rigid and twirls her pearls around her forefinger. "I want to discourage you from signing the contract and passing the funds. In fact, I won't accept them."

"Look, Thistlena, we are both ladies from the East—gloves from Bonwit's, tea at Schrafft's, blue-chip stock portfolios. That is still the core of me, but today I'm a new woman."

"How do you mean?" She wipes her palms on her skirt.

"Oh, I'm still Evelyn Henderson of Hackensack, New Jersey, but I've changed. I can feel it. I've met new people, tried new things . . ."

"But the money?"

I stand and begin to walk back and forth at the foot of my bed. "I don't know how to say it. When I arrived in Reno, I wore blinders, like all of those horses I saw at the rodeo. I viewed the world through a narrow lens. I was judgmental. I saw everyone and everything with a critical eye. I imagine this was a cover for my fear of this new place, of this new experience. My reference points were all back in Hackensack."

"And that's the world you're going back to."

"True enough." I stop and face her. "Now I've taken those blinders off, and my peripheral vision has broadened to accept—heck, even *admire*—people of all kinds. I'm open to new possibilities I never dreamed of before. According to my sister, I am the biggest scandal in town. Wait till I tell my friends that I'm an investor in a hotel and casino project." I laugh and hug myself. "I can imagine the looks on the faces of the Ladies' Aid Society."

Thistlena clears her throat, wets her lips. "One doesn't choose an investment in order to shock her friends."

"I know that," I say. "I expect to make money."

"I need a drink of water." Thistlena clears her throat again and sits in the chair.

I tap on the bathroom door, and hearing no reply, I fetch her a glass of water. As I run the faucet, I think, *How come this one-eighty?* Don't they need a certain number of shareholders in order to resume building the hotel and casino? Madeline, Tessa, and Flo have already signed on. Beatrice—having recovered her joie de vivre, thanks to Madeline's devoted attention—is leaning in that direction (to catch Nat, if for no other reason). And those are only the ones I know personally. Thistlena hasn't tried to discourage *them*.

Her hand trembles as she reaches for the glass.

"We all want to make money," she says.

I sit again on the bed. "I know I won't earn any income from this— you're not going to pay dividends—but I'm still young. I've got time. And I've got a hunch that we'll get a big payoff in a few years. So I'm confused. Is the project in trouble?"

Thistlena squares her shoulders. "Heavens, no. Nothing like that. It's just that . . . I know you. You're cautious."

I take a deep breath. I wonder what Thistlena would think of my acquaintance with Miss Helen or my horizontal encounters with Sundown. I sigh again. "Yes, I *am* cautious and have considered your project *very* carefully. You completely lost me with the revoking of water rights, but you have cleared that up. I'm certain I want to be included."

"Very well," she says, standing to leave. She walks to the door and pauses to look back. "You know, Evelyn, I'll never be able to repay you."

I must have looked perplexed.

"For accompanying me to the reservation . . . for holding my hand." She opens my door and leaves. The last thing I see are the seams of her nylon stockings, slightly askew.

I had tucked her abortion into a remote corner of my mind. It was a scandalous thing to be part of, and I prayed for God's forgiveness. I will always believe she had other choices, but I rationalized that I responded to a friend's desperation. What if it was me? I can't imagine such a scenario, but life is full of unexpected turns. Madeline still worries that Owen lurks behind every corner, and Beatrice is terrified of being alone. What am I afraid of?

I have small worries, to be sure. Sharing a home with my sister, who finds fault with my every move. Returning to the modeling agency and learning there is no work for me.

Losing the love and respect of my children for divorcing their father.

Is my choice to come to Reno a mortal sin? It certainly is, according to my parents and Marion. I suppose I will return home with an incurable contagion, "divorcée." But Mother and Father are dead now, and I have the financial means to live comfortably. Simply. And on my own terms. That is all I ask.

Blotting my face with a cool washcloth, I am saved by images of Sundown. Gazing in the bathroom mirror, I see goose bumps multiplying across my neck as I conjure the feel of his arms around me on the dance floor. I can practically smell his aftershave.

# CHAPTER 34

*Tuesday, November 10, 1931*

It is long after breakfast when I come downstairs wearing my desert walking shoes. I intend to have a cup of coffee, bundle up against the increasing November wind, and enjoy one of my last desert rambles. Instead, I find Arthur, Ramona, the sheriff, a deputy, and Little Hawk standing around the dining table, looking at a map.

Seeing me headed to the kitchen, Arthur says, "Thistlena has decamped."

I grab the back of a chair with two hands.

"Skedaddled," says the twig-thin deputy with wire-rimmed glasses.

"We are certain they took off by plane; I'm guessing to Mexico," says the sheriff, eyes squinting, scratching his jowls.

Madeline is seated, crying into her hands. Ramona, expressionless, stands behind her, rubbing her shoulders.

"The casino, Evelyn," Madeline says between sobs, "it was a scam. They have no water rights." She dissolves into more choking sobs.

So Mr. Anderson at the Bureau of Water Restriction was correct. The state has, indeed, taken back the land.

Savannah comes out of the kitchen with a tray of coffee mugs, the whites of her eyes as big as boulders. Neppy follows her with milk and sugar. I manage to let go with one hand and grab a mug.

"Miss Henderson?" I hear the sheriff say.

I jerk from my stupor, and he hands me a large, fat envelope. Everyone is silent while, fingers shaking, I unfasten the flap and remove the contents. On top of the pile lies the check from the Hackensack Trust Company for $5,000, payable to Twin Arches Hotel and Casino. Across the signature of the bank president is a large stamp: VOID AND CANCELED. Thistlena didn't deposit my check.

A car motor sounds out front, followed by screeching brakes and rapid footfalls mounting the steps.

"I came as soon as I heard," Candace Niven says as she bursts into the house with her camera, her short hair standing straight up.

My first instinct is to hide in the kitchen.

"This is a criminal investigation," says the sheriff. "No press allowed."

Candace creeps to the dining table and quietly takes a seat.

Turning to me, the sheriff says, "I need those papers as evidence."

*Did he say criminal?*

I hand him my envelope, collapse into a chair, and clutch my coffee mug. Everything comes rushing back. While Madeline continues to sob, I recall Thistlena's visit to my room and her insistence that the project wasn't an appropriate investment for me. I insisted that I wanted to be a part of it.

"We know she is Mrs. Sessions," the sheriff says, jotting in a small notebook.

Thistlena married to Ray? Not possible. I can't believe it. I try to bring the coffee mug to my lips, but my hands tremble too much. Does this mean that Ray was the father of her unborn child? If the child didn't belong to her former husband—is there a former husband?—why did she want to terminate a pregnancy by her *current* husband? I try to remember. Did Ray and Thistlena behave like man and wife? And if they are really married, why did Thistlena board alone at the ranch?

"Does Tessa know?" I ask.

Everyone looks at me. "Tessa Marquand. She's our friend and an investor. Different ranch."

The sheriff looks at his clipboard and makes a check mark. "There are two hundred and ten names here, and each one of them is out five grand."

I do a quick calculation. That amounts to over $1 million—a fortune! "How do you know Twin Arches is a scam?" I ask.

"We got a call from the bank," the sheriff says. "The trio withdrew every penny from the account yesterday afternoon."

Madeline continues to sob. "What a fool I was."

"Wait a minute," I say. "How do we know they didn't withdraw the money so they could pay the builders? You know, finish the project?"

"We checked with the powers that be at city hall as well as the state building," the sheriff says. "There is no water access. Not one drop."

I think of Tessa and Johnnie, of their plan to marry. Will this make a huge dent in their future? Obviously, Tessa believed she could put $5,000 aside for a future payoff. That was my rationale too.

Why didn't Thistlena deposit my check? Again, I recall how she came to my room and told me not to invest, but I opposed her. All this is *after* I told her about the water-rights problem. And they answered the question. Was their new document a forgery?

Out of the corner of my eye, I notice Candace fiddling with her camera. Does she have the gall to capture Madeline's anguish? I want to choke her! I glare at Candace, hoping my eyes portray my loathing.

I'm vaguely aware of the men talking in the background. The sheriff has to inform all the investors from the other ranches and from the hotels in town. Arthur and Ramona are instructed not to disturb Thistlena's room; the sheriff will come back later to collect evidence. The last thing I hear him say is "But they're probably already in Mexico."

And I was seduced like the rest of them, yet Thistlena chose to safeguard me. How will I explain this to the other investors? What if they suspect me of conspiring with Thistlena?

She said she would never be able to repay me for accompanying her to the reservation. Well, by God, she saved me from myself, and like my check, her debt is voided. Nevertheless, her deception leaves a foul taste in my mouth and a huge despondency in my soul—like the massive sinkhole I came upon on one of my desert walks.

⁓

One morning in Hackensack, as I poured household trash into the receptacle outside the kitchen door, I spotted many pieces of crisp but crumpled white stationery. Pausing to examine them, I found perfectly typed letters signed by Dean and addressed to school heads in New York, New Jersey, and Connecticut. Why hadn't he mailed these? The letters showed intention. What had changed his mind? I also discovered several newspaper classified ads with secondary schools circled and notes scribbled in Dean's hand. At the bottom of the basket, my eyes fell on a plain white envelope addressed simply to "Dean." The envelope, from the Gramercy Park Hotel, was not sealed, the back flap merely tucked in, and so I read the letter.

June 13, 1931

Dean—
Our time yesterday evening was a high point in my long and discouraging days. I feel reinvigorated by all that we shared, and I greatly anticipate our next meeting. Thank you for your thoughtful listening, wise counsel, and deep understanding. I feel a connection with you that I've never felt before.
I am profoundly grateful.
Yours, T.

My hand began to tremble. I set down my empty basket and felt an overwhelming need to walk, to get away—fast. I desperately wanted to avoid notice and tried to slow my steps to a casual stroll. I didn't know what to do with my hands, as they were twitching so badly. I finally stilled them by clasping them behind my back. I lifted my chin to look confident when, in truth, I feared I might crumble onto the sidewalk. Perspiration gathered at my armpits, but what was soiling a new gabardine jacket compared with the realization that my husband was having an affair?

Fortunately, no one engaged me in conversation as I made my way along the path that circled a pond in the park. A few men tipped their hats; a mother and daughter said, "Good morning"; and a mutt sniffed my heels. Everyone was outside enjoying a fragrant morning in June, but the scent of blooming jasmine bushes made me nauseous. I had to reach a toilet or vomit into the greenery.

Arms pumping as I raced home, I reviewed what I knew: First, Virginia tells me about running into Dean and a young man outside the Gramercy. Second, I find and read the letter. Perhaps I shouldn't jump to conclusions. Maybe this was all very innocent. I resolved to do my own sleuthing. I couldn't confront Dean until I had the facts. Having a plan of action calmed my stomach. Yes, I would learn the truth, so help me God.

Businesslike, I approached the front desk of the Gramercy. I knew my way around this hotel since Dean's brother William and his wife, Jane, had always lived here.

"Good morning, Mrs. Henderson. Shall I ring your brother-in-law?" Fastidious as always, Mr. Finch pulled down the lapels of his cutaway while he expanded his chest.

"Not today, Mr. Finch. I am meeting my husband, Dean Henderson . . ."

"Is he expecting you?"

"Oh, no," I replied. "I know he slept here last night after the meeting of school directors . . ."

"School directors?" Finch said.

"Am I mistaken? Dean attends regular meetings of school administrators, but perhaps I have the wrong hotel."

Finch lifted his eyebrows and said, "No meetings here last night, or in the past, for that matter. Last night he dined here with Mr. Wilder." Finch extended one arm toward the dining room and smoothed his goatee with the other.

"Mr. Wilder?"

"Yes, Thornton Wilder," Finch said, "the playwright."

"Oh, y-yes," I stumbled. "Mr. Wilder. We're old friends. He taught French at the Lawrenceville School while my husband worked there."

Did that sound promising? I didn't recall where Thornton had landed after all his publishing success. Maybe Dean was being considered for a position.

"Yes, I believe Mr. Wilder is on sabbatical, but he is our guest here at least once a week."

Dean had been spending the night at the Gramercy once a week. To meet with school personnel, he had said.

"Excuse me a moment." I took off at a clip for the ladies' lounge, fell into a toilet stall, and retched. I lost my breakfast and what felt like everything I had eaten for a week. I was stunned by Dean's lying, and his betrayal burned me to my core. Further, Dean had been using his "job-seeking allowance," which was begun by my father, continued by my mother, and now maintained by me, for these "meetings." But the lies, the out-and-out lies. I heaved again, but I had nothing left to expel. Eventually, my breathing slowed, and I blotted my face with cooling towels at the sink.

Inhaling to steady myself, I squared my shoulders. Perhaps I had heard wrong. Maybe Dean had been attending meetings and staying at a different hotel. He always said he was staying overnight with William and Jane, so what was I missing?

I started for the front desk. The sound of Dean's laugh startled me, and I ducked behind a cluster of potted palms. I expected to see him with another woman, but Dean and another man exited the elevator, upper arms touching, chuckling as if sharing secret intimacies. I remained hidden, trying to identify the stranger. Someone from church? A former colleague from Lawrenceville? Someone entirely new?

Dean gripped the elbow of the man as they walked toward the exit. They stopped to face each other and continued their animated chatter. This man was not a new acquaintance. He was Thornton Wilder. The same height as Dean, he had youthful eyes that twinkled with admiration and something else—attraction? They left the hotel, talking all the while, and turned north.

I wasn't sure how long I remained behind the palms collecting myself. Visions of Dean and Thornton continued to lodge in my mind. Eventually, I descended the marble steps and exited the revolving door.

A taxi carried me up Lexington Avenue and west on Thirty-Third Street. As I inhaled, I feared my lungs would burst. Exhaling, I blotted the spittle that had collected at the corners of my mouth. Closing my eyes, I willed my breathing to slow.

Dizzying thoughts tumbled in my head as my train left Penn Station. When I pondered a slew of questions, answers eluded me. One certainty I could not avoid: Dean's lies were the final straw. Nausea teased the back of my throat as I tried to imagine the reason for Dean's frequent overnights in New York. I recalled the letter I had found, signed "T." Did *T* stand for Thornton? I pulled down my hat's veil as low as it would go and quietly wept.

When a passenger smiled and said hello, I turned away. I wanted to appear relaxed, dozing, but underneath my skin, my muscles were jumping. Placing the back of my hand against my forehead, I suspected that I had a fever. The lies that I had discovered were making me physically ill. At this exact moment, I began to imagine a new life alone. I would leave a loveless marriage, a partnership into which I had been forced. I had lived a lie for years. Wasn't lying a mortal sin? And how about Dean with T.? I felt so injured, as if I had been dragged through thorns. T. had said he felt a "deep understanding" and "connection" with Dean. I, on the other hand, felt like I had been struck by the ultimate betrayal. I had tried so hard to bring an end to my purging, but I was on the verge of retching again.

⁓

Now I am confronted by a second treachery. Even though my check was voided, I, too, feel as though I were stabbed in the back. Oh, sure, I won't have to explain to Marion how I was taken for a fool. Thistlena, whom I helped in her time of need, had broken a trust with me. First, she had chosen to confide in me, though she had known me so briefly. Sensing her desperation over her pregnancy, I had finally given in to her urgency and held her hand throughout her abortion. I still wonder if God will forgive me. Does she honestly believe that returning my check erases her betrayal?

As the sheriff and deputy prepare to leave, Candace stands. "I'd like a picture of the investors."

The sheriff remains inches from her and snarls. "I said no press. Understood?"

"Yes, sir." Nevertheless, Candace follows them outside and leaves the ranch, her car trailing behind theirs.

I insist that Madeline accompany me on a walk. We meander slowly, each kicking up stones, each lost in our own thoughts. When we return, we find Beatrice on the couch in front of the fire, swiping at tears and whispering to herself: "He's gone. Nat's left me. How could he leave? We were getting on so well. We were going to marry. I know we were. A little more time. He needed a little more time, that's all."

Madeline and I slump down on the couch, one on either side of Beatrice. "I am still dumbfounded that Thistlena and Ray are husband and wife," I say.

Beatrice and Madeline stare at me blankly. "Ray is handsome," I continue. "I'll give her that. But do you recall how they went everywhere as a threesome? And with them, it was all business. They didn't dance very often."

"You're right," says Madeline. "They spent all their time moving around the six-weeker tables, selling their scheme."

"And when Nat and Ray did get up to dance, it wasn't with Thistlena," I say. "They were soliciting investors."

"I should have bought shares," Beatrice murmurs. "Stupid me. Nat would still be here if I had signed up."

Madeline touches Beatrice's arm. "Have you heard anything we've said?"

Beatrice looks at Madeline vacantly.

"It was all a scam," says Madeline. "There was never going to be a Twin Arches Hotel and Casino."

"Every day," I continue, "Thistlena would leave the ranch with Ray and Nat and deliver more prospective buyers to the development site. And they had all their folders and their drawings."

"Yes," Madeline says, "it was a very slick operation, and a lot of us fell for it."

"I feel so abandoned," says Beatrice as she falls over her lap and cries.

Conversation at dinner is minimal, although Arthur tries to distract us. While we three pick at our stew, he recalls life in Reno before 1931—before the legislature lowered the residency for a divorce and legalized gambling. As in so many other cities in America, investing in land development with borrowed money was the downfall of many a speculator. "I could take you to many piles of rocks that were once going to be another Taj Mahal."

Beatrice—who, for the most part, has been pushing her food around her plate—asks to be excused.

"Oh, Beatrice," Arthur says, handing her a small bottle, "I believe you left your medicine on the table again."

Beatrice looks at the bottle. "I wish I could say this calmed my stomach." As she walks to the stairs, her posture epitomizes a cactus flattened in a dust storm.

⌒∂

As for me, I need to change into an evening gown. The cowboys won't be in town tonight, and I have finally accepted a date with Boyd Whitaker, my Reno attorney, who will bring me to the Willows. I guess this will round out my Reno experiences, and I will bring home anecdotes to share with Sally and Betsy. I have even less appetite for dancing than I have for my dinner, but a change of scene will take me away from Thistlena's deception, I hope.

∽

"I swear, Miss Evelyn," Boyd says as he reaches for my gloved hand when I come down the front steps of the ranch house.

"Oh, you mustn't swear," I say, cutting him off while raising a fore-finger as if to scold a child.

"You are a vision of loveliness tonight," he continues, licking his lips.

Perhaps I made a mistake in agreeing to this outing. Maybe this man in a fine cutaway is as sleazy as so many of the other dandies I've seen outside the casinos. Unwilling to set aside my curiosity or excitement, I push my doubts away. Not all of the women who visit the Divorce Colony get invited to the Willows, so I resolve to press on and see what the night will bring. Putting on my best imitation of a giddy, coquettish flapper, I chat amiably while Boyd drives his Duesenberg west.

After closing for updating and remodeling, the Willows reopened last January to great fanfare and write-ups in all the papers. Supposedly, this is where the wealthy divorce seekers come to see and be seen. For this occasion, I had shopped for a long dress, choosing a form-fitting design made of pastel pink satin and chiffon. It hangs from spaghetti straps with a plunging neckline. A chiffon ruffle outlines my hips, while the same fabric gathers below my knees to the floor. It is pure Jean Harlow. This is an extravagance, to be sure, but I suspect I will have something extraordinary to tell my friends back in Hackensack, if they dare to listen.

Approaching the Willows, we are greeted by hundreds of tiny lights scattered over the surrounding grounds and a twinkling path that leads to the main entrance. After I leave my wrap with a scantily clad coat-check girl, Boyd offers me his arm, and we begin to tour the interior. I muster my best eastern-girl sophisticated charm when, in truth, I am aghast by the opulence. While the rest of the country endures the depression, Reno, it seems, is a land of extravagance.

The Chinese Room, where people gamble, is painted with red and blue lacquer. We find gold tablecloths, upholstery, and draperies in the dining room, where waiters in white tuxedo jackets dart like dragonflies to refill champagne glasses and serve entrées. We come to the entrance of the Blue Room, where Boyd whispers something into the ear of a tall majordomo in white tie and tails.

"George, may I present Evelyn Henderson," says Boyd.

The legendary George Hart, eyes opening as if to devour me, appraises my figure from head to toe, then bows and kisses my hand. "Follow me," he says.

With his hand at the small of my back too familiarly, George leads me to the grand piano. "Ladies and gentlemen," he says, projecting his deep baritone across the room, "may I present Evelyn Henderson from Hackensack."

Everyone standing around the room turns and gawks. I fear I might melt into a puddle but find the courage to lower my eyelids and make a little curtsy.

"Tell us, Miss Evelyn, are you married or divorced?" George asks.

Certain I am going to faint as I feel the blood drain from my face, Boyd comes to my rescue, placing my hand in the crook of his elbow. With his support, I manage to wiggle my fingers in a wave and say, "Married for a few more days."

As Boyd and I move toward an empty table at the edge of the dance floor, George flips up his tails, sits at the piano, and launches into a suggestive rendition of "If You Knew Evelyn Like I Know Evelyn, Oh, Oh, Oh, What a Girl." The other guests chuckle but appear blasé about the whole thing, thank goodness. While I wonder if every other woman is introduced in this manner, Boyd spins me onto the dance floor. Truth be told, he is a good dancer, and he doesn't try to talk at the same time, so I can observe the scene.

Such an assemblage of fashion finery I have never seen before in one place. Diamonds and other precious stones adorn many women's necks and wrists. Small hats with fancy plumes embellish their heads, and I chuckle when one slips onto the bridge of a nose. As for me, I choose two rhinestone combs. For this occasion, I don't want my hair flattened under a cap. All the ladies wear long gloves, and even a few hide behind sunglasses. Perhaps I am in the midst of Hollywood stars who prefer to hide their identities. Meanwhile, I wonder how they can see where they are going in this dimly lit room.

The orchestra—twelve strong—is larger and better sounding than those I've encountered in Reno's dance halls, and while many musicians rotate in and out, the group never takes a break. I am working up a thirst and crave a cold ginger ale, but Boyd continues to steer me around the dance floor and greet his friends in turn.

Meanwhile, I think I recognize Clara Bow, or a petite curly top who looks like her. Looking off to my right, is that Greta Garbo, a tall, slender beauty? I saw her in two films, *Anna Christie* and *Romance*. What is she doing here? I guess I've caught on to Reno's favorite pastime—celebrity sightings. Boyd continues to plough me toward his friends, so I can't be certain. One thing is indisputable: there are no cowboys here. Whoops, I brush elbows with a tall, mustachioed gentleman—Ronald Colman? His look-alike for sure.

In spite of these new surroundings, images of Sundown invade my brain, and I see in my mind's eye his handsome face. I must be careful not to slip! This elegant scene hasn't been my regular playground in Reno. I try to take it all in, but the people, the decor, and the music are bewildering. My brief thought of Sundown flies away.

A waiter carrying a tray of filled glasses walks behind Boyd. My hand leaves Boyd's shoulder to grab a glass, and I take a sip.

Boyd smiles and releases his tight hold on me. "Miss Evelyn, please forgive me. I am neglecting your refreshment."

"You're a wonderful dancer, Mr. Whitaker, but I could use a ginger ale."

"Waiter, a bottle of champagne," Boyd says as he leads me to our table.

"Ginger ale," I mouth to the waiter, who nods. When he returns to our table with our drinks, I feign ladylike sips while Boyd pops up and down to shake hands with friends who approach and demand an introduction to me. Despite their well-tailored cutaways and manicured nails, I am put off by their too-obvious interest. I excuse myself to visit the ladies' lounge.

I sink onto a velvet-covered settee and retrieve my handkerchief to blot my shiny face. As I powder my nose, a waiter pushes open the door and shouts, "Fire! Everyone out!"

At first, the women stare at each other, stunned. Is this some kind of sick joke?

"Ladies! Out!" the waiter shouts again.

Everyone rises in unison, grabs evening bags, and hurries out amid calls of "Where's the fire?" and "How will I find Harold?" and "How did the fire start?" and "Where should we go?"

I am carried along by the crush of women, now joined by hundreds of men. I can see an open door up ahead. Once outside, ladies gather up their skirts and hurry away from the Willows in every direction. Where is Boyd? I am bumped, kneed, elbowed, and shoved on all sides, finally coming to rest across Verdi Road, where everyone turns around to watch the inferno rising to the sky. A trail of pink chiffon streams from my hem. I rip it off.

We stand frozen in shock, holding handkerchiefs over our noses and mouths while the Willows burns to the ground in less than two hours. Crystal chandeliers explode, sending shards of glass into the air. Walls and ceilings collapse in ground-shuddering booms. Fresh winds feed the fire while a huge cloud of smoke attracts many cars from town, choking the road. Nearby ranchers run to help the firemen pump water from the ditch across the road, but the fire's heat is so intense everyone must stay back. It is too late to save this famous roadhouse.

All of the guests and workers escape in time, but tears wet my cheeks when I think of all the equipment and expensive furnishings that are lost. Scrutinizing several hundred black cars now clogging the road, I take off at a jog when I see Boyd Whitaker waving frantically beside his Duesenberg. As I take one last look at the Willows before getting into the car, all that remains among the embers are a piece of wall and one tall chimney. We ride in silence back to the ranch. I thank God that my life was spared, as well as the lives of all the others in attendance. But here was so much opulence, now destroyed. Is it insured? Will the owners rebuild again?

In time, will I consider this outing a complete waste of time? Or, in my scrapbook of Reno experiences, will I remember that I saw celebrities while I danced at the famous Willows? Of one thing I am certain: I have witnessed the complete annihilation of a famous resort. What a waste. The sight of that fire will haunt my dreams.

# CHAPTER 35

*Wednesday, November 11, 1931*

I call the A Bar Ranch and leave a message for Sundown. "See you in town tonight. Urgent news to share." After breakfast, I plan to read my book by the fire. As I am pouring coffee into my mug, there comes a high-pitched moan from the other end of the house. Madeline comes flying down the stairs in her nightdress.

"Beatrice won't wake up," she cries. "She's as limp as a dishrag. I can't get her to come around."

I hold my breath but force myself to follow Madeline to Beatrice's room. A streak of light coming from an opening between the shade and the window slices across Beatrice's face. She lies on her back, her mouth open, with one arm extended toward the floor.

I touch Beatrice's cheek, tentatively at first, but then leaning over her face, I shout, "Beatrice! Beatrice! Wake up!" I grab her shoulders and shake them. I feel for her carotid pulse, but there is nothing, and her skin is ice cold.

"Go find Ramona," I rasp. "Savannah, Neppy, Little Hawk, anybody!"

Madeline runs out and down the stairs. While trying to calm my nerves, I lift the window shades to let in more light. As I bend down to lift Beatrice's hand and put it beside her on the bed, I notice a glass bottle lying on its side. Hyoscine the label reads. Oh, Beatrice, what have you done? Then a wave of rage and grief slams me. *How dare you? We've come this far, but you gave up in our final inning.* It takes all my strength not to grab her by the throat and scream.

The rest of the morning is a blur. I lean against the windowsill with Madeline, quiet tears falling, while Neppy, Little Hawk, Arthur, and I-don't-remember-who-else come and go. There is much shouting back and forth. The sheriff arrives, followed by the coroner, who takes possession of the glass bottle I hold. He squints at the label and shakes his head. "A very little can settle your stomach," he says. "A lot will kill you."

The same questions fill my head, over and over. What could I have done? What could any of us have done to prevent this? Our six weeks are almost finished. Beatrice was so close to getting that piece of paper, that decree that would free her from Francis and all the ways that he had betrayed her. How could she give up so close to her goal? One look at Madeline's face tells me she is as confounded as I am.

We should have been more vigilant. Everyone knew she was extremely depressed after the square dance. Someone should have been with her every minute. I should have been a better listener. Lord knows I tried. She told me she was terrified of being alone. I suspect that every six-weeker in Reno feels that terror at one time or another. But Beatrice's fear was like a cloud that surrounded her. She couldn't get free of it.

After the attempted rape at the square dance, she was terribly ashamed and downcast. But after a while, she seemed to snap out of it. She started paying attention to her grooming again—wearing colorful dresses and even buying a new hat. Madeline and I were relieved that she was trying to put it all behind her. Instead, Beatrice became fixated on Nat. She chased him in the dance halls every chance she got. Madeline and I were fearful when she drank too much and laughed too loudly, but she appeared happy. And now I realize: When Nat escaped with Thistlena and Ray, that was the final straw.

I have never known anyone who took her life. Every once in a while, I heard about a suicide—a distant relative of a friend—and many years ago, there was a funeral service at our church for a woman with cancer who killed herself rather than face the ravages of the end. After the stock market crash two years ago, I read of investors who had lost everything and leaped off buildings, but these happenings didn't occur close to me. They were always something I heard about or read about, never within my close circle of friends or acquaintances. Did this happen more often in Reno?

"I feel like I should have been able to save her," Madeline says, startling me out of my thoughts. "And I'm angry! How could she leave us?"

"I feel that way too," I say. "We've all been through so much together, and our six weeks are almost over." And then I remember Beatrice's words from yesterday morning: "I feel so abandoned." That is exactly how Madeline and I are feeling. There's a huge stone in the pit of my stomach.

I need to get away from the ranch and all of the sadness here, so Madeline and I get a lift into Reno with Arthur. Madeline has an errand to do at Burke and Short, and I tell her I will meet her at the Monarch Cafe at noon. I try hard to stand up straight and not drag my feet, but I feel like all the stuffing has been kicked out of me. Collapsing onto a bench outside the beauty salon, I watch the other six-weekers strolling by, but in my mind's eye, all I can see is Beatrice's white face—eyes closed, mouth open.

A scent of perfume awakens me from my daydream as the local madam, Miss Helen, emerges from the salon, freshly coiffed under a stunning black hat and looking Fifth Avenue smart in a black-and-tan suit and matching shoes. She remains in place, looking both ways as if she is contemplating where to go next. She looks down and recognizes me.

"Miss Evelyn, Miss Evelyn, are you all right?" she asks. "You . . . you appear very sad."

I sit up straighter and determine that no one else is nearby. "The six-weekers at the Flying N have experienced a big loss," I say.

She steps closer to my bench. "May I?"

I gesture with my hand that she should sit down. "One of our women took her life."

"I see," she says staring straight ahead. She sighs deeply, then turns to me. "It happens."

"She was so close to the end of her stay. She had come all this way and made it this far."

"Not every six-weeker makes it to the end," Miss Helen says.

"I've come to realize that the women who come to Reno are all united by courage. They make the journey to escape unhappiness or worse . . ."

"You are right, for the most part. Unfortunately, suicide is an unpleasant fact here in Reno." Her blue eyes look at me tenderly. She puts her hand gently on my arm. "You have probably not heard of a place here called the Stockade."

I shake my head.

"Simply put, my dear, it is Reno's largest house of prostitution, and it's a bad place."

"There are streets we have been told to steer clear of."

"Good," she says. "The ranchers do a very thorough job of telling their guests what to avoid. The poor girls there have reached the end of the line. Two or three times a week, a girl overdoses on laudanum."

I gather Miss Helen can see the shock in the whites of my eyes. "I imagine it doesn't happen in . . . in your establishment."

"No, it doesn't," she replies, "but I have the incredibly sad duty of having to turn away girls from the Stockade. They wash up to my door, two or three a week. I wish I could take them all in, but I can't. I have petitioned the town bosses—many times—to take down the Stockade or at least clean it up, but they turn their backs on me. All they want is their money. They have no social conscience whatsoever.

"I started a home for the ones that get pregnant. Unfortunately, after good nutrition and a safe delivery, most of them return to the Stockade.

"I'm sorry," she says. "I can see I've upset you more."

"No," I reply. "I admire your compassion. God bless you for looking out for . . . for . . ."

"The bottom rung of society?"

I have never met a woman like Miss Helen. She could not do what she does in any other state except Nevada, but with her profits, she provides for those less fortunate.

"And your six-weeker who took her life . . . ?" she asks.

I look down at my gloved hands in my lap and sigh. "She was terrified of being alone."

"Ahhhh. Some women haven't thought it through," she says. "They find the pluck to get here, but they don't think about what comes after." She sighs and stares at the faraway mountains. "Once upon a time, long ago, I came to Reno for the same reason we all come. I almost gave up too. But instead, with a lot of courage and a lot of luck, I saw an opportunity and grabbed it."

We sit in companionable silence. I hear the last of the dying honeybees buzzing around flowerpots.

"What about you, Miss Evelyn? Will you return back East into the arms of your next husband?"

"Ha!" I laugh. "There's no one waiting in the wings. I plan to return to modeling, if I can."

"That doesn't surprise me. I hope everything works out for you."

"Thank you," I mouth, unable to refrain from blushing.

Seeing Madeline crossing the street, Miss Helen stands. She acknowledges Madeline with a nod and says, "For some women, the freedom of divorce is terrifying. Suicide has happened before, and it will happen again, but I'm sorry you lost your friend."

Madeline keeps a safe distance, but I stand and shake Miss Helen's hand. To hell with what other people think. It is clear I catch her off guard; she opens her eyes wide, as if to fight back tears. I have no words, but I hope she understands that I hold her in the highest esteem.

⌒☉

Sundown and Red recognize how downcast Madeline and I are when they greet us at the door to the Silver Slipper. Tessa and Johnnie come up alongside us.

"What's happened to you?" asks Johnnie. "You look like you've lost a dear friend."

Madeline's face is ashen. "We have."

The four of them stare at us open mouthed as we tell of Beatrice's suicide, and of Thistlena's escape. "Let's go in," I say. "We'll fill you in. I could use a *drink*."

We check our coats inside and make our way to a table beside the dance floor. I can't help but notice that the hall is only half-full. It is early yet—Kenny and His Boys are tuning up—but many tables are empty. I would have thought that, for the last night before this bunch of six-weekers returns East, the dance halls would be jumping. Maybe the gals are busy packing. Then I recall there were 210 investors in Twin Arches. Perhaps they, too, are devastated by the scam and too shocked to think of dancing.

Madeline and I relate the sad events of the last two days. Tessa and Johnnie are well aware of the con artists' escape to Mexico, the sheriff having visited Tessa's ranch yesterday morning. Sundown and Johnnie listen attentively as we reveal the details of their betrayal.

"We feel as if we've been run over by a train," says Tessa, who, along with four ranch mates, is out $5,000. "We not only feel double-crossed, but it's as if we've been touched by *evil*."

Sundown squeezes my hand under the table. He is as shocked as we are—about the bogus development, about Thistlena's marriage to Ray, about their fleeing to Mexico.

"They didn't take Evelyn's money," Madeline says.

"I'm still very confused about that," I say quickly. I never told a soul about Thistlena's abortion. What would they think of me, condoning such a decision, let alone holding her hand?

To change the subject, I say to Tessa, "The Twin Arches default won't cause you to cancel your plans, I hope."

"Not a chance," she replies through a clenched jaw. "I wouldn't give them the satisfaction."

The band begins a bouncy rendition of a Jerome Kern song.

"C'mon, fellas," says Sundown, standing, his eyes reflecting the sun-washed blue of his denim shirt. "Let's try to distract these gals."

As the evening moves along, I find that my mood lifts by dancing. Sundown doesn't try to fill our time with conversation. Instead, he keeps me kicking and twirling and spinning. Breathless, I laugh in spite of myself. Madeline does too.

For a moment, so beaten down by Thistlena's sellout and Beatrice's death, I had forgotten how gorgeous Sundown is. My eyes sweep over his earnest, caring face. As he holds me tight and I find my favorite place in the crook of his neck and shoulder, the tautness of my muscles loosens, and I relax into our familiar rhythms. Next the band takes up a medley by the Gershwin brothers. These are new tunes for us, but Sundown is in top form. He spins me out, draws me in, and dips me low, and soon the dance floor is ringed by couples watching us, a generous smile on every face. Suddenly I have never felt freer. At the end of the theme song, he lifts me in the air, and I cinch up my knees onto his hip and throw out my arms with a schoolgirl's delight.

Seated back at our table and gripping Sundown's hand, I say, "You have been the bright spot in this tumultuous excursion. If not for you, I might not have made it."

He covers my hands with his. "Of course you would have made it. Not only are you beautiful, Evelyn; you're *strong*."

"I am a fool."

"Nonsense. I remember how carefully you checked everything. Phone calls with your lawyer, trips to the bank, visits to all those offices in city hall. How many investors did you say? More than two hundred? If you were misled by their scheme, so were a lot of other six-weekers."

"I feel so betrayed."

While rubbing my hand, he asks, "Have you noticed I never gamble?"

I nod.

"Well, I used to." He edges his chair closer to mine and speaks in my ear.

"I lost a horse in a poker game. My brother lost a farm. Now I let off steam by drinking and dancing." He smiles and kisses my neck. "It took me a while to recover from my stupidity. A cowboy without a horse? Well, I wasn't much good for anything for a while."

"Sundown, you're good for many, *many* things. How 'bout that bull riding of yours?"

"Yeah, I like that. And I'm good at it. But it's dangerous, and there's no money in it unless you come out on top. I've entered many a contest and come away with nothing but bruises."

"But you still get back on the bull."

He smiles. I lower my chin and bat my eyelashes. He kisses my hand. "You say you wouldn't have made it without me. Well, I'm grateful for knowing you too."

I must look perplexed.

"It's true," he says. His eyes flash sapphire, and gold flecks radiate from his pupils. "I've never known a woman like you. I tried to tell you on our trail ride. Knowing that I can attract a woman as lovely as you—as beautiful inside as you are outside—has caused me to think beyond range riding. Can I do something more with my life? I don't know. But from spending time with *you*, I've learned I can look beyond those mountains if I want to."

"Maybe you could have your own ranch, find a wife, settle down, have kids . . ."

"Whoa, Evelyn!" He laughs. "I've only stepped off the range. Who said anything about a wife and kids?"

"Sorry," I say, putting on my most sheepish face.

"Well," he says, "knowing you has caused me to think about things. Maybe I've got some other choices."

"With your good looks and dance moves, where you really belong is Hollywood."

"Come with me?" he asks with a playful wink.

I laugh heartily. "Now that's the best offer I've had all night." Then I recall the conversation I had with Madeline. "In the *next* life," I had said.

"I have two wonderful children in college I have to get back to, and with whom I have some repair work to do," I continue, "and a sister who shares my house. I have plans to return to modeling, if the agencies will have me.

"What I'm trying to say is I'm a range rider too, but my range takes up New York to Philadelphia with Hackensack, New Jersey, in between. And from now on, I will roam it freely, thanks to the courageous examples I've observed here—the Anselms, Miss Violet, Miss Helen, and all of you cowboys. I will have to mind my p's and q's because *everyone* back East will be watching, but I will have relieved myself of a huge burden—a loveless marriage and the very stringent boundaries erected by my family." I wonder if there is anything Sundown avoided by taking to the range. Does he wonder about other people's opinions? Probably not.

"I admire your confidence," he says. "You seem very sure of your plans."

"Boy, have I got you fooled!" I say, shaking my head. "Nothing is certain, but I have faith . . . a *new* faith in myself, in fact. I've survived so far, including six weeks in this foreign land—complete with shootings, suicides, and shysters—so I'm going to give it my best effort. That's all I can do."

# THE TRAIN GOING EAST

# CHAPTER 36

*Thursday, November 12, 1931*

I wake feeling melancholy, but there is no time to dwell on gloom. Breakfast is waiting on the sideboard in the dining room for Madeline, Neppy, and me. We plunk down our luggage at the foot of the stairs, and Little Hawk carries it outside and puts it into the back of the truck. Arthur is chatting with the cowboys in the side room while Savannah hums a country tune.

I sit dreamily savoring my last taste of one of Savannah's biscuits and push a bit of egg around my plate. Ramona approaches with the registration pages we completed the day we arrived.

"I will come into the court with you, but you will need to show this to the clerk," she says.

As we go out the front door, a cold wind and a sky that threatens snow greet us. Savannah and the cowboys follow us. Henry, Smoky Joe, Zack, and Gerry step forward in turn, tip their hats, and shake our hands, one or the other mumbling goodbyes: "Have a good trip." "Nice to meetcha." "Come back and see us." I suspect none of us will.

Standing closest to Savannah, I extend my arms to give her a big hug. "You're a treasure," I say with a sob, smelling her lavender toilet water. I swipe the corner of my eye, and she reaches into her bosom to retrieve her hankie and blot her eyes. I want to say so much more—that she is a gifted chef, that I'm so grateful the Anselms found her, and that I hope, someday, her "demons" will disappear—but I can't find the words.

"You're a beauty, Miss Evelyn," she says. "Don't you forget it."

"Thank you," I mouth as I descend the porch steps.

Savannah hugs Madeline and Neppy too, and we climb into the back seat. When I turn around as Arthur drives away, the last thing I see is her white hankie waving to us. As we pass through the entrance to the ranch, the flying *N* swings noisily from its crossbar, an eerie screech in the wind. We ride in silence, each of us locked in our private thoughts, the only sound being the car tires on the stony desert ground.

Today I will officially become a divorcée. A shameful badge, according to many, but for me, it will mark the beginning of my independence, my new life. I have made it to the end. That is good, but also swirling in my head are feelings of loss—loss of this strange but beautiful land, of the people I have come to know, of the awakening of physical pleasure. And tickling my brain, off in a remote corner, are questions about my future: Will I survive life with my sister, Marion? Will my children accept me? Will the agencies have modeling work for me when I return to Philadelphia and New York? I won't find the answers until I try.

Arthur drops us off at the courthouse and bids us a perfunctory goodbye. I wonder if he feels relief over our departure. They will have a couple of days' rest, then begin six weeks all over again.

There is a lot of commotion among the women waiting their turn on the steps of the courthouse. I stay back, taking in the scene and bracing myself to accomplish my final task. I clutch my handbag, which contains the papers prepared by my attorneys and the ranch registration from Ramona. The ladies standing in the blinding sun have rouge-colored rivulets running down their faces, and there is a low hum of chatter. Several ranch owners, whom I recognize, stand stoically beside their charges, nudging them forward, three abreast, while the deputy in his Stetson hat bellows orders in the foyer.

Now inside, I look up the long marble staircase to the second floor and inhale. Grabbing the banister, I pause. This is the last obstacle, my final climb. Crossing the landing in the middle, passing colorful murals, I fix my eyes on the brilliant blue dome at the top and put one foot in front of the other.

Ramona, her unpowdered, chiseled features contrasting with the made-up faces crammed into the waiting foyer, steps forward to the courtroom railing. "Evelyn?" she says.

Aroused from my dream state, I place my papers on the judge's table. His ruddy face behind a pair of Ben Franklin glasses, he examines my materials. Without looking up, he says, "Raise your right hand. Swear to tell the truth, the whole truth, so help you God?"

"I do."

"You have resided at the Flying N Ranch for six weeks?"

"I have."

"And who vouches for this residency?"

"I do, Your Honor," says Ramona.

"And you wish to dissolve your marriage to Dean Henderson?"

"I do."

"So moved," says the judge. "Move along."

I hear the slams of rubber stamps on ink pads, and a clerk shoves the papers into my hands.

"Next," the clerk shouts.

That's it? I'm done?

I swallow with difficulty and once again gird myself to negotiate the crowd in the lobby while Ramona continues her duties for Madeline and Neppy.

As I exit the courtroom, I almost fall over my Hackensack acquaintance, Gwyneth Armstrong, who has collapsed in a heap on the marble floor.

". . . can't do it," she mumbles. "I can't do this."

I confess that my first thought is to kick her when she's down. I want her to feel some of the humiliation I felt when she demanded to know why I was in Reno.

Instead, I push away these thoughts, hand my papers and pocketbook to a waiting six-weeker, and lift Gwyneth to standing. While she sobs, I put my hands on her shoulders and, putting on my sternest face, say, "Yes, you can, Gwyneth. You're almost there. You can do this. You *will* do this."

I hear the judge say, "Next," and I nudge her through the door.

Holding fast to the stair's railing, I begin my descent down the marble steps. As I glance over my shoulder, Gwyneth is swearing her oath to the judge.

I feel considerably lighter than during my ascent and stumble into the blazing sun outside. Shielding my eyes, I find a bit of shade in the shadow of the building and observe the spectacle. Exiting six-weekers kiss a column on the courthouse portico, skip down the steps, and whoop "Yahoo!" Girls push and shove one another onto the Virginia Street Bridge and, on the count of three, fling their wedding rings into the Truckee River.

Some gals run with their beaus—several of whom I recognize as "cousins" from the train ride west—into the chapel across the street. And, yes, as Ray told Madeline and me during that first lunch at the Grand Café, the couples emerge minutes later swinging their hands, the bride carrying an artificial bouquet.

Neppy and Madeline squint as they come out of the courthouse, followed by Ramona, who points toward the train depot. She is to meet Arthur there, and Little Hawk has already deposited our luggage inside the building.

Tessa comes running up to me, holding her hat on her head, smiling broadly, and carrying a skimpy bunch of flowers. Her mauve shirtwaist, blown against her by the wind, outlines her youthful figure.

"Evelyn," Tessa says, out of breath, "please come into the chapel with me. I need a maid of honor."

I gulp air, but before I can speak, Ramona says, "Go ahead, Evelyn. We'll meet you at the depot."

Tessa gives me her bouquet, takes my hand, and pulls me to the chapel door. Coming inside after the intense sunshine, I pinch my eyes closed to adjust to the darkness. Tessa sets out for the front of the church at a tiptoed run, her spectator pumps scraping the rough tile floor. I follow as fast as I can, still dazed by the dark interior. I step into the second wooden pew and find myself looking down on Sundown. I gasp. Thank goodness I have the pew in front of me to grab on to. I didn't expect to see him again. I smooth my skirt, sit down, and exhale slowly. He reaches for my hand. Facing straight ahead, I give him a quick wink with a smile. Now I can make out rows of flickering candles along the side walls.

"I now pronounce you man and wife," says the robed man at the front. His too-large black costume reaches the floor. "Next!"

*My goodness,* I think, *it's an assembly-line wedding mill.* The just-married couple runs hand in hand down the aisle while a heavyset fellow comes forward with a fleshy gal a head taller than him.

I will my heartbeat to slow down. "Are you standing up for Johnnie?" I whisper.

Cupping his hand to one side of his mouth, he says, "Felt I couldn't say no."

"I was pulled in off the street." I cover my nose and mouth with my hands to stifle a giggle.

While the black-robed cleric intones, "Do you, Rosina, take this man . . . ?" I look at Tessa and Johnnie, shoulder to shoulder in the chairs in front of us. Tessa smiles serenely while Johnnie brings her gloved hand to his lips. These two are clearly in love. If Tessa has any doubts, I can't see them.

*Where are they going to live? How are they going to live?* Tessa has been burned by Thistlena's scheme.

I don't ask these questions. I don't want to appear as a naysayer. Or is there a part of me that is a little bit jealous—jealous of their obvious devotion and unquestioning commitment?

I told Sundown that I have a new faith in myself—a conviction that I will be able to make my way along the path that I choose. I hope that Tessa and Johnnie share the same belief, no matter what happens. And who am I to question their assurance? As Madeline and I agreed, Tessa emerged from her Reno tenure as if from a cocoon, now a colorful butterfly ready to fly. I wish nothing but the best for them.

Tessa and Johnnie stand, walk forward, and motion for Sundown and me to follow. Tessa hands me her flowers. I stand beside her, and Sundown stands next to Johnnie. We witness the exchange of vows and then of rings. After the minister says, "You may kiss the bride," Johnnie and Tessa embrace, and then Sundown and I hug them both.

I catch the minister tapping his foot while he peers out at the rows of couples waiting. "Next!" he says.

Tessa and Johnnie join hands like children and fairly skip down the aisle. Sundown and I follow, tiptoeing as quietly as we can.

"I don't know," Sundown whispers, shaking his head.

"That was my first thought too," I say, "but today they are *so* happy, and who are we to judge? They might make a success of it."

The four of us join Ramona, Madeline, and Neppy outside the depot. Both girls appear timid and bewildered, as if they have just arrived. We are all seasoned six-weekers by now, but perhaps they are uncertain about what lies ahead—Madeline in San Francisco and Neppy back on the farm in Pennsylvania. I shiver. Thankfully, I have several days on the train to contemplate what awaits me in Hackensack.

We wave to Arthur, who sits in the shade inside his car, waiting for Ramona. Sundown kisses me on the cheek, then kisses Neppy and Madeline. Adjusting his hat, he backs up to Arthur's car while smiling his delicious smile. I think I'll always remember how he looks at this moment—movie-star handsome, my dance partner and my lover during this unimaginable visit. *Oh golly, should I be leaving?*

We jump at the sound of a loud whistle and great exhales of steam. The train to Oakland is pulling in. I grab Madeline into a bear hug, my handbag slapping her bottom, but who cares? My eyes well up while

Neppy embraces her too. Ramona opens the door to the station. She shakes our hands, gives us each a peck on the cheek, and wishes us Godspeed.

Swiping my cheeks and struggling for words, I want to say how much I have come to admire her and appreciate all she and Arthur have done for us, but she lets go of Neppy's hand as another group of six-weekers bursts through the door. The last view I have of her is as I will always remember her—calm, erect, her thick gray braid against her back as she walks to the car.

The next thing I know I am standing on the platform beside Neppy, waving and blowing kisses to Madeline as her gloved hand reaches out her passenger window.

"Good luck!" we both shout. We walk beside the train as it begins its slow chug-chug. At the end of the platform, we wave for a long time, as does the small hand from the window. Finally, the train rounds a bend and disappears.

I shudder for Madeline. She has lost her investment money, is traveling to an entirely new city, and, although completely divorced, still lives in fear of her ex-husband. I recall she has her cousin, with whom she will stay at first, but what fortitude she shows.

Neppy and I go back inside the station to check on our luggage. Although both the front and back station doors are open, six-weekers are tightly packed like a corral full of cattle, flicking their fans and blotting their faces. I think back to the chill that blasted us this morning as we left the ranch. Once again, the Reno sun penetrates the cold like a sword.

Eventually, the train from Oakland going east arrives, great ghosts of steam coming from its engine along with ear-piercing screams from its brakes. Neppy clutches my hand while holding on to her blue straw hat.

Porters descend from the train and hoist the bags the women point to. The crowd inches forward like slow but steady snails. Neppy and I grab brown hands that pull us aboard, and we step sideways into the first car. We each throw a small bag onto opposite seats and wait while the porters stow our cases on the racks above. Finally seated, Neppy and I look at each other and heave a simultaneous exhale. "We made it," she says, and closes her eyes as if in prayer.

I wait for feelings of elation, giggly glee, a euphoria over my mission accomplished, but all I feel is numb. But as I sit quietly, a cacophony of shouts around me—"Sit here, Ann," "That's my bag, the brown one," "Over here, Herminie, over here"—I realize I'm not numb. In fact, I'm profoundly sad.

The train lurches. Neppy and I pitch back and forth, then resettle into our seats. The cars chug-chug along, slowly picking up speed. This car is unusually quiet. A train full of garrulous women would ordinarily produce a din of chatter. Perhaps today each woman is quietly contemplating all that has happened, or all that might happen on her return. Neppy, her hands folded neatly in her lap over her return ticket, stares out the window. Her simple brown dress drapes her graceful legs, and I smile as I recognize the silk stockings that I purchased for her. I suspect, from her dreamy countenance, that she isn't really seeing the ragged shacks that line the tracks leading east. Perhaps she imagines instead the rolling hills of Pennsylvania or the little boy who counts the days until her return. Does she dread the farm chores that await her? The task of raising her son alone?

"You know, I seriously considered staying in Reno," she says.

I look at her open mouthed.

"Honestly, I did."

"Actually," I say, "I considered it too." Sundown's smile flashes across my mind.

"I don't know how to explain it except to say I felt safe there."

"Safe?" I ask.

"Oh, I know, we had that tragedy with Beatrice. And Owen showed up to kidnap Madeline."

"And don't forget the shameful business with Thistlena," I add.

Neppy continues to gaze out the window. "Maybe *safe* isn't the right word. Maybe I felt free—free from all my cares at home."

I recall all the fears I carried with me to Reno when I arrived more than forty days ago: Who are these women I will be living with? What will my accommodations be like? Who are the Anselms and how will they treat us? What will I do all day for six weeks? How will I occupy myself?

Perhaps what Neppy said about feeling free has gradually come to me as well. Although in a new and strange land and constantly having to adapt, I was far away from Dean and all the disappointments of my marriage. I no longer felt suffocated by the emotional distance between us. I also left behind the daily outbursts and finger wagging of my sister. No doubt I will have some fence-mending to do with Charlie and June, but yes, it is freeing to be far away from what hurt me so much.

Will I ever understand the significance of T.? The thought of Dean with a male lover is more than I will ever comprehend, let alone accept. Whether T. is a close friend or something more, Dean's deceit regarding his reasons for staying at the Gramercy overnight is unforgivable. And I had come to realize that he was often just *pretending* to look for work.

But freedom is more than an absence of hurt. It is elbow room to try new things. Plenty of rope, as the cowboys would say, to play, and no doubt stumble, but with the license to get up and play again. Yes, I have been bucked and thrown to the ground, but absent the constraints of Hackensack—my town, my family, my history—yes, Neppy is right. I have acquired a new freedom.

In Hackensack, there were whispers in parlors about friends who "fell on hard times and had to take in boarders" to pay the bills. This was viewed as a big comedown. However, I have nothing but admiration for Arthur and Ramona, who provide so well for so many six-weekers. Yes, they dress differently than easterners and work at a livelihood that I can't imagine for myself. But they work tirelessly—from sunup to sunset—and have their own definition of a family to support. Little Hawk and Savannah and the cowboys.

And what about Savannah and Little Hawk? No one ostracizes them for their skin color or their size. They are good at their work and devoted to the Anselms. What's more, Savannah's demons are not only accepted but forgiven.

I suppose that the Anselms watch the six-week lodgers pass through their doors like a faceless blur, perhaps numbering in the hundreds, too many to count or remember. But I will always cherish Arthur and Ramona and be grateful for their selfless examples of pioneer spirit.

Madeline. Dear Madeline, who has become my dearest friend during this adventure. I recall the disdain I felt for her at first—all teary eyed and three chinned on the train coming west. I wasn't keen to be her companion, but having been rebuffed by Thistlena, I reluctantly let her cling to me. And nervous? Afraid of her own shadow, she was. But we had all come to understand her terror of Owen. And yet she stood up to the men who wanted to abuse Beatrice. She told me she learned that behavior from how I confronted Owen. Perhaps it was true.

Madeline, who knew about real estate, asked intelligent questions about the hotel and casino project. Even though she was fooled by their scheme, I am certain of her success going forward. I, too, learned from *her* example—she accepted with grace her failed investment. I have every confidence that she will retain her lessons and grow in wisdom.

And Beatrice, poor Beatrice. Married to a womanizer but panic stricken to be alone. She had enough stamina to get to Reno but not enough desire for freedom to finish the job. I will never forget the stomach punch I carried after her suicide. That event will take a long time to recover from, but I found the strength to set aside my guilt, thanks to Miss Helen. Sometimes a six-weeker brings greater challenges than "the Reno Cure" can repair.

If ever there was a transformation from a homely stalk into a radiant flower, it is Tessa Marquand. When I recall my first impressions of her on the train, I am ashamed. Her gray clothes and gray pallor soon remodeled themselves into western costumes and then colorful shirtwaists for doing the Charleston at the dance halls. Tessa was schooled in the same manners as I was, but her naturally outgoing nature hastened her changeover. How I envied her when-in-Rome attitude. She kicked up her heels but never ceased to be a well-bred lady.

Always the first to try new things in Reno, Tessa is now Mrs. John Wiggins. I'm still shocked and quite possibly a tad bit envious. Free from the constraints of her upbringing, she has chosen to judge Johnnie for his goodness, competence, and resilience rather than his social position or family background. She has cast her lot with a good man, even after losing her investment. I wish her nothing but the best.

And Thistlena Duncan? It will take me the rest of my life to process my encounters with her, from my first impression of her as an aristocratic queen, to an aloof businesswoman desiring to end her pregnancy, to what? Runaway con artist?

What is her real story? Has she really been married to Ray Sessions all this time? Was there an ex-husband before him? Was Ray the father of her child? If not him, then who? Where are they now? Since I am still in shock over Thistlena's abrupt disappearance, I haven't taken the time to express relief that I'm not out $5,000. Madeline didn't shed any more tears after that first morning of discovery, but I'm certain that the loss will force her to adjust her plans in San Francisco.

And me? That money not spent in Reno will be used for college tuition for my children, as well as on updating my modeling portfolio. Yes, I am beaten down by Thistlena's betrayal, but she has indeed erased any obligation to me. Grateful to have my funds in hand, I will be more than cautious concerning any future investments; of that much, I am certain.

～⑨

Neppy and I are back from supper in the dining car. We sat with Jennie Newcomb and Rachel something or other—I don't recall her last name, or care. By this time, no one is a stranger. Even if we don't know each other's names, we recognize faces from Virginia Street or the dance halls, from Miss Violet's or the tearooms. However, tonight the passengers are quiet. I had anticipated boisterous celebrating and much raising of glasses, be it water or "grape juice," considering how far we have come and all we have accomplished. Instead, perhaps like me, each one is sifting through her emotions—from joy to sadness, from relief to fear of what is to come. All I hear is the clink of forks on porcelain plates. Eyes stare past one another, as if daydreaming. On the train west, we acknowledged to each other our families', and society's, expectations, which we had chosen to defy. Today, we recognize the finality of our actions. How will each one deflect the arrows of shame?

A trainman hurries down the aisle shouting, "Penn Station! Coming into Penn Station, New York City! Make sure you take all your belongings. Penn Station! Coming into Penn Station!" He vanishes into the next car.

We have arrived in New York in the morning. I'm grateful I will not have to make my way back to Newark after dark. The passengers, burdened with luggage in both hands, descend from the train cars, impatiently yanking their valises through the narrow doors. Another train journey of four long days has made most of us cranky. We are anxious for this episode in our lives to be over.

Plodding up the iron steps from the lower level, I pause to view the train concourse, covered with acres of glass in domes, arches, and vaults. Taking my last step up, into the main concourse, I draw in a long breath—the knots of steel ribs are so high, the space so vast. I shiver despite the warmth from the sunlight. The huge expanse overwhelms me. I've come so far. I've met my goal. What is this sudden fear?

Which way do I go? How do find the local trains for New Jersey? I've done this thousands of times with Mother, Marion, and my friends. I move aside so as not to block others coming into the Main Waiting Room. The sun shines bright on a million dust motes. I can't see through them. It's so crowded. People are everywhere.

What will I do tomorrow? How will I begin my new life? Who am I now? Am I still Evelyn Henderson? Blinking through the brilliance,

I see the opening to the General Waiting Room. That's where I see the signs for Newark. I have wired Marion to meet me and bring me to Hackensack. Straightening my back and inhaling some new fortitude, I forge ahead. I am jolted from the left by a man in a cowboy hat. "Sundown?" Flustered by my error, I mumble, "Sorry," and refocus on the train signs.

Despite the jitters I felt when I first arrived in Reno, and the unexpected disasters that almost caused me to abandon my mission, Sundown is, without question, the highlight of my journey. From a sea of six-weekers, he chose me, and as our dancing evolved into lovemaking, he taught me the joy of letting go and trusting my heart. To hell with the confines of convention! And whose conventions are they anyway? From now on, I am determined to judge people for their goodness rather than their appearance, for their competence rather than their social position, and for their resilience rather than their family background.

As much as I did not want our passion to end, I thank God that we both had the self-possession not to lose our heads. We were generous in our support of Tessa and Johnnie, and who knows where that will end? I saw plenty of six-weekers throw themselves at cowboys, as well as the gals who emerged from the chapel on the arms of their "cousins." But for me, I am an easterner through and through, and I will return to the environment I know. Do I have unfinished business in Hackensack? To be sure. But of one thing I'm certain: I am now unfettered to set goals for myself beyond the restrictions of my family's, or husband's, rules. I am free to try new things, and perhaps fall down, but continue to stay my course on my terms.

# ACKNOWLEDGMENTS

Like my protagonist, Evelyn Henderson, who defied the odds and secured a divorce in Reno, Nevada, in 1931, I, too, was victorious after three months of rejection. Pitching my query letter to agents in the summer of 2023, I collected many "thank you, but no thank you" responses. I contemplated giving up and embarking on another route to publication. One morning in September, I received a call from agent Marlene Stringer, who said, "Lucy, I *love* your book." I was stunned. Approval? What was that? As we say in publishing, "All it takes is one," and I am indebted to Marlene for negotiating my contract with Lake Union. I would be remiss if I didn't acknowledge the superb editing of Jane Rosenman, who got my novel in shape for agents.

Along the way, many reading friends gave me feedback, especially Wendy Dingwall and Eleanor Brackbill. I am especially grateful to several critique groups, including my Connecticut girls—Penny, Helen, and Prill, my Connecticut teachers—Jessica Bram and Suzanne Hoover, and my Sisters in Crime group in Florida. Lake Union provided me with the superb talents of developmental editor Charlotte Herscher. Together we made the manuscript shine.

To all my friends to whom I talked ad nauseum about *Six Weeks in Reno*, thank you for putting up with me and for encouraging me at every turn. I couldn't have completed this journey without you.

Last but not least, I wish to acknowledge my grandmother Evelyn, who loved me and encouraged me, and who was an invaluable role model. In the historical struggle by women for independence and freedom, I have the utmost respect for her resilience, strength, and determination.

# BOOK CLUB QUESTIONS

1. What do you think of Evelyn's reaction to the Reno environment, both the desert and the town?
2. In your opinion, does Thistlena's decision not to deposit Evelyn's investment in Twin Arches even the score?
3. What do you think of Arthur and Ramona Anselm, their quiet ways reinforced with western resilience?
4. Sundown Ahrens is changed from knowing Evelyn. How is she transformed?
5. Evelyn and Miss Helen establish a tentative friendship. How does it affect Evelyn?
6. Evelyn wants to return to modeling. Will she be successful?
7. Discuss the theme of freedom, desired by most of the six-weekers.
8. Evelyn's relationship with her mother is complicated. What do you think of Evelyn as a mother?
9. How is Evelyn affected by knowing Madeline, Beatrice, and Neppy?
10. Evelyn is often critical of others but also kind. Do you like her?

# ABOUT THE AUTHOR

Lucy H. Hedrick is the author of five works of nonfiction. *Six Weeks in Reno* is her first novel. Born in Chicago, Lucy attended Goucher College in Maryland, where she majored in music history and sang in the glee club. She has roamed the Eastern Seaboard ever since. Marriage brought Lucy to Old Greenwich, Connecticut. Shortly thereafter Lucy gave birth to her son, Tod. Today, Lucy lives in Sarasota, Florida, where she devotes herself to writing women's fiction. She is a member of the National League of American Pen Women, Sisters in Crime—Florida Gulf Coast Chapter, and Sarasota Fiction Writers. For more information, visit www.lucyhedrick.com.